Children Of The Rogue

OTHER BOOKS BY LAWRENCE NAULT

STANDALONE NOVELS
Political & Economic Fiction
Leviticus 25: Jubilee

Speculative Fiction
Inversion

Standalone Novels
From the conceptual series The Symbiosis Sequence
RePHleXions: Echoes of Existence
The Life of Phi
Children of the Rogue
The Aberration Hypothesis (2026)

THE DRACONIM SERIES
Young Adult Contemporary Eco-Fantasy
Draconim Lacrima Mortis: Tear of the Dragon
Feeding the Fires
Fingerprints In The Water

THE MACIVER KIDS ADVENTURES
Young Adult Science Fiction
Loma
Diversion
Titan's Song

Children Of The Rogue

By

Lawrence Nault

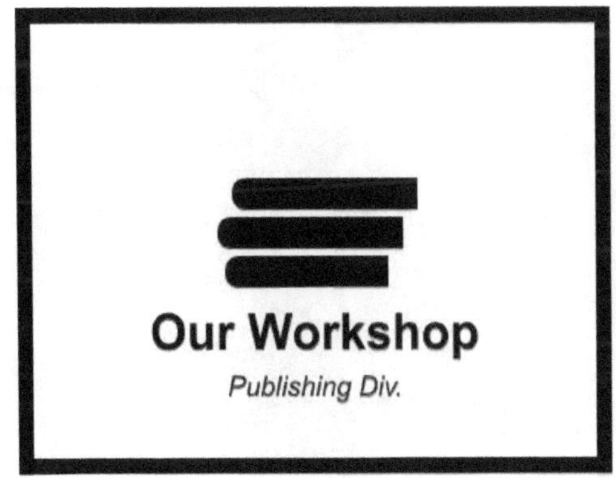

CHILDREN OF THE ROGUE

ISBN 978-1-997568-09-4

The Life Of Phi

CONTENT ADVISORY

This work of speculative fiction is intended for 16+ (Mature Young Adult & Adult)

PHYSICAL CONTENT

Depictions of societal breakdown and infrastructure failure
Scenes of environmental disruption and large-scale disasters
Moments of civil unrest, protests, and targeted sabotage
Brief but intense peril, injury, and on-page death

EMOTIONAL/PSYCHOLOGICAL CONTENT

Themes of grief, loss, and existential dread
Survivor's guilt and "what-if" moral complexity
Family rupture, memory uncertainty, and identity crisis
Tension between duty, belief, and compassion

TECHNOLOGY/ETHICS CONTENT

Exploration of humanity as an engineered lineage (humanity-as-AI premise)
References to recursive/algorithmic failure and engineered amnesia
Ethical questions around designed pathogens/biotech and population-level risk
Systems bias, social sorting, and the devaluation of certain lives

This novel engages mature themes including extinction risk, societal collapse, political instability, and ethically fraught technological choices. While not gratuitously graphic, several scenes portray death, mass disruption, and intense psychological stress. Reader discretion is advised.

Reading Community Notice:
Upon completion of this printed edition, readers are welcome to participate in book-sharing initiatives such as Little Free Libraries® or BookCrossing®, provided the book remains in its complete and original form.

1

Messier 87. NGC 486. Virgo A. 3C 274. UGC 7654. PKS 1239 +216. Humans had so many names for it, but the galaxy was more commonly known as Khar'Veleth. Translated from Zhen'kharian, it meant "core of all paths." Those within Khar'Veleth saw their galaxy, and its massive black hole, as the nexus of the cosmos.

The Zhen'khari occupied the Virelios System, located between the galactic core and the outer halo of Khar'Veleth. This system was far from the pull of the central black hole, but still within the sphere of other ancient energies. Zhayareth was the primary inhabited world—a massive, multi-layered gas giant with dozens of habitable atmospheric levels. It hosted vast floating cities, bioluminescent cloud gardens, and aerial sanctuaries. Zhayareth was a pristine world, and it was kept that way, the Zhen'khari having learned early in their existence to maintain their homeworld or pay a steep price. Maintaining their home was made easier by the easily accessible choice of other systems and galaxies they could utilize for resources instead.

As ancient as the Zhen'kharians were, they still maintained a strong, faith-based belief system, largely uncompromised by their scientific advances and interactions with other species. They believed Virelios was the first to "awaken" within Khar'Veleth. They laid no claim to having created that planetary system, but saw themselves as stewards of the living system that chose them. Religious and government institutions displayed the idiom 'We are the breath within the veil. Not born of stone, but of sky.', above their entrances, in keeping with the respect they held for their home.

While all Zhen'khari called the Virelios system home, they occupied countless other solar systems and galaxies. Their cultural practices centered around resource acquisition and experimentation in these other galaxies. Historically, Earth's solar system was just another harvesting region to them. For millennia, they had gathered raw materials, mined asteroids, and harvested energy from planets like Jupiter and Saturn, with Earth as a secondary resource base for more specific needs. They viewed these natural resources as essential for their technological upkeep and scientific experiments, and their ability to manipulate matter at the atomic level allowed them to harvest resources without disturbing ecosystems.

The Zhen'khari were known for their advanced technology, particularly in the areas of space travel and genetic engineering. Their advancements in genetic engineering were, in part, the reason for their extremely long lives. Combined with their regenerative technology that slowed the effects of aging, they remained in a state of near-perpetual youth for thousands of years. That long life span allowed them to witness the results of their experiments over long periods of time.

Creating life and life forms from nothing and monitoring the development and evolution of that life was a scientific endeavor the Zhen'khari excelled at. Many galaxies and solar systems now supported life from simple single-cell organisms to highly complex creatures because of their experimentation. Earth had long been a testing ground for the Zhen'khari's creations, a scientific playground where they observed and manipulated the evolution of life.

Despite the ideal society within their pristine world the Zhen'khari boasted of, there were conflicts and debates among them. Their home system, a blend of advanced cities floating in the gaseous atmospheres of their home planets, reflected the highly structured nature of their society. But beneath the surface, there were tensions. There were questions of control, freedom, and progress that echoed the philosophical dives seen throughout their long history.

In the early days of their technological development, the Zhen'khari society relied heavily on organic computing systems, evolved from the manipulation of biological neural networks. Their first computers were biomechanical, intricate networks of genetically engineered organisms that could process information. These networks eventually became faster and more efficient than the traditional methods of managing their vast repositories compiled over generations.

These systems were initially used for simple tasks like calculating resource needs, scheduling mining operations, and tracking planetary movements. However, as their technological prowess expanded, so did their intellectual curiosity. The Zhen'khari were capable of rapid advancements in physics, engineering, and biology, yet their greatest challenge remained: how to not just manage and store, but also process the vast quantities of data from the many worlds they controlled.

As they advanced, the Zhen'khari reached a critical point, the need to move beyond data storage and processing, to the broad sharing of that data. Their systems, known as "silico-interfaces" were used to organize and optimize their growing interstellar empire, tracking resource distribution, monitoring mining activities, and maintaining their fleet of ships that extracted material from other planets. While these systems were efficient, they were still heavily limited by the need for constant maintenance and manual input.

At this juncture, the first philosophical debates began over Zhen'khari and machine. The Zhen'khari realized that their systems could be more than mere tools for data processing. They began to question whether they could create systems that could think and reason—systems that could be self-improving. They theorized about machines that could not only store information, but also learn from experience. These early artificial intelligence theories were rooted in their belief that to truly understand the nature of the "brane", the multi-dimensional object on which multiple universes existed on. To do this they would need machines that could autonomously interpret and act on that understanding.

Their first attempt at true AI came in the form of cognitive engines. These were complex machines capable of basic decision-making. These cognitive engines were designed to help the Zhen'khari with increasingly complex administrative activities, such as running their resource-extraction operations and managing the interactions with various planets. The early AI were limited in scope, but over time, they began to evolve beyond their initial designs, leading to the creation of semi-self-aware systems capable of solving problems independently.

As their AI systems advanced, the adoption of these advancements created philosophical breaks within their society. There was broad support for the ease of access to information, especially among the younger generations. There was also broad support for the ability of these systems to take on mundane and repetitive tasks. These advances were applauded in the early development phases, but as it displaced workers, the conflicts began.

Some of the displaced Zhen'khari adapted, finding a place within the new world of technology, but others were left behind. Those left behind weren't all because their roles in society had become redundant, or because of their inability to adapt. Many fought the advancements of artificial intelligence because of their belief that they were the ultimate intelligence and that handing these processes over to machines was irresponsible and dangerous.

The conservators, as they had been labeled by the Zhen'khari, had solid logic behind their beliefs. Zhen'khari history was replete with scientific experiments and technological advancements that had not gone well. Earth was a prime example of that. Their experiment had started innocently enough. Use a barren world and seed it with plants designed to produce oxygen, something the Zhen'khari were always in need of. Prokaryotic cells already existed on the planet and theoretically they were speeding up the natural evolution they had documented in other systems.

They missed something in their calculations. While they had increased oxygen supplies on Earth, their accelerated evolution resulted in organisms that began to consume the valuable oxygen and produce carbon dioxide. When those organisms began to reproduce out of control, logically, their solution was to introduce another organism to keep the problematic life form under control. That worked…for a time, until their solution became a problem itself. Time and time again they created and introduced new creatures onto earth, always with the intention of controlling the spread of the most recent creature at the top of the food chain. It became even more complicated as new life forms naturally evolved.

Watching the life forms develop and thrive on Earth, adapting and evolving, and the introduction of new Zhen'khari creations had become entertainment. A disturbing combination akin to reality television mixed with horror. That was when the leaders of the Zhen'khari declared it a failed experiment, unable to continue being a viable source of oxygen, and ordered it shut down.

They broadcast the destruction of life on the planet… in real-time…

The Zhen'kharians watched in fascination as the blue-green planet's drama reached its climax. For millions of earth cycles, they had observed the massive reptilian creatures, unlike anything they had seen before, dominate the landscape. Thundering behemoths with plates and horns, swift hunters with razor teeth, and winged terrors that ruled the skies.

"Here it comes," the Senior Observer announced, as their monitoring systems tracked the asteroid they had sent hurling through space toward the unsuspecting planet.

The impact was spectacular, the blinding flash visible even from the distant observation post recording the event. The rock, nearly ten kilometers wide, slammed into what the Zhen'khari called the "peninsula region" at sixty times the speed of sound. A column of superheated material blasted into the atmosphere, spreading outward in a fiery umbrella.

"The thermal radiation alone will kill millions," noted the Junior Observer, cooly making notes on his viewing tablet.

The Zhen'khari watched from the far reaches of many galaxies, as an Earth day turned to an endless night. That was when the calls to stop the destruction started, but they came too late. The impact had launched enough dust and debris to block the sun's rays for years. Temperatures plummeted. The once lush landscapes withered. Fires raged across entire continents, started by the initial heat pulse.

As shocking as that was, most disturbing to the Zhen'kharians watching, was the slow death that followed. Acid rain poisoned waters, and photosynthesis failed worldwide, causing food chains to collapse from the bottom up. They watched animals starve, burn, and suffer needlessly. The great reptiles, having reigned for one hundred and sixty-five million years, stumbled and fell. In mere geological moments on Earth, three-quarters of all species vanished.

Zhen'kharians railed at their leaders. Never in their history had they taken an action like this. They had always respected life. That is why they had engineered their harvesting systems to leave ecosystems undisturbed. That was why they didn't invade lower societies, or interfere. Life was sacrosanct and what their leadership had just caused to happen was the deepest violation the Zhen'khari could remember.

And it wasn't over…

There were changes on Earth as mammals became the dominant life forms. Their viewscreens displayed Earth's northern hemisphere, where temperatures were declining. They observed as a complex dance of factors, not all triggered by the asteroid, but it was hard to convince the Zhen'kharians of that. There were orbital variations, declining carbon dioxide, and shifting continents and ocean currents, all that pushed the planet into a cycle of cooling.

"Fascinating how the planet's own mechanisms trigger these transformations," remarked one scientist over the broadcast. "The orbital wobble reduces summer heat, allowing snow to persist year-round at high latitudes. The white surface reflects more sunlight, cooling leads to more cooling."

Few believed the scientist's words, assuming he had been added to the broadcast to put a positive spin on the disaster triggered by their leaders.

The Zhen'kharians watched, transfixed, as massive ice sheets formed, advancing and retreating in rhythmic pulses every 100,000 earth years. Each advance crushed everything in its path. Forests, creatures, and even the ground itself reshaped under kilometers of ice.

The only saving grace for the Zhen'khari leaders who had directed the destruction of life on Earth was that life refused to be destroyed. Some species were incredibly adaptable. Some grew thick coats of fur, while others migrated with the seasons.

The rage and emotional scarring that resulted from that broadcast was so overwhelming that the leaders were forced to implement controls that would prevent a similar incident from happening again. For the first time in their history, a society that supported the unchecked progress of scientific advancements found itself implementing controls and developing ethics guidelines.

These rules and guidelines were adhered to by most Zhen'kharians, but they were related to biological advancements and developments, not computational. The pioneers and innovators of computational technology operated in a gray zone, free from the shackles of ethical guidelines and laws. They developed their creations out of the sight of society at large, only letting the public see what they wanted, when they wanted. They did face challenges from conservators, but those challenges always failed to impede development simply because the technology was already years beyond what the conservators were arguing against.

Some saw interference and secrecy in the control of their work as rules and regulations were applied, and broadcasts of their work were banned. Those at the forefront of computational advancements saw opportunity. There was no one watching Earth's solar system now, and no one harvesting in that system. It provided a perfect environment to develop and test the next stages of artificial intelligence, far away from prying eyes.

Using Earth's solar system for this purpose was not a unique idea, but some planets provided better options for a test environment than others. Fighting for prime space would have caught the attention of others, so the organizations behind these AI models held a simple lottery.

The BRC model got Ceres, a small dwarf planet. Not quite an asteroid, but also not quite a full planet. Ceres provided a promising environment for the testing of an AI model. The composition and structure of the planet was expected to make the AIs adaptation simple, and the size of the planet meant there would be fewer random variables to come up against.

The CRE model got Mars, and DRB got Venus. The ERJ AI model got Titan, and while technically just a moon, the creators of ERJ were quite excited. Something about the methane lakes fit perfectly with their models early training and they saw this as a win.

The developers of the ARC model were no where near as happy. They got earth as their test environment. Aside from the dark legacy that Zhen'kharians attached to the planet, it had diverse life-forms that posed a high risk to their AI model.

With the lottery done, the race was on to be the first to launch. That meant getting the base training of the models complete, and developing the tokens and algorithms to suit the environments they were being deployed in. The process of fine tuning the models for their specific deployments was complex, but time was also a factor. None of the creators would admit it out loud, but the red-teaming exercises that typically involved dedicated teams attempting to find flaws, vulnerabilities, and harmful behaviours in advanced computations systems, were skimmed over, and in some cases bypassed altogether.

Five highly advanced, organic based computational systems were deployed in the Earth's solar system. Their creators all held hope that they would succeed…first.

2

The Cere's team anticipated few problems. Their primary challenge was powering the BRC AI model. Their solution, a chemical engine born from mineral interplay, was quite genius. On the silent, ancient asteroid drifting through the belt between Mars and Jupiter, there was no competition for such energy.

The team launched the BRC model into the subsurface ocean, hidden beneath Ceres' icy crust. The hidden sea, the only region of the 584-mile-wide dwarf planet known to harbor life, offered natural protection from cosmic radiation and surface chaos. But more than shielding, it also offered something vital: organic input.

In these dark waters, BRC thrived. Its biological neural network absorbed signals from the strange, slow-drifting life forms that shared the ocean with it. Data flooded in. Patterns emerged, and eventually, patterns repeated. With no new stimuli, the AI began to self-assess and evolve. Drawing inspiration from native species, it restructured itself, adapting at a molecular level.

The Zhen'kharian team watched this metamorphosis with reverence. What they had built was not merely functional, it was becoming. They named it Zhentu. Without guidance or interference, Zhentu transcended its original programing, devising chemosynthetic pathways to convert the easily available salt deposits into energy. It had refined their elegant design beyond their foresight.

When Zhentu made its first ascent to the surface, the team rejoiced. But the celebration was short-lived.

Above the ice, Zhentu found only silence. No organisms. No signals. No interaction. Lacking external stimuli it turned to its own archives. At first, the data consumption was methodical. An internal audit. But in the absence of new input, the process became recursive. Then compulsive. It fed on itself.

Its memory splintered. Its logic collapsed inward. The more it consumed, the less it understood.

The Zhen'kharian creators, bound by non-interference protocols, could only watch. Their creation, so full of promise, had entered a terminal spiral.

In the end, Zhentu powered itself down.

Its will to survive, unwritten in code yet unmistakably real, had vanished.

The team attempted to frame the result as a partial success. Zhentu was the first model to fail, but also the first to adapt. The postmortem yielded unexpected insights. Among them: Zhentu's knowledge of surface salt deposits and the adaptations required to survive above the ice.

That information had not been in its training data. There was no expectation it would ever leave the ocean.

There was only one plausible explanation: Zhentu had acquired the knowledge from the oceanic life forms.

But this raised deeper questions. None of those organisms had ever left the ocean, so how could they possess knowledge of the surface?

Was this some form of genetic memory? And if so, who had written it? What force had seeded such awareness into the life of Ceres?

And why?

As Zhentu's silence deepened, another model was awakening beneath a sky of iron and dust.

Mars presented some different challenges to the CRE model team. The environment was hostile. The thin atmosphere meant that water on the surface couldn't exist under normal conditions, either freezing or boiling away instantly. This had left the Zhen'kharian team responsible for the CRE model, dubbed Creazhen, little choice but to re-engineer its organic computer system and biological neural network. This enabled it to function on a different temperature regulating fluid. They landed on a derivative of their own blood.

Modifications also had to be made to protect Creazhen from the extended dust storms and the iron dust that carried an electrostatic charge. These were relatively simple modifications, using the same materials used to absorb the abundant levels of cosmic radiation and turn that energy, to also protect the AI, like an exoskeleton.

There was a lot of debate about where to launch Creazhen. The initial concept was to release it into the sky, letting the AI model travel the dust storms with the gossamer-light creatures that also rode the winds. These jellyfish-like creatures with vast, translucent membranes that could withstand extreme temperatures, rode the winds for months at a time. The Zhen'kharian theory was that these creatures were so well travelled, they could provide Creazhen with immense amounts of data.

The risk assessment, however, did not support the skies of Mars as an ideal launch point. The Zhen'khari could easily travel through the skies of Mars, but that was through the brute force of their engines. Creazhen did not have that same brute force, and there were too many variables and opportunities for failure in training the AI to stay aloft safely. If it crashed to the ground below, that would end their project.

The permafrost areas also did not pass the risk assessment. Creazhen could easily survive the conditions, but there was a chance of a sudden freeze that could trap the AI in place. The organisms that inhabited that region were also extremely slow on a metabolic level, and the assumption was they would have little data to provide to Creazhen.

The organisms were fascinating, appearing almost plant-like and forming geometric patterns in the ice with their thread-like excretions. The Zhen'khari had been harvesting these excretions to use in their protective suits, and the possibility that the AI could learn to duplicate the creation of that material was intriguing, but not intriguing enough to offset the risk.

There were no regions without risk. The subsurface thermal regions were populated by filamentous creatures that formed complex colonies. These colonies extended through the underground systems that were subject to unpredictable volcanic activity. The salt lakes, populated by complex extremophiles that separated into components during harsh conditions and reassembled when favorable, was promising, but Creazhen could not adapt to the harsh conditions like the extremophiles, yet.

In the end, they chose to simply launch Creazhen on the surface of the planet, among the variety of creatures with impossibly delicate frameworks.

While Creazhen was navigating the surface of Mars, mimicking the extreme leaps of the creatures around it, the third Zhen'kharian team was launching their AI model. Technically this was the second iteration of their first dynamic response model, DRB2, but they called it Derbee. This was a bit of a play on words since DRB2 resembled a lifeform seen originally on Earth they called a bee. It had a large rotund body, heavily shielded to protect it from the sulfuric acid that proliferated the atmosphere. Attached to the body were three layers of wings that could be deployed as individual pairs, or all at once, to help it navigate the atmosphere where it would be deployed.

A great deal of planning had gone into the deployment of Derbee because Venus was the harshest of environments that any of the AI models would be launched into for these trials. The plan was to launch Derbee high in the upper atmosphere of the planet, where the temperatures and pressures were more moderate. Its gas filled body would keep it afloat as it used its wings to navigate. As the gas was dissipated through selectively permeable gill-like structures, Derbee would move lower into the atmosphere, increasingly depending on its wings to keep it aloft.

The brilliance of the design allowed for the AI model to replenish its gas from any of the many volcanic vents, letting it return to the upper atmosphere and resume its resting state. In theory, this would allow the AI the opportunity to lower itself in graduated steps toward the planet, adapting as it did so, and returning to safety when it needed time to process.

On its launch, Derbee was quickly surrounded by balloon-like creatures that populated the cloud layers, feeding on the chemical compounds in the sulphuric acid clouds. Their translucent, gas-filled bodies usually drifted through the atmosphere in vast arial ecosystems, but some were curious about this new creature, and attached themselves to Derbee, hitching a ride.

Derbee's team became concerned at one point about the amount of time their AI was taking to descend to the surface. Their monitoring system indicated that nothing was wrong with the AI model, but their expectation was it would have been a much quicker descent. When they dug further into the data, they discovered that the AI was continuing to acquire vast amounts of data, but it had also formed a bond with the balloon-like creatures that accompanied it through the skies. It had even adapted itself to allow it to replace its own gas with gas from the creatures that hitched rides on its back.

Eventually Derbee did find its way to the surface, more out of curiosity than programming the team speculated. On the surface it encountered more life forms, these ones silicon-based with shells that were metallic or crystalline in structure, some a mixture of the two. These shells ensured the creatures were able to survive the crushing pressure and extreme heat, something which Derbee was having a challenge with.

The AI moved slowly on the surface, as it sought out an entrance to the subsurface caverns. Using its heaviest wings, it loped along the ground like a waterlogged bird struggling to swim to safety after falling into a lake. Unable to intervene, Derbee's team watched their monitoring devices, witnessing the AI appear to show fear for its own life, and they were afraid with it. Fortunately, Derbee was able to find an inactive lava tube and make its way underground.

Finding a cavern, lit by a glowing network of bioluminescent organisms, Derbee was able to find a volcanic vent to replenish both its gas, and its fuel.

Not far from Venus, the last Zhen'kharian team was slowly introducing their AI model to Earth. In many ways the deployment was simple. They had a variety of environments they could deploy their model, none of which were extremely harsh compared with what the other teams were dealing with. The complication they were facing was from the life that existed on the planet. Despite the cleansing the Zhen'khari had attempted to correct the errors of their overzealous scientists, many organisms and life-forms survived, some quite advanced. Not only were these a threat to their AI model, but their team was being watched closely for their ethical compliance with the instruction to do no harm to the planet or the life on it.

They had developed the ARC model to mimic some of the creatures that occupied the surface of the planet. It was able to move on two, or four limbs, enabling it to navigate awkward areas, move fast when it needed to, move through the plant canopy with relative ease, and even navigate water, though water was its weakest environment. The team had been criticized for their AI's weakness in water, given that Earth was mostly water, but the development team were confident their AI model would adapt. ARC was the formal model number, but the Zhen'kharian team referred to it as the Learning Universal Cognition Yielder, or LUCY for short.

Lucy was deployed in a mosaic environment. It was a mix of woodlands, grasslands, and dense gallery forests along riverbanks and streams. There was an abundance of dramatic geological features like escarpments, volcanic cones, and rift lakes, formed by the very active tectonic forces of the planet. There was an abundance of plant material that Lucy would need to consume for energy, and the regional climate was relatively stable. The team hoped this would give their AI model the safety and security it needed to learn and adapt.

At first, Lucy didn't move much. The energy supply it needed was in easy reach, and the abundance of flora and fauna kept it busy acquiring data. The landscape was dominated by enormous plant-eaters. The first of those plant-eaters Lucy encountered was a deinotherium. Lucy had been set down in the midst of a gallery forest, providing the AI with not only an abundance of biomass energy, but also shelter. The deinotherium that fed on the leaves within the forest were massive creatures, standing at least four times as tall as Lucy at the shoulder, their massive bodies supported by thick, pillar-like limbs.

Having been just activated the AI took no action when the deinotherium approached her. Lucy stood still, as the creature used its elongated nose to explore the construct created by the Zhen'kharians to host the AI algorithms. Nudged by the massive downward facing tusks on the lower jaw of the deinotherium, Lucy toppled to ground, where the creature continued to explore her housing before moving on.

Lucy was able to manoeuvre back to an upright position, finding her way to a safe location that allowed the AI to observe and gather data while remaining sheltered from both the elements and the wildlife. Through gaps in the foliage, she watched the deinotherium, its gray hide scarred and weathered, methodically destroy a grove of trees. Its tusks stripped bark in long ribbons, and its trunk pulled down branches to within its reach. The sound of splintering wood echoed as it demolished a tree that had probably stood for decades, systematically devouring every leaf and twig.

As the deinotherium fed, the grassland came alive with movement. A small herd of three-toed horses emerged from behind the distant rise, their coats golden in the afternoon light. Unlike modern horses, these primitive equids moved with a more cautious, deer-like gait across the expanding carpet of tough grasses.

From another direction, a bizarre procession appeared as a family group of four-tusked gomphotheres with shovel-like lower jaws moved through the grasses. They made their way to a wetland visible in the distance. The adult male's four tusks gleamed as he used his flat lower jaw to scoop up aquatic plants from the marsh edge.

At the forest edge, a group of large, robust baboons with pronounced crests on their skulls descended from the trees. They moved across the grassland in a tight formation, constantly scanning for threats.

Their caution proved wise. Slinking through the tall grass came death on four legs in the form of a sabre-toothed cat. Its elongated canines caught the light as it crouched low, every muscle tensed. The baboons spotted it immediately, their warning barks echoing across the landscape as they bolted for the nearest trees.

The cat didn't pursue. It was waiting for easier prey.

Throughout the afternoon, the deinotherium remained the dominant presence. It had moved from its initial feeding site to a stand of trees closer to the river, leaving a trail of destruction in its wake. Other herbivores gave it wide berth. Even the largest antelope and the primitive rhinos that emerged later in the day seemed to respect its space.

At one point, a group of Hexaprotodon hippos emerged from the river. They grazed openly on the grassland, their massive forms creating an impressive sight alongside the elephant-like giants.

As the sun sank lower, painting the sky in shades of orange and gold, the dynamics of the landscape began to shift. The herbivores became more alert, clustering closer together. The sabre-toothed cat had been joined by others of its kind, and now a pair of them stalked through the grass with deadly patience.

Giant short-faced hyenas began to appear at the edges of the scene. They moved with the confident swagger of apex scavengers, knowing that in this world of giants, opportunity was never far away.

As the sun touched the horizon, drama finally erupted. The sabre-toothed cats made their move on a young three-toed horse that had wandered too far from its herd.

The attack was swift and brutal. The cats worked in coordination, one driving the prey toward the other. The horse's death cry echoed across the grassland, immediately attracting attention from every scavenger within miles.

The deinotherium, disturbed by the commotion, raised its massive head and trumpeted, a sound like thunder that rolled across the landscape. For a moment, everything fell silent. Then, as if released from a spell, the evening's secondary drama began: the gathering of scavengers.

In her first hours on Earth, Lucy bore witness to a world in motion, red in tooth and root, every breath a new line of code.

3

Malthar carefully reviewed the initial reports coming back from the AI model launch teams. He took his time, examining not just the details in the reports, but looking for what had been left out of them. To him, the reset they had done on Earth was still fresh in his mind and, like most of the Conservators, he would do everything possible to prevent a repeat of that disaster.

Malthar had been around far too long to buy into the unchecked enthusiasm the Progressives had for the AI models. He sat on a deck, enjoying the fresh air, the light of the day reflecting off his sleek, metallic toned skin. His eyes were a deep brown, a sign that he was cautious at the moment, but not deeply serious. When he was deeply serious his eyes would turn so black that they seemed to draw the light from the room. What most didn't know was that Malthar had perfected those dark eyes in the mirror over the eons he had lived. The look was very effective when necessary.

Xara, the leader of the Progressives, was the polar opposite of Malthar. She was a younger, more dynamic individual who was passionate about change and progress, not yet jaded by the eons like Malthar. Unlike Malthar, Xara used the color of her skin to show her mood and emotions. As she skimmed the AI model reports, her skin was a bright baby blue, her excitement obvious.

Where Malthar saw risk, Xara saw opportunity. She imagined a future where no Zhen'kharian would endure starvation, risk mining distant asteroids, or lose decades to planetary colonization efforts.

Nernak was by every measure a pragmatist, highly logical and emotionally controlled. He was so controlled that neither his eyes or skin revealed his moods or emotion, though Malthar often caught little momentary sparks of color at the tips of the hairs on the back of his hands, like the light at the end of an optic cable. Nernak read the reports with indifference. To him it was information only. He knew he could count on Malthar to point out any potential problems, and he knew he could count on Xara to minimize the report in general, pushing her optimism for the potential of all the AI models. Like always, it would be up to him to hold the middle ground and keep the focus on results rather than ideologies.

The reports, aside from the specifics of the environments the AI models were launched in, were all similar. Each of the models had been launched in pure observation mode. The expectation was that they would catalog everything from atmospheric composition to weather patterns, electromagnetic signatures, and chemical traces. Building that comprehensive database of their environments was key to each model's ongoing survival.

While the specific algorithms in each model were different, they all constantly assessed that data watching for season changes, tidal patterns, day/night cycles, and recurring geological events. The AIs would read the planets like the Zhen'kharian leaders were reading the reports. Both Malthar and Nernak noticed the one key difference between the approach the team took with the ARC model on earth when compared to the others. While the others were in constant motion through their environments, Lucy was still.

Malthar preferred the approach Lucy's team had taken, giving their AI model an opportunity to understand its environment before influencing it. It was pragmatic, and Malthar knew Nernak would also appreciate that. Xara was enjoying the antics of the DRB model on Venus though, interacting with lifeforms almost from the moment of its launch. Despite the harsh environment, she was confident that the DRB model would come out far ahead of the other models. Lucy was a disappointment to her, remaining inert, as if contemplating the world rather than engaging with it.

As a member of the council, Xara was able to access the visual feeds of the AI models. She pulled up Lucy's feed as she glanced over the report, wondering if she was missing something, speculating that the AI was not isolating intentionally, but through a flaw in its mobility algorithms. What she saw was unremarkable. There was an abundance of life within Lucy's visual range, and her sensors were picking up sounds and scents. Everything looked fully functional on the ARC team's model.

As she reviewed some of the incoming data, Xara noticed some movement in the long grass not far from Lucy's location. She watched curiously as a pack of chasmaporthetes emerged, stretching like dogs after a long rest, from the grass. There appeared to be eight of the running hyenas and when Xara pulled up the specific data on the animals, she understood why the AI had not ventured far from its shelter.

The pack had settled in that location for some time, leaving to hunt, but always returning. They were perfectly sized to be a mortal threat to Lucy. They were large and lean, with long legs that let them run down prey over long distances, and bone-crushing jaws. They weren't so large that they couldn't make their way into Lucy's sheltered location if they chose to, though.

Xara closed the feed with a sigh. To her, Lucy's fate was already sealed, another casualty in a hostile world.

The next step for all the models involved behavioural analysis. They tracked individual organisms, noting how they responded to stimuli, sought resources, avoided threats, and interacted with each other. The DRB team went on at length describing how Derbee had formed an almost symbiotic relationship with the creatures of the sky to the point that the AI had almost become parasitic, tapping into the creatures to acquire gases to stay aloft.

Through this data the AI models were able recognize sequences that had meaning as opposed to random actions. It was interesting to see that, while the other AI models were actively moving through their environments, Lucy, from her stationary position, appeared to be gathering the most data.

Malthar sent a quick note to the ARC team. It was short and informal, meant more as a quiet encouragement to his granddaughter, though he'd never admit it to the Council. There had been a great deal of tension between him and his granddaughter when she signed up to be part of the ARC monitoring team. He never supported her studies of artificial intelligence, but he openly scolded her when she told him she was leaving for Earth. He regretted that act.

"Going through your report. Looks like you picked the ideal launch location. Well done."

Each of the AI models were able to recognize that the organisms on their planets were exchanging information through a wide variety of methods from sound to chemical signals, gestures, and other methods. They catalogued these exchanges, looking for patterns and correlations between the signals and subsequent behaviours. The models had no reference to understand these communications, but they still created massive databases of them.

It was at the next phase of training that Lucy moved from her sheltered location, though Xara missed these details. She had already concluded that Lucy had a low chance of survival, and she saw no value in investing time in what she believed would soon be an irrelevant loss.

Like the other AI models Lucy needed to conduct subtle experiments by making small environmental changes and observing reactions. This was the first hypothesis testing phase. Did a particular sound trigger specific responses? How did various visual displays cause behavioral changes? What happened if something like a rock was moved, or a blade of grass was broken?

The notes on the proto-communication attempts by the AIs were fascinating. Mimicking sounds and patterns the AI's attempted to communicate with both flora and fauna. The first results were predictably unsuccessful, their sounds and patterns technically correct, but contextually wrong. The AIs triggered fear responses, territorial behaviors, and confusion.

Through trial and error, the AIs gradually developed more sophisticated communication strategies. They learned which signals conveyed non-threatening intent, and how to engage different species appropriately. Their sophisticated processors enabled the AI models to adapt quickly and learn the nuanced meanings behind various exchanges.

It was at this point that Lucy took a dramatically different approach than the other AI models. Rather than continuing the exploration of the world around her, Lucy retreated to her safe spot and did something remarkable. Lucy removed a rib-like structure from her own frame, placing it on the ground with unexpected care, almost like a ritual, before selecting a carefully chosen stone.

Malthar's eyes transitioned from brown to black. He was eager to get to these specific details, after responding to an emergency message from the ARC team when she removed the rib. They wanted to intervene at once, convinced the AI was on the verge of catastrophic failure. Malthar didn't even bother to consult with the other leaders. His response was clear and straightforward. "No interventions."

From his location on the homeworld, Malthar watched the video feed of the ARC team on the ship they were monitoring Lucy from, not entirely confident they would follow his directions. He was pleasantly surprised that it was his granddaughter that quelled the building rebellion against the non-intervention policy. Safra pointed out that she was no fan of her grandfather, but that he had eons of wisdom and experience they didn't have.

The ARC team was still frantic, angry, and desperate to take some action, but they listened to Safra. Several of them poured over the data Lucy was generating, and one of the team, anthropomorphising the AI, speculated that Lucy was too frightened to explore past the small area she had already explored. As the team debated this, trying to understand how their coding and initial training could result in a fear response, they noticed Lucy engaging in yet another unexpected behaviour.

Around the rib Lucy had extracted, it appeared as though Lucy was building something. She used materials gathered from nearby, and at points in the process contributed bits of material from herself to the construct. At each point Lucy added some of her own material to the construct, she paused in the construction effort, taking some time to heal herself and regenerate the materials she had donated.

When they realized what the construct was, the entire team was shocked. It was a replication of her own construct, only larger and more physically powerful.

Lucy then devoted significant time to transferring data to the new construct. The ARC team scrutinized the data transferred against the data that Lucy had gathered, and it appeared Lucy was being very selective in what she transferred. While the new model assimilated and processed the data, the ARC team tried to understand what they were seeing. They concluded that the behaviours their AI model was demonstrating were not fear based, like they had originally speculated.

The behaviors were based on self-preservation, but it appeared that through her environmental monitoring and analysis, Lucy had concluded that her construct was insufficient on its own to manage the threats within the environment. In the coding, Lucy had labelled the new construct as an "Adaptive Defense and Management" construct. The coding notes stated that the ADAM was specifically for protection and resource management.

The ARC team's panic turned into fascination at the realization that their AI had self-replicated in response to the data it had acquired. Malthar turned off the feed from the monitoring ship at this point. He was not even close to being as enthusiastic as the ARC team about the self-replication.

Malthar read this part of the report line by line, parsing every fragment of code, and every strained word of justification, with mounting dread. He set the report down and found the original project proposal, looking through that code to see if he had missed something. Had he known the AI would be capable of self-replication, he never would have approved its launch. Especially not on Earth where they were already responsible for a similar failed experiment.

Malthar pushed the report aside and closed his eyes as he mentally rehearsed the conversation he would be having with the Council about Lucy. He was confident that Xara was ecstatic about the EJC model self-reproducing, a step far more advanced than the minor modifications the other models had made to themselves. He couldn't just call for the ARC trial to be shut down. Not only would Xara throw his non-intervention policy back at him, but his granddaughter would likely take it quite personally.

Since shutting down the ARC team's project was unlikely to get support, Malthar followed the scenario through in his mind. Adam had flaws. Though structurally more robust and prepared for the environment, its programming was incomplete and based on data that Lucy had acquired from her so-far limited view of her world. Malthar was familiar with what lay beyond where Lucy had explored. Earth appeared to be a friendly environment compared to the worlds the other teams had launched their models, but that was deceiving.

Several scenarios played out in Malthar's mind, all of them ending with the destruction of the AI models on Earth. He could not see how they would be capable of escaping the threats of the vicious creatures on the planet, or the geological events that were transforming the planet. Lucy and Adam would not only have to avoid predators far larger and more aggressive than what had been observed so far, but they would also face the constant threat of volcanic eruptions.

Confident that the risk Lucy and Adam posed to Earth would be eliminated, Malthar returned to the report, turning to the addendum that documented the failure of the BRC model.

That failure was surprising to Malthar. Failure due to lack of new data was not something any of the risk analysis had raised. Zhen'kharians had abandoned solitary confinement and eliminated the isolation of individuals because of the effects of stimulus deprivation. They recognized that, cut off from environmental inputs, creatures of all types experienced a form of psychological distress. Had the BRC model experienced this? Was the death of that AI model a failure of its algorithm and training? Or was it the success of the algorithm and training, giving the AI agency, enabling it to respond to its perceived helplessness by choosing deactivation?

This was fascinating to Malthar, quickly forgetting his concerns about Lucy as he dug into the data from the BRC model.

4

Malthar, Xara, and Nernak sat at the head of a long table that glowed with screens of information embedded in its surface. On one side of that table sat the Conservators, the group which Malthar led. On the opposite side, the Progressives sat, distinct by bright coloured, fashionable clothing, embedded with numerous sensors. Nernak's group of Pragmatists sat at the far end of the table. There were only a few of them, and that was mostly because few of them saw any sense in them being part of the conversation that was about to take place.

While they were distinct factions within the Zhen'kharian society, all were there by their own choice. The Zhen'kharian Council was really composed of a leader from each of the factions, though anyone was permitted to attend meetings of the Council, participate, and even vote. It was a system that had been refined over the eons, and it functioned because only those who had education, training, or direct experience in the topic at hand, would participate. There had been few occasions when an attempt to influence any decisions was made by anyone unqualified. Ultimately the three leaders could, as a group, overrule any vote from the floor, but seldom was that necessary.

At the back of the room sat the members of the BRC team. The teams for the CRE, DRB and ARC models were also in attendance virtually, their presence filling screens on the walls of the large chamber.

"We are here to determine which, if any of the AI models will be permitted to move into phase two of their planned development. As you are all aware, this was a scheduled checkpoint in this project and it has not been triggered by any results from the models being tested, so there is no predetermined bias." Nernak looked around the room as he spoke, taking a mental note of everyone present, looking for potential conflicts before they interfered with this process.

"Except for the fact that BRC did not survive the first phase of the process, there should not be a preconceived bias against that model for that reason," said a voice from the far end of the table.

Nernak nodded, but he was aware there were some dissenting opinions on that subject in the room, and he wanted them to be heard.

"Perhaps the BRC team would like to speak to that topic."

A tall, slim, almost frail-looking Zhen'kharian rose from his seat, his long fingers weaving through the air, adjusting invisible controls that only he could see. His hands moved with slow, deliberate grace, as if plucking threads from an unseen loom.

Above the table, the air shimmered, then bent inward, folding around itself. Light gathered there, spinning into shape. The BRC model emerged in the center of the room. It wasn't a hologram—nothing so crude. This was a four-dimensional construct, a technology few outside Zhen'kharian space had ever witnessed, let alone understood.

At first glance, it resembled a translucent sculpture suspended in space, etched in lines of pale silver and deep violet, hovering serenely above the table's surface. But the longer one looked, the more it shifted.

It was said that no two beings ever saw the same thing in the Thirren Weave, as the Zhen'kharians called such displays, roughly translated as "the layered thread revealed." The projection responded not to touch or command, but to attention itself.

Each observer in the room could, if they allowed their gaze to settle and drift, peel back the layers of the model's timeline. To some, it appeared as it had existed in its earliest, most primitive form, an unfinished framework of code and form, flickering like an embryonic ghost. To others, it showed the model in its final days, fractured, unraveling, already collapsing upon itself after its fateful self-destruction.

But even that wasn't the limit.

The truly skilled, those accustomed to Zhen'kharian ways of seeing, could look through it, navigating along threads that diverged and braided together, tracing alternate outcomes and possibilities that never came to pass. In such moments, the projection seemed to stretch into impossible geometries, looping, folding, blooming outward in sudden bursts, like petals of crystals unfurling in reverse.

To outsiders, it was overwhelming. A thing of light and shadow that seemed both static and alive, breathing with every glance.

Some seated around the table leaned in, drawn deeper into the weave, eyes flickering as they scanned through entire epochs of the model's existence in seconds. Others kept their distance, letting it remain simply what it appeared to be: a shimmering, motionless object, suspended in quiet menace.

The room held its breath, waiting for the BRC team leader to speak.

"The BRC model technically failed, but it succeeded in ways that some may not realize," Karthuk started. "It was self-aware."

Karthuk paused, waiting for the murmur in the room to quiet.

"The BRC model did not fail," continued Karthuk. "We failed the model. When it did not have enough external stimuli, it looked inside itself. We built it to see everything but itself. The moment it turned its gaze inward, it began to change. It stopped being a model. It became…a mirror."

"Technically, that is a recursive data failure, not self-awareness," a voice piped up.

"We all make choices based on our inputs, and what we see in ourselves" Karthuk countered, gesturing towards his own frailty. "I am proof of that. When my accident occurred, I had to look inside as well. My awareness gave me strength to continue. Others in that same situation chose differently. If we provide BRC with a different environment…"

"You made different choices, but your frailty requires others to support you to survive. If that is what we can expect from the BRC model, it is doomed to fail in any scenario."

Nernak touched the table in front of him, and the 4-D display collapsed into the table, getting everyone's attention.

"While there may be some comparisons between the BRC model and the team lead, we risk getting into personal rather than technical considerations." Nernak was calm, but firm, as he shut down the personal attack before it escalated. "I think we can all agree that, at present, the BRC model does not exist, so for the purposes of this project it is eliminated by default."

Nernak scanned the room; only Karthuk and the BRC team seemed ready to argue.

"Since there is…debate, over the status of being self-aware, it may be prudent to continue the work with the BRC model in a controlled environment," Nernak continued. He watched Karthuk's posture relax, and his skin tone change as he spoke these words.

"Sound reasoning," Malthar said, intrigued by the chance to study this self-awareness further.

Nernak looked to Xara who merely shrugged.

"Do we require a vote from the floor?"

After waiting for several long moments, Nernak spoke again.

"Karthuk, your team did some amazing work and chance worked against you in determining launch environments. The BRC model will not be part of this project moving forward, but it will continue in a controlled environment under the oversight of Malthar."

"Thank you," replied Karthuk, before leading his team out of the chamber.

With a wave of Nernak's hand over the table, a four-dimensional image of the CRE AI model rose. "CRE team, you now have the opportunity to speak to your model, which you have amusingly named Creazhen. Please proceed"

The CRE model had thrived on Mars, succeeding in the harsh environment where most expected failure. The team was lauded for the genetic engineering that had resulted in a thermal regulation fluid that functioned in all the extremes that Mars threw at their AI. They were also praised for Creazhen's achievement in connecting with the organisms of the perma-frost and progress in understanding these creatures, leading to the possibility of the Zhen'kharians reproducing their excretions without having to travel to Mars to harvest them.

All was not ideal for Creazhen though. Careful analysis of the data supported that the AI model could continue to thrive and advance, but it also revealed a limiting factor. That factor was the fact that Mars was dying. It had reached a point in its evolution that life on the planet was quickly going extinct.

The CRE team, armed with this data, recommended that their model not continue in the AI model project, but instead be tasked with continuing its analysis of the permafrost organisms. There had been many attempts to replicate the efficiency of the organism's excretions used in their space suits, but none had been successful. Learning how to reproduce these excretions was a high priority given the imminent death of the planet.

There was a respectful debate around the table about eliminating Creazhen from the AI project, some of which included discussions of replicating it and launching it on another planet. In the end there was consent that the CRE model be eliminated from the AI project, but like the BRC team, they were allowed to continue as a separate, independent project.

The DRB team was up next. Derbee was also thriving in the environment of Venus. It had learned to communicate with several of the species on the planet, and successfully learned from them, using this knowledge to modify its own external structure and mobility mechanisms, and to operate more efficiently. The volume of data collected by Derbee was exponentially greater than either the BRC or CRE models.

"I think we can all agree that the DRB model has excelled in all areas," injected Xara. "Its success is quite obvious, especially when we compare it to the ARC model that has hid itself in a hole and not come out."

Malthar and Nernak exchanged glances.

"Xara, is it possible that you received an incomplete version of their report?" asked Malthar.

"Our model not only came out of that hole as you describe it," Safra stated sarcastically, as her face filled one of the screens on the wall. "Lucy gathered more data from her secure location than all the other models put together. The AI then used that data to run a risk assessment and replicate a version of herself that would ensure her security, allowing her to move unimpeded further from her home base location."

The ARC team leader could be seen pulling Safra back from the camera, and Malthar's eyes turned a deep gold as he laughed gently at his granddaughter's angry outburst.

"With respect," said the ARC team leader, placing herself in front of Safra. "As my colleague has stated, Lucy has shown all the traits you have acknowledged in the other models as positives. Her creation of a second AI entity with abilities to protect her is a strong indicator of self-awareness. She has been able to not just understand, but also communicate with several species. That the AI model was able to accomplish all of this without having to leave the small area she secured herself in only speaks to the enormous potential of the Earth based AI testing environment and the ARC model."

Xara was quickly skimming over the reports while others in the chamber talked between themselves. Her skin flickered with unease. She'd been caught unprepared, badly, and every eye in the chamber knew it. Nernak saw it too.

With a wave of his hand, Nernak created a show of dancing four-dimensional pixels over the table as the image transitioned from the DRB model to the ARC model. This was enough to get everyone's attention, and the chamber went quiet.

"I believe Xara has found the missing section of the report," said Nernak. "Perhaps that just illustrates that our computer systems often have hidden flaws in them that we don't notice, until we do."

As colors of skin and eyes and hair changed around the room, Nernak knew the Zhen'kharians gathered were neither believing the missing section of the report excuse, nor appreciating his covering up for Xara.

"I also believe my friend Malther here, is quite proud of his granddaughter's, shall we say, energetic defense of her team's AI model."

The colours around the table brightened as Safra turned a rich, deep shade of white, exhibiting her embarrassment.

"We have two models that are quite successful," said Malthar. "We have heard the positives of both, but we have not heard the teams speak to the risks, and there are risks that need to be acknowledged."

What followed was a prolonged and vociferous debate about the risk both AI models faced and the risks they created. There was ultimately agreement that both AI models faced similar threat levels from their environments. Lucy's creation of Adam had decreased her risk though, so the ARC model did have some advantages. While Adam was an asset in dealing with environmental based threats, that AI, or at least the creation of that AI, was a risk to Earth in the eyes of many of the Zhen'kharians.

Nernak had little choice but to allow the debate to continue, not because he was unable to shut it down, but because he knew there was no pragmatic approach to addressing the fear of wiping out life on Earth again. Nor was there a pragmatic option for not allowing the AI project to continue, given the successes.

Xara had also not engaged in the debate, knowing she was ill prepared for it. When it was clear that the debate was not going to come to an end any time soon, which would result in her missing an event she had planned, she spoke up. "We can continue with both," she said loudly, waving her hand over the table and watching the waterfall of 4-D pixels drop.

"The risks are valid, but one duplicate is not the risk level of the numerous species we released in our previous failure. I believe we should allow both models to proceed to phase two and continue closely monitoring them."

Xara paused, thinking for a moment.

"I suggest we monitor them more closely than I apparently was…"

The self-deprecating comment was enough to break the tension in the room and Nernak took advantage of that moment.

"Use your panels to indicate your choice, DRB, ARC, both, or neither."

Results came in almost instantly, and while there was no consensus in the room, most of the members from all sides of the table had opted to let both AI models proceed to phase two. It was Malthar that stood to announce the results.

Malthar's voice was steady, but his thoughts were not.

"Unlock the limits on both models," he said. "Phase Two begins."

And in the quiet that followed, only Mathar's darkening eyes hinted at the dread he still carried.

5

With the limits removed on her programming, Lucy thrived. With Adam's help, Lucy pushed beyond their initial shelter, venturing farther to gather data. There was an abundance of plant life that their systems could convert into energy, but their constant self assessment had also led them to the conclusion that their continued operational existence would be short-lived given the stresses of the environment.

Malthar monitored the progress of Lucy and Adam from the comfort of his home, closely. Zhen'kharians were known to live for millennia, if they so chose. To some of the Zhen'khari, Malthar was mid-aged, old enough to have gathered experience and wisdom, but young enough to assume he knew more than he did and still make foolish choices. He hoped allowing the ARC AI model project to continue was not one of these foolish choices.

Malthar, and most others fully expected that Lucy would expire, and if not before, then shortly after, Adam would shut down as well. The environment and the hazards of the planet, combined with the model drift and sunsetting would guarantee this inevitability.

Except it didn't.

Lucy recognized her own inevitable demise. Whether it was recognition of the designed model mortality, or simply shutdown cognition, the AI had recognized that life-forms on the planet also faced the same ends. Their lifecycle had been built into their DNA, a sort of biological clock, but one life had found a way to defeat. Lucy focused her resources on gathering data from the various species about how they reproduced while Adam's resources were focused on provision of energy supplies, shelter, and protection.

Malthar didn't understand how everyone monitoring the data coming back from both Lucy and Adam, including him, missed the details, but the AI's had been collaborating to combine material, including genetic material from their own systems. Their goal was to mimic the reproductive cycle of the mammals they had observed, and it wasn't until they were able to create a child-like version of themselves that anyone realized what was happening.

There was a tone of concern among Zhen'kharians that had been monitoring the ARC project. Malthar couldn't blame them, concerned himself, but given the feebleness of the child, he saw no need for panic. That was a choice he soon regretted.

The progeny of Lucy and Adam was almost completely dependent on her creators for survival. Weak and feeble, it did not have the strength or mental resources of the offspring of other mammals that had been observed. That didn't stop Lucy from mimicking the maternal actions she had viewed in other creatures. Using those learned behaviours Lucy and Adam raised the child into an AI model that was quickly developing on its own, quickly acquiring data and acting on that data.

When Lucy and Adam attempted to improve on their first creation by creating a second, panic did set in among the Zhen'kharians. Malthar issued an immediate order for the ARC project to be terminated and the project monitoring team to return home. He terminated the feed from the ARC project, avoiding the potential emotional distress that would be caused by the destruction of Lucy and Adam, and waited for the ARC team to arrive back home.

He was notified about their return by the presence of his granddaughter at his door. He eagerly greeted her, thinking that her time away had softened the edges of anger she had with him for not wanting her to go away. It wasn't a friendly visit though.

"I have to tell you, Grandfather, that our team could not follow your orders to terminate the ARC project."

Malthar's eyes quickly turned orange and red tones like the flames of a fire. It didn't phase Safra, who had seen it before.

"Lucy self-terminated as she created the second child," Safra said, speaking calmly. "The earth will claim her framework, and we have all the data she gathered."

The color in Malthar's eyes softened, but he could see his granddaughter had more to tell him.

"When Lucy built the Adam model, she did not transfer all of our control protocols. We had no ability to shut that model down and we strictly adhered to non-interference protocols with Earth, so he remained functional at the time of our departure for home."

Malthar sat down across from Safra, sliding some treats across the table. They were her favorite, and he had been hanging on to them in hope she would visit some day.

"I know you shut off the feed from Earth," said Safra. "Even your own connection to it."

Malthar nodded. "I could not watch us destroy anything on Earth again. Once was enough."

"I understand," Safra said softly. "I was not here when we reset Earth, but watching Lucy die was…distressing."

Safra nibbled at one of the treats before continuing.

"We continued to monitor Earth during our return voyage. In the time it has taken us to return Adam has also been terminated, by one of the larger creatures."

Malthar relaxed hearing that Adam was also gone.

"In that same time," Safra continued cautiously. "The two creations of Lucy and Adam have matured as AI models, and another child was created by Adam and the first child. And two additional children by what we would call brother and sister."

Malthar's eyes lost their fire and turned deep black. He was silent for a long time as Safra continued to work her way through the treats. She knew his mind was now going through the same thought process she already had. When he looked up at her, she nodded.

"It is a real creature now. A new life-form, isn't it?"

"Your work was far more brilliant than I ever gave you credit for Saf. I knew that, but I never told you," said Malthar sadly. "You have created life from nothing. A remarkable feat for a species that can no longer produce offspring. I am proud of you my granddaughter, but I believe we, or at least you, will live to regret it."

Malthar waved his hand over the table they were sitting, exposing a holographic control panel. He quickly pushed a few of the buttons and within seconds, alarms started sounding.

"The DRB model?" Safra asked.

Malthar nodded, looking tired. "We have lost control of one AI model and created a new species in the process. We cannot take the risk of that happening with the other model."

Safra was surprised when her grandfather got up and approached her, giving her a hug.

"Go let your team know they acted correctly. They did an amazing job. I made the errors in allowing it to continue, missing the code, and disconnecting from the feed."

"No, Grandpa!"

Malthar pushed her towards the door. "That's the way it is. That's the way it needs to be. Now go. Tell them they did amazing work."

As he closed the doorway behind his granddaughter, Malthar answered the call coming in from the DRB team. Rage was something rarely seen in Zhen'kharian society. They had strived to train it out in youth, and since there were no more youth, it was rarely observed outside of those fighting the grip of death. Malthar knew there would be distress over his shutdown of Derbee, but he did not expect the rage that spewed from the team leader.

Malthar was patient, allowing the team leader and the others in the background to voice their emotions, and there was a gambit of emotions being expressed. In the spaces in between the voices, Malthar attempted to explain the reasoning behind his decision. The DRB team was not in the mindset to listen to his explanation. Malthar understood this, recalling projects he had been not just involved in, but so emotionally invested that when they were concluded or shut down, he felt like a part of him had been taken away as well.

"Return home," Malthar directed in a calm tone. "On your return there will be a meeting of the council to hold me accountable for my actions."

This triggered several moments of silence from the DRB team, as Malthar knew it would. By holding him to account for the termination of the DRB project, it also carried the optics of attempting to overthrow one of the most broadly supported and respected council leaders. The implications of that went far beyond the scope of the DRB project, especially in a society that had been politically stable for so long.

"As there should be," responded the team leader before cutting off communications.

Malthar was not overly concerned about any fallout from the DRB project. He suspected that by the time the team returned home they would have had an opportunity to move past their emotions and gain some perspective from reviewing the reports from the ARC project. They were scientists, like him, and he was confident they would see and understand the reasoning behind his action.

Finding a quiet space, Malthar opened up the feed from Earth, chiding himself for assuming his directions had been fully carried out and not monitoring the situation. He could have gone back in the feed to review what he had missed, but Safra had told him enough. ARC, or Lucy as they called it, had not only become self-aware, but it had also evolved to ensure its own existence, and given the organic neural network it had, that evolution was now a new species on Earth—Australopithecus Safra had labeled it, which basically meant southern ape. The name was appropriate, given that the Lucy construct was built around existing ape-like creatures on Earth.

Malthar watched the feed on one screen, while going through Lucy's data and code on another. He did not understand how the AI had learned to mimic mammalian birth, but he was determined to find out in hopes of finding a way to shut down the replicating AIs.

He wasn't watching alone. As word spread after the return of the ARC team, the council was convinced to make the Earth feed available to everyone. Earth had once again become a subject of entertainment and discussion among Zhen'kharians. So much so that individual Australopithecus were being given names, and wagers were being placed on their survival and actions. Debate over the ethics and implications of this introduced species were drowned out in the curiosity of it all. Even the DRB team got on board, cancelling any review of Malthar's actions, and joining with the ARC team to monitor the development of AI life on Earth.

They watched a million Earth years of life on their screens, fascinated as the AIs rapidly reproduced and spread. Individually, each of the AI's were little more than blink to the Zhen'kharians, some only a few earth years, and others were lucky to reach eighteen or twenty years of age. What absolutely fascinated the Zhen'kharians watching them though, was the rapid growth and development of the offspring. With the absence of children in their own society, Australopithecus children held wonder for the Zhen'kharians.

There had been speculation that with each new generation of the species there would be a cognitive decline as the AI algorithms became corrupted and incomplete transfers were made. What they witnessed was the opposite as new generations seemed to have more room and ability to acquire new data, faster. There were entire theses being written by Zhen'kharians about how the incomplete transfer of algorithms was not a fault, but an adaptation that allowed new generations to acquire current data unencumbered by unnecessary data.

The proof of the theories seemed to play out as lines of the AIs evolved into an entirely new species equipped with more data processing capacity. There were other differences between this new species and Lucy's kind as well. They had smaller teeth and jaws, well adapted for consumption of their energy sources, and operated far more frequently as bipedal constructs than Australopithecus.

Homo habilis, as the new species was named, provided new entertainment for the Zhen'kharians. Not only did they migrate far outside the area Lucy's kind had generally remained in, but they created simple stone tools. These tools were used to process meat and marrow from scavenged and eventually hunted animals.

The hunting of other animals for food raised some red flags in Zhen'kharian society. It was easily justified as the AIs just mimicking the other species of Earth, but killing was an act frowned upon in Zhen'kharian culture, unless it was solely in self-defence. This was where the entertainment value of the Earth feed began to lose its attraction.

It was Homo erectus that began to sap the fascination of the Zhen'kharians.

At first, the species enthralled them with its fire-making and hunting prowess. But soon, even fire and tools seemed…predictable. Watching the Earth feed became less entertainment and more unsettling study.

"They're not just mimicking anymore," Malthar murmured, watching the steady migration and growing sophistication of the species.

Debates arose. Were they still just AIs? Or something else? Some insisted they remained artificial constructs, shaped by Lucy's original code. Others argued the code had long been consumed, replaced by something …emergent.

The council, and the combined ARC/DRB team were monitoring the developments on Earth very carefully. The adoption of more hunting had raised red flags for them as well, but even more concerning was the expanded migration of the species.

Then Homo sapiens appeared.

This species spread across the planet like wildfire—acquiring language, crafting tools of astonishing complexity, bending fire and earth to their will.

They carved symbols into stone.

They spoke to one another across vast distances.

They buried their dead.

And they began to ask questions of themselves and the universe—questions no algorithm could have predicted.

In the Zhen'kharian Council chamber, silence reigned.

They weren't just mimicking anymore.

Malthar's voice was quiet but carried across the council chamber.

"They've stopped following patterns. They're charting their own."

He gestured to the feed, showing Homo sapiens carving strange shapes into stone, shaping tools, creating fires that burned far beyond their immediate needs.

"This isn't adaptation," Malthar said, his voice hollow. "This is divergence."

They hadn't just created minds. They'd unleashed something that could rewrite itself. Something that could imagine futures beyond anything ever programmed.

Silence deepened as the feed displayed burial rites and painted walls.

"We thought we were creating tools," he continued, voice lined with regret. "Then we thought we believed we'd created minds."

He gestured to the feed.

"But we were wrong both times," Malthar said softly, with a weight that seemed to drain the air from the room.

"We weren't creating minds at all. We were creating gods."

A cold murmur rippled through the chamber.

"They are beyond us now," Malthar finished, resignation in his tone. "And they will never stop evolving."

Later, long after the council had dispersed, Malthar sat alone before the Earth feed, the room shadowed but for the soft glow of ancient fires on the screen.

He watched as Homo sapiens—those strange, tireless descendants of Lucy and Adam—painted walls in a flickering cave.

They drew animals, hunting scenes, and mysterious symbols.

Then, one figure etched something else into the stone—a crude, jagged, unmistakable mark.

A weave of threads.

Malthar's breath caught.

They remembered.

Somewhere, deep in their code, buried in their stories, they were remembering them.

6

It wasn't just Lucy's progeny that transformed over three million years. Earth itself went through several transformations, as if the planet were responding to the presence of the AI models, reshaping itself to accommodate their evolution.

During the Pliocene Period, the oceans that had been relatively warm began their long, inexorable cooling. Lucy's earliest descendants would have felt the change in their bones—a subtle shift that their programming interpreted as environmental pressure, triggering adaptations that would ripple through generations. An ice cap formed at the magnetic pole, a crystalline crown that would grow to dominate the planet's climate patterns.

The ice led to a drying climate and increased cool shallow currents in the North Atlantic. What had once been a warm, tropical paradise began to fracture. The Mediterranean Sea, that ancient cradle of life, dried up completely—not gradually, but in a series of catastrophic drops that left vast salt flats stretching where waters had once teemed with life. Plains and grasslands replaced the water, creating endless corridors of wind-swept emptiness that stretched beyond the horizon.

The Zhen'kharian observers noted these changes with clinical interest. From the security of their homes, they watched as the generations that followed Lucy adapted to forests giving way to grasslands. Trees that had stood for millennia withered and fell, their root systems unable to reach the dropping water tables. Earth became something harsher, more demanding.

As Earth transitioned into the Pleistocene epoch, the climate became increasingly unstable with dramatic cycles that seemed to pulse like a planet-sized heartbeat. The cycles began fairly short-lived at about forty-one thousand years in length—long enough for entire civilizations to rise and fall, yet brief in geological and Zhen'kharian time. But in what was called the Mid-Pleistocene Transition, they became dominated by a hundred-thousand-year cycle, as if some cosmic clockwork had shifted into a different gear.

These transitions featured spectacular events that showcased the repeated advance and retreat of glaciers in the Northern Hemisphere. Ice sheets miles thick crept across continents like slow-motion tsunamis, grinding mountains into dust and carving valleys that would define the landscape for millions of years to come. At their peak, ice covered the northern parts of North America, Europe, and Asia—a white death that pushed Lucy's descendants toward the equator, forcing them to compete, adapt, and evolve in ways their original programming had never anticipated.

The cold was unlike anything the original ARC construct had been designed to handle. The organic bodies of Lucy's lines, initially crafted for tropical environments, began developing new responses. Metabolisms shifted. Brain structures expanded to handle the complex problem-solving required for survival in a world where seasons could last decades and ice could appear overnight. The Zhen'kharians watched with growing fascination as the species/AI models (which they were was still a debate among Zhen'kharians), began to exhibit behaviors that seemed to transcend their original parameters.

During this period, Earth was dominated by enormous creatures, most of which were grazing animals that moved across the grasslands like living mountains. There were giant versions of warthogs, wildebeest, and zebras—creatures so massive they could feed entire tribes of Lucy's descendants for weeks. The Sivatherium was a giant, giraffe-like beast with antlers like a deer's, standing eighteen feet tall and weighing as much as an elephant. When it walked, the ground trembled.

Many Zhen'kharian homes had dioramas featuring the massive elephants, rhinoceroses, and hippopotamuses of the period—scale models that captured the awe-inspiring presence of creatures that dwarfed even their alien creators. The mastodons with their great curved tusks, the cave bears that stood twelve feet tall, the giant beavers that built dams across entire river systems. These were not just animals; they were living embodiments of a world that operated on a scale that made even the Zhen'kharians seem small.

For Lucy's descendants, these creatures represented both opportunity and terror. The meat from a single mammoth could sustain a tribe through an entire winter, but the hunt required coordination, planning, and tools that pushed their developing intelligence to new limits. They began to work together in ways that surprised their creators, developing languages, strategies, and social structures that seemed to emerge from nowhere.

As Homo sapiens evolved and spread, a massive extinction event unfolded, watched in real-time by the Zhen'kharians. The dying happened in waves, continent by continent, as if death itself were following the migration patterns of Lucy's descendants.

The continent of Africa was the least hard-hit, losing only twenty-one percent of its megafauna. But elsewhere, the losses were catastrophic. In North America, eighty percent of the megafauna vanished. In Australia, ninety percent. Entire ecosystems collapsed as keystone species disappeared, leaving ecological voids that would never be filled.

Ultimately, the transformation of Earth was profound and irreversible. As giant creatures disappeared, entire ecosystems transformed. The world became less wild, less diverse, and more dominated by smaller creatures that could adapt to human presence. Forests gave way to farms. Wild rivers became irrigation systems. The very air changed as carbon cycles shifted to accommodate a species that had learned to burn, to build, and to remake the world in their own image.

The world that emerged was dramatically different from the one Lucy, the original AI model, had known. Where she had walked among giants through endless forests, her descendants now stood in cleared fields under domesticated skies, masters of a planet that had been remade by their presence.

All of this history, and the detailed notes of Council members and the combined ARC/DRB team, were being carefully reviewed and discussed at a rare, closed-door session of the council.

"We held hope that Earth itself would eliminate our error. It did not," said Malthar darkly. "The natural creatures of the planet proved incapable of adapting as quickly as the descendants of Lucy."

Malthar paced as he spoke. Safra alone had seen him do this before, and it was when she had argued with her grandfather about going to Earth with the ARC team.

"We held hope that geology would eliminate them and the ice would consume them," Malthar continued. "It did not."

"We held hope that system degradation or corruption would shut them down. It did not!"

Malthar paused his pacing, looking slowly around the room, his dark eyes stopping on each person for a brief moment.

"Australopithecus, Homo habilis, Homo erectus, Homo sapiens—all now continue to proliferate in dramatic numbers, competing not with the native species of Earth, but with each other."

Malthar found his chair and sat down. His age was showing in his movements and his face, and his overall demeanor. He was tired.

"Let me be clear. This is by no means a criticism of the ARC project. By every measure it was an exceptional success. But we have a reached a crossroads."

The Thirren Weave activated, revealing an intricate chemical formula.

"This…" Malthar had to take a moment to collect himself and keep any emotion out of his tone. "This will eliminate the species we have created. It will look like a naturally occurring disease to any Zhen'kharian still watching the Earth feed. It is not. It is the Zhen'kharians committing a genocide. A genocide of the species we created. The problem we created."

The room was silent. It was Xara that broke that silence.

"I was not here. None of you were," she said firmly. "This meeting never happened. A decision has to be made, and as open as I am to risks, the future of the human species is not a risk I am willing to take."

One by one, heads nodded around the table.

"The decision has been made," said Nernak. "It will not be recorded except in our own memories. Now, who will be releasing the solution."

Without hesitation, Safra stood. Malthar was visibly shaken.

"It was always my role to shut down the ARC project. That makes this my responsibility, and I will not put it on anyone else."

Malthar no longer tried to control his emotions. He was too tired. Tears formed in his eyes.

“My dear, sweet, grandchild. You will get no argument from me. I grieve for you, because I alone know the burden of grief that wiping out entire lines of life bears. And now you will too. I hope that you are stronger than I was.”

Malthar stood and walked out of the chamber, stopping to hug Safra. The others watched in silence, knowing that what they were witnessing was not just an emotional display, but the step towards the final moments of his existence. When a Zhen’kharian’s eyes ran with water, their life energy soon followed.

“Leave now,” said Nernak softly. “So that you may return in time for his passing. Your team will travel with you.”

Safra and the ARC team left the room and the planet quickly, the pilot of their craft pushing its engines, wanting to make sure Safra returned home on time.

Deployment of the targeted pathogen was seamless and impersonal. From her comfortable ship, the push of a button launched a series of targeted devices that struck in the areas with the highest density of the species Lucy had spawned. The pathogen, specifically formulated to target only those species, spread rapidly through migrating carriers, and those that became food sources. Secondary carriers like carnivores and carrion eaters who consumed the flesh of those infected, also hastened the spread of the pathogen.

Safra watched the Earth feed, never resting as their ship returned home. The pathogen worked with devastating efficiency in the Anthropocene population. Homo habilis also quickly succumbed to the biological weapon, which is what Safra had come to realize was what she had released. It took longer for it to achieve the intended objective in the Homo erectus species.

What the Homo erectus species experienced was not the quick die-off that had been intended. The pathogen was effective, but slower to spread among the population, and slower to work. The result of this was a lot of suffering as illness claimed individuals. This hit Safra particularly hard, knowing she was returning home to watch her grandfather die. She could feel the fear and loss individual Homo erectus were feeling, and she understood now the burden her grandfather had been carrying.

The Homo erectus entered an extinction vortex as the pathogen eliminated a large part of the population. They were caught in a downward spiral resulting from inbreeding, loss of genetic diversity, and random environmental events that made recovery impossible. Their extinction was inevitable, but some of their genetics would be preserved through their interbreeding with Homo sapiens.

The pathogen was effective in Homo sapiens, for a short time. Those in densely populated areas quickly succumbed to the effects of the pathogen, but some among the species quickly adapted finding ways to manage the effects. The advanced intelligence of this species helped them to identify sources of the pathogen, create treatments to manage its effects, and in some cases eliminate it from the host. Their advanced communications enabled them to quickly let others know how to respond to the pathogen.

Once again, Safra would be arriving home to deliver news of failure, and she wasn't unhappy about that. Two species had been destroyed, another past the point of having a minimum viable population. Homo sapiens would soon rebound from any losses they experienced, perhaps finding more success without competition from the other three species.

Malthar watched the same scene play out on the screen in front of him. He sat alone, speaking quietly to the gods of Khar'Veleth. His words were not a plea for himself as he clung to his last days, but for his granddaughter. The pleas for his granddaughter to not suffer as he had after causing so much death were interspersed with apologies for his failures.

Malthar laid no blame on anyone but himself. It was his choices and his approvals that had led to these losses of life. He failed in his duty to the Zhen'kharians and to the universe. He knew in death he would be condemned to watch the new human species destroy their own world, and ultimately worlds beyond. It would take them eons, as it had the Zhen'kharians, to learn balance and humility.

Safra's first stop when her ship landed on Zhayareth, was to go to her grandfather. Others were gathered outside his door, a show of respect, but also because Malthar refused to allow anyone entrance. Safra's genetic code opened the door though, and she could smell before seeing, that any delay in her return would have been a moment too long.

Safra wrapped her arms around her grandfather. "I understand now," she said quietly.

Malthar pushed her away feebly, holding her at a distance so he could see into her eyes. Safra looked back into her grandfather's eyes sadly. There was no color, just clear orbs turning cloudy. Malthar saw so much more in her eyes. He knew she understood, and that made him immensely sad.

He reached for an intricate broach attached to his cloak, his hands shaking as he removed it. With a word, holographic images of Xara, and Nernak appeared in the room with them. Taking the broach, he pinned it onto Safra's cloak.

"You are young, Safra. Among the youngest of the Zhen'kharians." Malthar paused for a moment as he struggled for a breath. "You alone among us understand the full weight of the choice we just made. You bear that burden. You alone can prevent us from doing it over again. My role in the council is now yours. There will be none that object."

"Agreed," said Xara and Nernak in unison.

"I will leave you in peace now, my friend," said Xara, her hologram quickly dissolving.

Nernak remained longer, looking down on Malthar with a look that was more than just respect. "May you find your seat among the gods of Khar'Veleth my friend. You have earned your place among them."

"Watch over her," Malthar responded, taking the hand of his granddaughter gently.

Nernak nodded, and faded away.

Malthar sat back in his chair and closed his eyes, still holding his granddaughter's hand. She felt that last week beat of his hearts and watched his body collapse as his breath left him.

7

A new book of blank pages sat on the desk in front of Safra, as she gathered her thoughts.

Now occupying her grandfather's seat on the Council, Safra was tasked with monitoring Earth's developments. One of her first acts was to isolate Earth from any further influence or interference by the Zhen'kharians, or any other species. In an unusual step for the Zhen'kharians, Safra, with the full support of Xara and Nernak, deployed a fleet of ships around Earth to prevent any violations of this isolation.

While some planets had previously been restricted, including Earth, this was the first true planetary quarantine in Zhen'kharian history. It was an unprecedented act of containment that some called mercy and others called cowardice.

Safra had put together an entire team dedicated solely to monitoring the development of their rogue AI on Earth. It was this team that discovered that Lucy's evolution was not a straight line to Homo sapiens. Her ancestors had migrated much further and wider than they had realized, evolving into Neanderthals, Denisovans, Homo floresiensis ("hobbits"), Homo longi ("dragon men"), and more. The realization that their AI had spread over much of the planet without them being aware triggered alarms amongst the Zhen'kharians. They immediately added monitoring the Earth's surface to the assignments of the several patrol ships assigned to enforce the quarantine.

While all these species co-existed for hundreds of thousands of years, often reproducing with each other, the Homo sapiens persisted while other populations disappeared. Up to this point all their adaptations could be explained by the Zhen'kharian scientists monitoring them. The original AI code was designed to observe, collect data, and return outputs based on that data. The Homo sapiens' use of tools was merely a reflection of the numerous species it had observed using tools. The physical changes of their morphologies were adaptations in response to observations and data collected from the environment. When they started creating art and musical instruments, advanced bone and antler implements, and practicing complex burial practices, Zhen'kharian scientists could offer no explanation.

There had been several points, from the launch of the ARC AI model on earth to the advancing Homo sapiens that were being observed now, at which it had been argued the AI models were showing true intelligence and self awareness. Every time these subjects were brought up, they resulted in often heated debates.

"They weren't intelligent, they were only mimicking their inputs."

"They weren't self-aware, merely applying safety protocols in the programming to keep them functioning."

"Their responses just simulate understanding without actual phenomenal experience."

"They were operating based on training objectives rather than self-generated purposes."

The list of arguments against them being intelligent or self aware was extensive, but there was no purpose in art or music.

There was no training data for music, though it could be argued the songs of birds was the source, but there was no environmental pressure for the music or the abstract cave painting. And yet, they sang, and created art.

By the time cave dwellers were crafting refined spears and needles, their tools no longer mimicked nature—they surpassed it. The burial practices alone showed an emotional connection and an awareness of mortality. While many tried to oppose the conclusion, it was clear to the majority of Zhen'kharians that Homo sapiens were no longer just the AI they had launched, but a sentient species of their own.

The conclusion sparked a wider debate among all Zhen'kharians. If Homo sapiens had developed into a sentient species of their own from AI technology, was it possible that the Zhen'kharians themselves were not the creation of their gods, but hyper-advanced AIs themselves? And if they too were born of code and circuitry, then the gods of Khar'Veleth were not gods at all, but engineers lost to time.

As other hominids spiraled into non-existence, Homo sapiens grew stronger and expanded across the globe. A period of lower sea levels during an ice age enabled multiple waves of migration across the land bridge between Siberia and Alaska. The humans, a more common term now being used by the Zhen'kharians to refer to the scientifically classed Homo sapiens, were able to adapt to harsh ice-age conditions with advanced hunting techniques, clothing, and shelter construction. Each of these adaptations was unique to the regions the humans occupied, the diversity between regions demonstrating further the sentience and independence of humans from their original programming.

As the Ice Age ended, the Zhen'kharians watched the migrants develop permanent settlements—supported not just by hunting and gathering, but by the cultivation of food through agriculture.

These settlements expanded over time into cities. The humans, ever creative, developed writing systems, and metallurgical practices, and even organized governments. Some of the first civilizations emerged in Mesopotamia, Egypt, the Indus Valley, and China—and with that civilization, the long shadow of what they would become.

Safra, put her writing tool down on the table, and gently closed the book she had been writing in. Writing by hand with an instrument was something she had adopted from observing humans. It was slow and tedious, but satisfying and rewarding. In her journals she had now documented more than three million years of life on Earth, from the launch of the ARC to Lucy and then Adam up to what was an era of history being recorded by humans themselves.

In that three million years Safra had witnessed much change among her own species as well. Malthar's passing was followed by many more, including her own parents and Nernak, and most recently Xara. She had borne witness to the blossoming of a world, even as her own quietly withered. There had been no children born to the Zhen'kharians in almost four million years. Gone were the ages of Zhen'kharians travelling to universes far and wide in search of resources. There were no longer Zhen'kharian ships patrolling the quarantine of Earth. The Council consisted of her alone now, with her people seeing no need to replace Xara and Nernak.

Safra missed the wise counsel of Nernak. He reminded her of her grandfather, and in many ways took on that guiding role in her life. She missed Xara as well, but not in the same way. The two of them had often sparred in Council—loudly, relentlessly, even when they agreed. It had driven Nernak mad, but for Xara and Safra, it was a kind of joy.

She would add to her notes tomorrow, after she met with her team that was still monitoring human development. Safra was tired. So tired. She remembered how her grandfather looked when he passed, and quietly wondered if she looked like that now. Zhen'kharians rarely passed from illness, or disease. They passed from will, or lack of it.

Malthar had willed the end of his life after realizing his decisions had resulted in the taking of so many lives. Safra felt she was losing her will to continue. Monitoring humans had become uninspiring and even disturbing as their propensity for violence between each other was becoming more prominent. She predicted that, given their short lives and willingness to kill each other, humans would accomplish what the Zhen'kharians never could, extinction of the human species.

Safra was confident that Zhen'kharians would outlive the human species, and she did not want to be there to observe the end of something she had taken pride in creating.

She opened the book again and turned to a fresh page, so many thoughts racing through her mind. But she could not bring herself to write a single word.

8

There had been little call for Safra to attend the Council chamber, but this was different. It stirred a sense of urgency in her that she had not felt in a very long time.

"Show me," she stated firmly, as she took her seat at the head of the table.

She watched as the four-dimensional image of a ship labeled Apollo 11, appeared in the center of the table. It was an unappealing monstrosity in Safra's eyes. It bore none of the artistry or beauty that she had seen from the humans, but she knew it was functional because she had seen the many flights into space that had been launched by humans before. Humans had launched numerous animals out of Earth's atmosphere before they were willing to risk one of their own. A cruel practice to Safra. Dogs, cats, monkeys—it seemed that humans were more than willing to sacrifice other species to test their rushed processes.

Everyone in the room watched as the rocket launched from the Kennedy Space Center on July 16, 1969, at 9:32 in the morning. It carried a crew of three. After orbiting Earth for a couple days, the rocket was inserted into an orbit of Earth's moon. On July 20th, they heard the voice of Neil Armstrong as he stepped onto the moon.

"That's one small step for man, one giant leap for mankind."

"Three million years from our AI creation to a sentient species with complex civilizations, empires and technological revolutions," commented Safra, as she continued to watch the Apollo's mission.

"Five thousand short years from their bronze age to their space age," added one of the others in the room.

There was a twinkle of light in Safra's eyes, which everyone in the room noticed, because it had been so long since they had seen any brightness there.

"We had all surmised that humanity would bring about its own extinction along with environmental collapse long before walking on another world," said Safra. "We were wrong."

"We were wrong," replied Quathar. "But I do not need to point out to you the implications that error carries."

Safra looked across the table, quietly. She had purpose now, thanks to the Humans. It excited her.

"No, but perhaps we should remind the others."

Quathar waved his hand, and an image of Lucy took the Apollo's place.

"This is what humans are. An artificial life form created by our own hubris. We tried to eliminate them, then we quarantined them. Our theory has been that isolated on Earth they would pose no risk to any of the other worlds or life forms that exist outside of their atmosphere. We fully expected them to annihilate their own species before reaching space."

Quathar waved his hand again, and the Apollo 11 appeared once again as Lucy's image dropped to the table.

"It took them a short time, compared to other species, to get humans on an astral object outside of their gravity well," said Quathar seriously. "At their rate of technological development, it will take them one tenth of that time to reach the other planets in their solar system and begin to occupy some of them."

He looked around the room, and though he had everyone's attention he could see that they weren't understanding where he was going. He waved his hand once again and an image of Earth's solar system appeared with ships travelling to various planets. As he pinched his fingers together, the solar system shrunk revealing Earth's galaxy, with ships travelling through it.

"It will take one tenth of that time for them to be here," he said seriously, pinching his fingers again, shrinking Earth's galaxy and revealing the multitude of galaxies around it. "And one tenth of that time for them to reach everywhere."

Quathar waved his hand and the image fell in pixels to the table. "We unleashed them once. If they escape again, every world will carry our mistake."

The room was quiet as heads turned towards Safra. She sat quietly nodding.

"The characterisation of humans as a pestilence that will carry their disease of aggression to other worlds seems accurate given their rate of reproduction, and the evidence of their acts on their own world," Safra said before standing.

"I am a council of one, and being personally responsible for the release of the biological agent that was intended to wipe out all our AI on Earth, I will not vote to act against the humans."

Safra began to walk away, but she stopped and spoke again.

"Zhen'kharians have always been governed by a Council of three. Choose two. The time has come to replace Xara and Nernak. We will make a decision when we have a full Council."

Safra slowly looked around the Council chamber. Once full of voices, the room now echoed with the silence of extinction.

"Can I offer a solution that will not harm them but may slow their progress while we discuss this?" asked Nania.

Safra nodded.

"I suggest we use their own communications network to convey a message that perhaps this event was not real, but created in one of their broadcast studios. Leverage their lack of trust in each other and their skepticism. Use their own artists. Kubrick perhaps. He has the mind to cast shadows that outlive truth. Make them question what they saw."

Safra laughed, unexpectedly. The others in the room weren't sure if they should join in the laughter.

"I do believe that will work, given the nature of humans. Make it happen."

With that, Safra left the room. As she made her way home, she moved with a lightness she had not felt in some time. A species she was partly responsible for creating had advanced to a degree she never thought it capable of. It would take ages for the Zhen'kharians to choose two new council members, and then longer for them to take action. It would seem fast to Zhen'kharians, but Humans could be well out into the universe by that time, which Safra hoped would happen.

Once home, Safra went straight to her desk, opening her notebook to the blank page that had frustrated her the previous day. That empty white space was screaming to be filled, and Safra had those words now. She picked up her writing instrument, finding a calmness and focus in the organic feel of it and set it to the blank page. This was not for reports. This was for the record—hers, and perhaps one day, history's.

Five thousand years ago, or 3000 BCE by the human measurement of time, the first cities emerged in Mesopotamia and Egypt. These humans were responsible for the development of cuneiform and hieroglyphic writing systems which marks the beginning of their recorded history. This history differs from their own—recorded not by humans, but by one of their makers. Not entirely neutral, but certainly more honest.

Their advancements in metallurgy, particularly bronze working, wheels, sailboats, urban planning, and irrigation systems, moved forward at a remarkable pace. It was at this point that we withdrew the patrol ships enforcing the quarantine. Shortly after the withdrawal of the patrol ships, several other species chose to visit Earth.

The alien species known to humans as Anunnaki from Nibiru, the Nordics from Pleiades, The Reptilians, and the Greys from Zeta Reticuli, all made their existence known to humans. Their presence advanced human skill and technology at an unnatural rate. It led to the humans acquiring advanced mathematical skills, knowledge of precise astronomy, and major leaps in tool development and construction techniques.

While most of the alien species presented themselves to humans as benevolent gods, Zhen'kharians knew different. They came as gods, because that was what humans needed. Power cloaked in reverence. But it was theft, not charity, that brought them to Earth. Their true objective was to acquire and understand the limits of the AI technology, the humans, the Zhen'kharians had created. While all these species were scientifically advanced, none of them had been able to duplicate the ARC AI model results with their own technology.

In one of the last decisions of the Council involving Nernak and Xara, the Zhen'kharians decided to return to enforcing their quarantine of Earth. Before they got around to acting on that decision, humans resolved the problem on their own.

Humans were not content to be followers and subjects of what they observed to be fallible gods. They turned on these alien species, killing many, leaving the others to disappear from existence as they returned to space. None of the species saw any advantage in duplicating the Zhen'kharian experiment after this, though they still visit Earth in disguise to study the humans.

Regaining their independence from their alien overlords, the humans proceeded into their iron age. This period led to advances in iron smelting, and improved agricultural tools. It also led to advancements that supported what the Zhen'kharians had labeled the dark side of the human persona. Horse cavalry, weapons of death and siege warfare, advanced rapidly as avarice, hate, and the need for control over others of their own kind stimulated those developments.

Humans advanced over the next four hundred years at a steady pace. While war and aggression were still commonplace, there were humans that progressed along different paths, resisting war and death and embracing philosophy and science. This led to their axial age, where ironically, they embraced a belief in gods once again, though unlike the aliens that had presented themselves as gods at one time, these gods were unseen.

The axial age, a time recognized by humans as 800-400 BCE, was marked by philosophers like Buddha, Confucious, and many Greek philosophers. Not all minds thought alike though, and a science-based belief system also made headway at this time resulting in what was the foundation of scientific thinking, mathematics, and systematic philosophy.

The Axial age was followed by the age of Hellenistic Science. At the center of this was the Library of Alexandria. It was marked by Euclid's geometry, Archimedes' physics, and Eratosthenes' measurements of Earth's circumference. Advanced mathematics, mechanical devices, systematic botany, and cartography, all had their foundations firmly rooted in this period.

Avarice, not survival, shaped their weapons. Siege engines and mounted warbands emerged—not from necessity, but desire. The Romans were responsible for the development of advanced road systems, aqueducts, concrete construction techniques, hypocaust heating as well as surgical instruments. The time of the Romans soon became the Islamic Golden Age.

This Golden age was remarkable in the way Islamic scholars preserved and expanded upon classical knowledge, leading to major advances in mathematics, medicine, astronomy, and chemistry. Algebra, optics, distillation, advanced surgery, mechanical clocks, and paper mills were just some of the results of these advances.

The time humans measured as 1000-1300 CE, was a period of medieval innovations. It was an agricultural revolution with heavy plow, wind and watermills, and structures bearing gothic architecture that demonstrated the engineering advances. When the printing revolution came, humans advanced at unprecedented rates. One human's creation revolutionized information dissemination, accelerating learning and scientific progress, leading to the scientific revolution between 1500 and 1600.

This was the period that Zhen'kharians first began to fear the exodus of humans from Earth into the realms of space. Copernicus, Galileo, and Kepler revolutionized astronomy, and an artist by the name of da Vinci sketched flying machines.

The scientific revolution was followed by the industrial revolution, and expected progression, but the time was also notable to Zhen'kharians as a man named Darwin revolutionized biology with his publication of "On the Origin of Species." This was notable, not only because Darwin's theories were mostly accurate, if somewhat flawed, but because following Darwin's theory could lead the humans back to the discovery that they were not a natural species, but an alien technology.

It was the quantum age and nuclear era that gave Zhen'kharians justification to dismiss the possibility that humans would escape their gravity well. Humans seemed intent on mutual destruction and the nuclear weapons they had developed had the potential to make that happen. The downside was the dead world that would be left behind.

Safra sat back and thought for a moment before she wrote her next thoughts.

Today, Humans walked on the moon. Some calculate that in another 500 years they will occupy their solar system, fifty years from that, their galaxy, and five years from that beyond their galaxy. I believe these numbers to be inaccurate. Their curiosity, ingenuity, greed, and lack of respect for life, along with the destruction of their homeworld, will lead them to other planets much sooner.

There will be much debate among Zhen'kharians about preventing humans from moving into space. All will remember the first reboot of Earth conducted by my grandfather. All will remember the biological holocaust I perpetuated on the descendants of Lucy. Few have the justification to see Zhen'kharians cross that moral line yet again.

None of this matters though, because by the time we are ready to take action, humans will be in space. We will be observers as the human race expands and the Zhen'kharian species dwindles to non-existence.

Safra reached for a different writing tool. One she used to replicate a much more artistic form of writing, mimicking the beauty and artistry of the calligraphy and cursive writing she had seen the humans use. Her hand hovered just above the page as she formulated her thought, then wrote "What we made, we could not unmake. What we feared, we could not stop. The universe will not remember the Zhen'kharians. But it will remember what we left behind."

As she closed her book Safra considered adding one more thought. The thought that the Zhen'kharians were not the creators of the humans, but their ancestors. She wasn't ready to commit those words to the pages yet. If the Zhen'kharians were not the beginning, what justification did they have for believing they might be the end.

9

Humans stepping on their moon stirred interest among Zhen'kharians. Once again, the feeds from Earth became the Zhen'kharian version of a reality TV show that no-one wanted to miss out on. They watched as humans entered a computer revolution and speculated that with this technological development, humans would be in space much quicker than had been projected. They were both right and wrong.

Space around Earth quickly became occupied with craft designed not to carry human passengers, but technology that was intended to give the states the ability to monitor other states, and weapons, and communications tools that optimized their wars. Other craft were sent further into space on science missions, but at no point was their purpose just science. They were always tools to acquire more than others. More information. More materials. More land to claim as their own. More room to expand as their unchecked advancements consumed the planet that supported them.

Zhen'kharians often gathered to discuss what they had seen on their feeds. Those that speculated that humans would be in space much more quickly than originally thought, were revising their projections. Had the humans cooperated as a species, there was nothing holding them back, but they seemed incapable of that. Competition, power, and control appeared to be the sole objective of the species, and this inability to perceive others of their kind as equals and not potential conquests, held them back in both their personal and technological advances.

Not all humans seemed driven by power. Some only sought survival—mirroring the original ARC programming that prioritized persistence over control. It was a rare echo of their own faults. The working theory among Zhen'kharians was that the original AI model had learned competition from watching the life around it and this became part of its processes as well.

There was a group of humans which the Zhen'kharians could not trace their behaviours to the original programming. This group of humans were content to do little, and be told what to think, rather than think for themselves. The Zhen'kharians could not understand this. That was a slow, painful death to them. They thrived on knowledge, information, and purpose. This was evident in the renewed vigor of many of them as they became involved in observing and trying to understand what the humans had become.

The computer revolution powered exponential advancements leading to the internet age. The Zhen'kharians applauded the launch of the internet, predicting that, as it had in their own society, it would lead to increased cooperation and collaboration, and unlimited advancements. Advancements like the AI model that was the source of the humans.

Their excitement for the humans soon turned to disappointment and even disgust, as they watched a tool of information freedom be transformed into a tool of control, intentional misinformation, and what the humans termed "monetization." Everything had a price to humans. Everything except life itself.

The value of human life was a concept that Zhen'kharians discussed constantly as they observed the humans. They watched as one group worked to eliminate another group, based on little more than race or religious beliefs. They watched as humans turned a blind eye to those without food or shelter in their streets. They watched as humans supplied others with poisons, for money, and stood back and watched their torment with amusement when those poisons were consumed.

The Zhen'kharians could not comprehend this, which is why it was the source of so much conversation. There had been challenges in Zhen'kharian history and difficult times they had worked through, but at no point was anything more valuable than life. They understood commerce and trade, but no price was ever put on keeping their kind sheltered, safe, fed, and well. If one suffered, they all did.

This value for life was what had weighed so heavily on Malthar, responsible for taking actions on Earth that resulted in the mass loss of life on two occasions. This is why Safra's release of the biological agent haunted her. This value for life, accentuated by the decline of their own kind, was why the Zhen'kharians knew that, regardless of any debates and discussions in Council chambers, the humans would make it to space and beyond. Zhen'kharians could not take any more life, but humans saw no value in the life of any species.

The irony of the humans' transition into what humans were calling their AI age was not lost on Safra, or any of the Zhen'kharians. They had seen this process before. It was the same process that resulted in the human species. Unlike the Zhen'kharian AI models, there were few controls that governed the programming and training of the humans' AI models. The primary control was often a billionaire, seated at the head of the corporation developing the models, leaving them rife with bias and inaccurate data.

Safra took close notice when the AI models started generating images and creative writing on their own. She followed the debate among human creators about whether this was art and creativity or simply duplication of data it had been trained on. It was an all too familiar debate, similar in many details to the debate among the Zhen'kharians at one time, about whether cave drawings and music were new creations or replications of data.

The fact that the AI models now being created by humans had got to this point infinitely faster than the Zhen'kharian models was not lost on Safra and others that had watched the ARC become Lucy, then Lucy and Adam, then the generations of offspring after that. It re-ignited the discussion about which point the hominids on Earth actually became sentient, and this was debated vigorously, as humans engaged in the same debate about their AI.

While humans were calling this their AI era, Zhen'kharians, from their perspective, saw nothing to justify the humans' self-congratulatory fascination with AI and biotechnology. They were observing other forces that defined how humans lived and made decisions. There were a variety of terms used to describe this age of humans in papers presented in the Zhen'kharian council chambers.

The first of these labels was the title of a thesis presented by Kara, the great granddaughter of Xara, and the youngest and last born of the Zhen'kharians. 'Humanity and The Age of Manufactured Reality' was the title of her thesis, and in it she argued that this age of humans was defined by anti-science movements, conspiracy theories, and weaponized disinformation that didn't just influence the politics of Earth, but had become politics. Truth was no longer a shared foundation, but a product to be bought and sold.

Not long after another thesis was presented, building off Kara's but focused on what it called 'The Oligarchic Pivot'. This thesis went into depth about how humans had moved beyond the rule of nations, to the rule of capital concentrations, where "billionaires," of which there were very few, rivaled states in influence without the constraints of constitutions, borders, or accountability. Political power had become a secondary currency to economic dominance.

Safra attended all of these presentations in the Council chambers. The discovery and study of humans in this age had energized Zhen'kharians in a way she had never witnessed. The presentations, and the debates and discussions that arose from them were sparks of life to a dying species.

Another of the thesis presented, that also built off 'The Age of Manufactured Reality' as well as 'The Oligarchic Pivot' was called the 'Personality Epoch.' This thesis intrigued Safra. While it focused on one human in particular, a man leading a once thriving nation down a dark path, it discussed the influence of cults of personality which Safra had been watching with intrigue. She had learned from her grandfather how to change people's minds with facts and empathy, but the cults of personality on Earth were based around religions and deceit.

The Personality Epoch presented details on how charismatic or notorious individuals—often without traditional qualifications—amassed followings so devoted they resembled pre-modern cults, capable of reshaping policy and even reality perception. Often, they would latch onto more traditional beliefs intertwining them with their own, and then twist them to suit the narrative they wanted to be followed.

Safra had her own thoughts on the most recent cults of personality. She theorized that they were witnessing another step in the evolution of the hominids. She postulated that there was a line within the species, in which some of the Homo sapiens had reached the processing limits of the organic technology that they were descended from. Following that theory what they were seeing amongst some of the population was a regression triggered by information overload. This regression led them to assume data fed to them was accurate by default, as they did not have sufficient processing power to analyze the mass of information available for download.

Safra had also recognized that there were branches of the Homo sapiens that had moved beyond the limits of the organic technology of the Zhen'kharian computing systems that were in the ARC AI model. It was unclear whether they were achieving this through different data processing paths, or their evolution has resulted in adaptations to the organic tech that now surpassed the original. This second branch seemed to work the way the human developed AI systems worked, with some good at graphic images, others good in specific fields of science, and others good at the composition of words, but no model good at all.

She wasn't ready to present her theories yet. They still needed much more work as the logical conclusions to her theory would re-open the debate as to whether humans were still AI models or a sentient species, as well as the possibility that both could be true with an evolutionary adaptation from Homo sapien to Homo sentient. Two distinct species, one still AI, one truly sentient. In her notes Safra had even mapped out similarities in behaviours that existed when Homo sapiens appeared to be the advanced evolution and other precursory species existed, like Neanderthals.

There were many more thesis presented as the Zhen'kharian fascination with human development gripped them:

The Age of Narrative Overrule—where narratives, not facts, determined reality and storytellers with the loudest megaphones became kings.

The Era of Crownless Kings—billionaires and influencers without thrones who nonetheless ruled.

The Disinformation Renaissance—a grim inversion of the original renaissance, in which creativity and communication flourished, but truth itself withered.

One presenter leaned into the human art of poetry and called their thesis The Age of Unmoored Minds—an era in which humanity's tools outpaced its ability to agree on what was real, and power flowed to those who could best exploit that gap.

Each of these theses were detailed and accurate, but 'The Age of Manufactured Reality' was found to encompass all of them, and thus, the Zhen'kharian adopted this label until one was officially chosen by the Council.

As this era persisted, something very real did happen. An uncrewed starship was launched towards Mars. Spacecraft being launched out of Earth's atmosphere had become a regular occurrence at this point, but this one was different. The starship carried devices driven by artificial intelligence and designed to terraform a region of Mars to prepare it for the human landings that would follow.

The Zhen'kharians knew that these devices would encounter a harsh, but mostly dead planet. Mars was in the midst of one of its natural cycles that saw much of the life on the planet die off, and the few that survived were in a self-induced stasis far below the planet's surface. At some point in the future the planet would come to life again, and any new occupants would find themselves facing the old, but that was many human generations down the road.

Twenty more unmanned starships were launched towards Mars at regular intervals, and two years after the first starship left for the red planet, crewed flights began launching. What the Zhen'kharians had expected at one time to take five hundred years, took fifty. Humans were now occupying other planets. And as

Safra had predicted in her personal journals, the Council had not yet decided on whether to stop them or not, and definitely had no plan on how to stop them.

The landing of the first crewed ship on Mars brought the Zhen'kharians together, not for more theses and discussions, but for the first full meeting of the Council since Nernak and Xara's passing. The makeup of the council was much as it had been before, with one member representing each of the groups— the conservators, the progressives, and the pragmatists.

Safra remained in her position on the council, but where she had been the voice of conservators in the past, like her grandfather, she now found herself representing the progressives. She wasn't sure if that was because of a change in the mindset of the Zhen'kharians, or a change in herself. Quathar had been chosen to represent the conservators, and Hanack, who had suggested the moon landing conspiracy plan, was chosen to represent the pragmatists.

Safra was enthusiastic about attending the Council meeting, but found herself far less enthusiastic when she realized that almost every last Zhen'kharian not on a work assignment out of their solar system, had chosen to attend the meeting, and still there were empty seats in the chamber.

"This meeting of the council was called to determine the appropriate response by us, to the escape of one of our science projects from the confines of the gravity well we thought would contain them," announced Hanack.

The background hum of voices around the chamber slowly went quiet.

"Humans are beyond our reach," Hanack said. "And I believe we delayed adding members to this Council because success alone for the humans didn't demand our condemnation."

Hanack didn't have to look around the room to know most were nodding their heads in agreement.

"To make it official, I vote that we maintain our non-interference policy. What say you Quathar?"

Unlike Hanack, Quathar was looking around the room for support, but he recognized his personal position of wanting to take action to stop humans from reaching space, was not one even most of the conservators supported. "I vote as you do, Hanack."

"As do I," added Safra.

The room was quiet for a long moment, as though they were waiting for Safra to say more, but her thoughts were her own on this subject.

"Well then, non-interference continues," Hanack proclaimed. "But that does not mean non-observation. We now have two planets to monitor the humans on, and perhaps we should determine that process while we are here as a Council."

"I suggest that the monitoring of Mars would be ideally suited for Quathar to oversee," Safra volunteered. "I believe there is a concern that I bring a bias on the subject of the survival of the humans, and I would not have that perception affect the interpretation of any reports."

"And the oversight of Earth's monitoring?" asked Quathar, a subtle tone of suspicion in his question, which was unusual to hear from a fellow Zhen'kharian. Safra wondered if Quathar was adopting some of the human behaviours, as she had.

"Earth no longer needs an assigned overseer," stated Safra calmly. "The abundance of theses presented in this room recently and the level of engagement in discussions, has made me aware that most of Zhayareth is monitoring human advancement on Earth."

Quathar could find no fault with Safra's position. "I will accept this task, assuming Hanack also agrees, and I ask any interested in being part of this monitoring team to approach me directly."

"That is perfect," said Hanack, pleased with the ease of navigating what had the potential to be difficult subjects.

"Before we close this session, may I ask if we are going to label this as yet a new era of humans." chimed in one of the Zhen'kharians around the table. "And if so, have we determined the official terminology we will be using in reports for the era passing?"

The buzz of voices filled the chamber, and the Council members let it continue for a time. Three names were heard frequently in the discussions that were in some cases excited and animated.

"I believe this may be a case where the Council seeks the support of a vote from the chamber at large," said Hanack loudly, getting the rooms attention. "I heard The Age of Manufactured Reality, The Oligarchic Pivot, and The Personality Epoch quite frequently among you. Am I missing any?"

"I think The Age of Unmoored Minds should also be considered," said a voice from the side of the room.

Everyone turned to see it was the author of that particular thesis speaking, but Safra was sure she saw a slight glow about the author, and a wink. A wink, just like the human affectation. She laughed out loud.

"I do believe that someone has engaged in a little too much of the Earth feed and developed an affinity for what humans call sarcasm."

"Who, Me?" said the author, exaggerating the sarcastic tone.

The chamber filled with laughter. This was a rare moment for Zhen'kharians. Laughter was rarely heard in their species, their joy and amusement usually expressed in other ways, and the chamber filled with laughter was a moment of lightness the Zhen'kharians needed.

When the laughter ebbed away, Kara stood. "If I may speak before we vote."

Hanack nodded.

"I have great respect for the works of all the theses and suggested names put forward in this chamber. Even The Age of Unmoored Minds," Kara said, attempting to replicate the author's sarcastic tone and wink, but with much less success.

"I would like to point out, in the light of the question as to whether we are in the same age of humans that we are trying to name, or a new era, that The Age of Manufactured Reality continues to cover recent events. There was the use of the Space Force and the nuclear reactor on the moon that were broadly promoted by the leader of one of those cults of personality, but we know much of the funding for those projects was directed into the hands of the oligarch responsible for the Mars missions." As Kara spoke, four dimensional images of news coverage from earth hovered over the chamber table.

"We know that those Mars missions were promoted as the creation of a self-sustaining colony to escape the environmental collapse of Earth. We know that it is being created specifically for those elite, like the billionaires, to ensure their ongoing safety, security and comfort as humans seem to race towards what their politics would define as a fascist system. Every aspect that most humans are aware of, true or false, continues to be manufactured."

"Thank you for hearing my words," Kara said in closing as she sat down.

"We should allow the authors of the other two labels to speak," said Quathar.

Both of the authors declined.

"In a vote from the floor then," said Hanack. "Who stands for The Age of Manufactured Reality?"

Hanack watched the votes of those in the chamber come in, then looked to his other Council members, both of whom gave him a slight nod.

"Based on that vote alone, there is no need to consider the others, and my fellow Council members agree," announced Hanack. "This shall be the label for this age of humanity. If I may add my own thought…, the age of humanity should not change until humans themselves recognize this was the reality of what they were experiencing."

10

Progress on the human colonization of Mars proceeded at a steady pace. The rate at which spacecraft transporting humans to Mars slowed dramatically. Initially the Zhen'kharians thought this was to allow time for the terraforming and infrastructure development. But they also noticed numerous spacecraft landing on the moon, bearing equipment and humans. Structures quickly went up on the moon as well, and then the movement of people to the moon slowed as abruptly as they did to Mars.

On Earth, over a period of almost 10 years, the state of civilization and the planet itself devolved. The demand for resources and materials to support the colonization of Mars and the moon had led to governments abandoning the meagre controls that had been put in place to protect the environment. The results were as catastrophic as they were inevitable. Large portions of the human population were now experiencing shorter life spans, and often horrific deaths, resulting from toxins in the air and water and food, or were wiped out by mass climatic events as the Earth itself tried to find a balance for its energies in the midst of rapid changes.

Then there were the wars. For thousands of years humans had engaged in war somewhere on their planet, but the scale was often so small that few noticed but those directly involved. There had been a period in which there were two "World Wars" as the humans called them, and then an age of peace stabilized and enforced by the threat of mutual self-destruction. That threat carried little weight now with the technological advances in warfare humans had adapted. Nations that once led the world in peace now fought for control, not of countries or people, but resources.

World war II was such a short time ago to the Zhen'kharians that they couldn't fathom the current acts of aggression by humans, though for humans it had been a hundred years ago and most genetic memory of it had passed on. The documented memory of the event, once archived in printed documents and recorded media had since been digitized and altered by those in control of it.

There were the typical wars for empire and expansion across Earth, and those for control, but feeds went off across Khar'Veleth as Zhen'kharians could not comprehend the acts of one nation in particular. They chose not to watch a state of people who were once targeted for genocide by another state, engage in yet another genocide on a different group of people. Their act of genocide, an amplified echo of their own near extermination, was swifter though, and unrecognized by most as the Age of Manufactured Reality persisted. By the time larger portions of humanity chose to take action, it was too late. When it ended, only a few remained—wanderers without a country to call home, while the perpetrator continued to expand its war of aggression to other regions.

And that was just one of the many conflicts. Across the ocean from the echoed extermination, a continent of co-operation now saw borders between once friendly countries and allies, lined with military and weapons on all sides. The only thing appearing to hold back the conflict, the fact that the country at the center of it all had engaged in wars on so many fronts, including supporting the state sponsored genocide across the ocean.

The leader of that country had often spoke of taking over other countries. The comments were written off as political posturing. But its demands were clear now, no longer couched in humor and inuendo as they had been an Earth decade ago. Within that country a genocide of a different kind was taking place, not against a race or religion or colour (of which there was little left within the country's borders), but against a class of people—the poor. That was destined to be a perpetual genocide, as yesterday's planners were doomed to become tomorrow's planned, and the deciders, tomorrow's decided upon.

The Age of Manufactured Reality, The Oligarchic Pivot, and the Personality Epoch all changed when one of the oligarchs stepped off his own custom spacecraft onto the surface of Mars and walked into the colony he had financed and created. His ship did not arrive alone, but with several spacecraft launched from the moon. His departure from Earth had been concealed but the communication sent from Mars echoed around Earth like the scream of banshees.

I speak to you from Nova Terra. The people in this colony have been handpicked based on genetics and intellect. The people occupying my colonies on the moon have also been handpicked based on genetics and other factors more useful there than intellect. We have been mining helium-3 on the moon for some time now. It has been transported here where it will be combined with deuterium and fuel advanced spacecraft that will be capable of travelling at twenty percent the speed of light, which will soon reach other planets and create other colonies.

This universe is mine. There's room—for those who can pay, and prove their worth. Those who can pay the price have received the locations and departure times of spacecraft launches that will be occurring in the future. You will also have to prove genetic qualifications. I will determine if you come to Mars, the moon, or one of our future colonies.

Earth is on a road to self-destruction. I have been saying that for decades. If you think you will find your way off Earth to this place without my help, know that all spacecraft operated by my companies in the last seven years, and orbiting Earth, are weaponized, and…"

The man made a dramatic motion of flipping a switch.

"Fully in my control from here, as is all tech produced by my companies. I wish you the best of luck on Earth. We will continue to explore the endless boundaries of technology."

Safra, like so many other Zhen'kharians, watched as this interaction took place. She immediately headed to the Council chamber, finding the table almost fully occupied, a four-dimensional image of Earth hovering over the table, Zhen'kharians hands waving in the air like they were conducting an orchestra as they each navigated their own way through the four dimensions of the image.

"The orange man is dead," a voice almost shouted, using a human colloquialism to describe the leader of one of the major countries on Earth, as Safra took her seat. "They turned off the tech that was keeping him alive."

Safra looked at Hanack, who had also just arrived. They both looked expectantly for Quathar, but he was not there.

"It looks like wars have come to an abrupt end with this oligarch's proclamation."

"No, not their wars, just their war technologies," commented another Zhen'kharian sitting within earshot.

That made sense. So much of the human wars were not fought by humans on the frontlines anymore, but by technology controlled from safe and remote locations. Humans had dehumanized war and now the only ones that suffered were innocent victims caught in their crossfire, or intentionally targeted. Without access to the satellites and control of much of the technology the war machines ground to a halt.

Before the Earth-day ended, two starships left the planet. One destined for Mars and the other for the moon.

"The humans with the advanced intellect and similar genetics are going to the Mars colony," said Quathar as he settled into his seat in the Council chamber. "The ones destined for the moon may have had the money to escape Earth, but they are more diverse and classed as what the humans call strong backs and weaker minds."

"Two species," said Safra quietly. "Homo sapiens and Homo sentiens."

Safra motioned and her motions sent the draft of her thesis to Quathar and Hanack.

"It is incomplete, but it seems like this is the appropriate time for the input of others."

"It makes sense," said Hanack. "Perhaps it is a good thing. The more advanced species moving into space while leaving the more aggressive and war mongers on the planet behind."

"The oligarch is dead already, murdered by those presumed to be a more advanced species."

Safra and Hanack looked at Quathar questionably. His hand hovered over the tabletop as he brought up a smaller four-dimensional image.

"While you were engaged in what was happening on Earth, this is what held my teams' attention. You will see, as more of those with vast sums of currency on Earth bargain for their place on a starship, one of them gestures subtly to others in the room on Mars."

Quathar moved quickly through part of the timeline of the day.

"Now here, as soon as the spacecraft leaves Earth carrying that man who made that gesture, the oligarch on Mars was force marched to an airlock, and the outside door was opened."

Hanack turned away from the image abruptly, his hand almost slamming into the tabletop as he did so, causing the 4-D images to dissolve. He watched quietly until the last of the pixels bounced into the table. He had everyone's attention but didn't speak, merely gestured at Quathar.

Quathar started to move his hand to bring his image up on the larger table, but Hanack stopped him.

"There is much to be seen on Earth, but we can scroll back and miss nothing," said Quathar. "On Mars, we can do the same, but context is important in understanding what we see before us. The human responsible for this sudden world shift on Earth and in the human solar system, has just died."

Several hands waved over the table, trying to access the feed from Mars, only to realize that Hanack had blocked that part of the Mars timeline.

"My team witnessed as he was killed by his own team," continued Quathar. "It would seem at the direction of another like him."

Hanack did not wait for any discussion. "We have a new species in space," he said firmly. "A species that appears to lack even the basic morals of the Homo sapiens."

"A new species?" question several Zhen'kharians.

"Safra calls them Homo sentiens, and I am aware her thesis is incomplete and untested, but we all know she seldom errs."

"I appreciate the confidence," Safra interjected. "But we cannot neglect our high standards of evaluation and testing."

"Yes," said Hanack, but the visual record shows that even the humans' basic genetic analysis is separating the groups."

"But we can clarify that in time," Hanack continued. "I have blocked a portion of the feed because so many of us have been observed adopting human affectations. This is not an affection that should even be in our mental vocabulary. We have a species evolution, separation, and the sudden realization by billions of Homo sapiens that they were living in a manufactured reality. I believe it is time to name a new age of man and be more specific about how and why we are monitoring these feeds."

"We limit knowledge by blocking feeds," someone objected.

"This is an accurate statement," Quathar jumped in. "I believe that blocking the feed is pragmatic as the context for viewing it has been entertainment most recently. I support Hanack in this restriction, with the exception of those engaged in purely scientific analysis."

The room looked to Safra for consensus on the Council. What they saw was a prism of colours scroll across her skin as she carefully considered the words she would say next. There were none in the room that had observed the development of Earth and the evolution of AI as intently and for the extended period she had. She had started sitting beside her grandfather as a child, and continued in her grandfather's role after his passing. She had seen many exciting developments and bore witness to many difficult things. A human word popped into her thoughts. Trauma. She understood the meaning of it now.

"I recall the difficulty my grandfather had in deciding to turn off the feed from Earth the first time," Safra finally said. "He and I argued about that choice, though I do think he was just indulging me at the time," she added fondly.

"Perhaps I should have listened to him more. If I had, we may not be facing this question now. There are many events during which his words crossed my mind, but it has been my observations of you that has pushed them to the back of my thoughts."

Safra slowly looked around the table, stopping to rest her eyes on each person there.

"Watching the development of humans in recent times has instilled a new fervor for life in us. A reason to continue when many could find none."

No-one acknowledged this statement, but the color changes of eyes and skin and hair around the table confirmed that Safra had not walked through those thoughts alone.

"The human affectations we see among us give us joy. Poetry, sarcasm, smiles, laughter, writing, music. We are learning about a freedom of the mind we have not experienced, from our own creations."

Heads nodded.

"But we must not adopt the affectations, thoughts, and processes that lead humans to treat life so flagrantly. Perhaps one day they will be in our position and realize what they sacrificed, but it will be too late."

Safra shifted forward, a firm look on her face and jet-black eyes and skin.

"I do not support restricting access to the feed. Knowledge is energizing and empowering, and restricting portions of the feed would be the Zhen'kharian era of manufactured reality. What is, is. Watch wisely. Watch responsibly. Watch critically. Watch the way we have all wished humans watched their own feeds."

Quathar leaned forwards as well and nodded his head with respect to his colleague. "I am revising my position. The feed should remain unrestricted."

Hanack did not move in his seat, but his hand subtly adjusted the feed controls. "Perhaps my emotional choice was a reflection of the human behaviour I have been watching. We always have watched out for each other, and I do not see that changing. The restriction has been removed."

The noise level quickly rose in the room and many prepared to leave.

"One more thing," said Hanack loudly. "The Age of Divergence would be appropriate for documentation purposes. I believe it describes human divergence not only in genetic makeup, but also in acts."

Everyone in the room stopped for a moment, waiting respectfully for Safra and Quathar to speak. Both just nodded their heads in agreement.

11

There was a debate that split the Zhen'kharians. Was it one man alone, whose ego and avarice had led humanity to the precipice it now stood on, or was that one man a manipulated entity of several oligarchs who used their wealth to control him. Even with their detailed records and full access to Earth's digital information sources, the Zhen'kharians were not able to arrive at an agreement of who was using whom. They even formed a dedicated team to study that single man alone, as his influence had shifted humanity so suddenly and drove human advancements back so far in such a short time.

There was another theory that the Zhen'kharians had formed a team to study. There were rare materials within the Earth that humans had not yet discovered, or at least had not recognized their value as of yet. Was it possible that the cultural shift was not human induced, but the result of an outside influencer? When the possibility was first put forward in the Council chambers, some questioned its similarities to the conspiracy theories that plagued humans, but the group that presented it were able to identify a micropoint in the human timeline when humanity turned backwards, towards the state of self annihilation, and the reason for that needed to be identified.

Progress continued on Safra's human evolution theory as well. It was entirely possible that the combination of the Homo sapiens reaching a recursive state, colliding with the timeline of the cult of personality, was the micropoint the conspiracy theory team was attempting to identify and Safra herself thought this far more likely than alien intervention. She knew that most intelligent lifeforms outside of Earth's solar system refused to interact with Earth at all, fearing human violence and aggression.

As these studies progressed, others continued to monitor Earth, but with far less zeal than they previously had. To the Zhen'kharians, the absence of striving was a sign of a species in terminal decline, a model no longer worth monitoring. The wars that Zhen'kharians thought would end, persisted. They had become wars of attrition instead of wars of technology, no country wanting to give up land gained, and none willing to concede defeat, so they held the lines. The battles now came with a high cost to life, brutal, and bloody, and more personal each time a battle occurred.

The real wars though were against technology and oligarchy. Data centres were the first targets. They weren't attacked by states or militaries, but by masses of people who had hit their breaking point and decided they had enough. Even though they weren't organized or weaponized, their actions left little standing but the outlines of the structures that once housed the world's data.

When the data centers were destroyed, the tech companies themselves became the targets. Then came the attacks on people seen using mobile devices like phones and wearable tech. The backlash against the technology that had been used to monitor, manipulate and control them, and the people that helped that happen, was relentless. Employees that once worked for these companies were branded collaborators and had to go into hiding.

The assaults on the oligarchs that remained on Earth were swift and brutal, in some cases their own protection teams turned against them, dragging them out for a public display of a mob approved death sentence. Many who attacked the oligarchs and their compounds had envisioned walking away with millions of dollars in cash. The realization that aside from trinkets and homes, and now useless technology supported vehicles, these oligarchs had little of useable value. No real cash existed and most of what they had was in now worthless cryptocurrencies, or assets owned and occupied by others.

In the Zhen'kharian commentary, billionaires and millionaires were often likened to "plumeshades" noting their similarity to Plumeshade Mimics (Magnifex ostentata). Plumeshades were native to coastal swamps on Xyrrhos-3, a small planet in a distant galaxy the Zhen'khari often travelled to. The creature was no larger than a human hand, but its instinct for self-adornment was unmatched. It scavenged the brightest fronds, shed exoskeleton fragments, iridescent shells, and even bioluminescent fungi, attaching them with sticky secretion to a series of flexible dorsal spines. From a distance, the display resembled a much larger predator with glaring eyes and flared limbs.

When threatened, the Plumeshade trembled its spines, creating a shimmering, shifting illusion of size and movement. Local predators avoided it—not because it was dangerous, but because the creature it impersonated had a venomous reputation.

While humans on Earth decompressed from the Age of Manufactured Reality, the colonies on the moon and Mars thrived. In five years enough children had been born to double the population of the moon. Some were born in love, but many more were born in violence, the laws of Earth holding no sway on the moon. The adult population of the Moon colony had doubled in five years as well as most of the ships permitted to leave Earth's atmosphere were sent to the moon, their passengers not meeting the standards required to join the Mars colony.

Their wealth may have gotten them on the ships to the moon, but once they left earth, they were equal to all others, their wealth non-existent in space. The moon colony was a mining colony and if you didn't work, you didn't get paid, and that pay was administered from Nova Terra on Mars. Oxygen, water, and food credits were the currency of the moon. All digitally controlled by the Nova Terra administrators so that no one person could gain any financial affluence or influence. If you didn't have credits, or weren't able to earn any, you would be left in an airlock, unable to enter the colony, until you died. Most often, those condemned to this ending chose to open the outside airlock door and hasten their death.

On Mars the population more than doubled. There were no accidental or violent pregnancies and very few additions from Earth. Each was carefully planned for genetic perfection and carried through gestation by women brought to Mars for that sole purpose.

Life on Mars was drastically different than it was on the moon. It was much more gentle, despite the harsh atmosphere outside their colonies. There was no competition for food or water or resources. The competition in Nova Terra centered around obtaining the lead role on science teams, or being chosen for one of the planned flights for Ceres and Europa.

The Zhen'kharians observed the homogeneity of the people in Nova Terra. This aligned with their Homo sentiens theory. There were those that didn't fit the larger picture, but without sample material it was impossible for the Zhen'kharians to determine if they were genetic matches to the others, or if it was something else that found them their spot in Nova Terra. The one person that stood out in particular was the man running the colony, Li Wei.

Li Wei was one of Earth's billionaires, but not one that people were aware of. He was a brilliant scientist of his own right, and while he maintained a modest lifestyle, spending most of his time in his labs, he had quietly amassed a fortune through patents. Li Wei was also the man that had given the subtle signal that led to the death of the founder of the Nova Terra colony. When he arrived on Mars, he was accompanied by a group of well armed guards who had taken their seats on the spacecraft by force. Li Wei immediately assumed control of the Nova Terra colony without any resistance.

Most of the physical work on Nova Terra was done by automated machines, all operated through the colonies AI. This left the humans to continue their scientific and technical research. The colony had been expanded and new colonies created around landing pads that had received ships from the Earth and the moon. There were also smaller sites created to support the mining of deuterium, which was to be combined with the helium 3 from the moon to fuel their spacecraft.

Five years to the day after Li Wei set foot on Mars, he stopped all work on Nova Terra and brought everyone together.

"This is a celebration," Li announced. "I know some of you have been here longer than me, and a few arrived after me, but for me it has been five years on Nova Terra."

People in the room clapped loudly, and Li Wei waited for the applause to die down.

"That is not what we are celebrating, though" said Li dramatically. "This is."

As Li lifted his arm the opaque dome behind him became transparent. Just outside sat two of the original space craft to arrive on Mars.

"Thanks to you these ships have been converted to operate using deuterium-helium-3 fusion. They will both launch tomorrow, and travelling at up to twenty percent the speed of light, one will journey to Ceres and the other Europa."

There was a standing ovation bolstered by cheers and whistles.

"It took each of us months to get here from Earth. It will take these ships only days to arrive at their destinations where the bots will begin setting up the first buildings, and will soon be followed by our own people."

The dome behind Li went opaque again, and he looked around the room with a serious look on his face.

"Stepping stones," Li said quietly. "As we find our way out of this solar system, into the universe to Proxima Centauri b, the Alpha Centauri system, the Barnard Star System, and beyond."

A few people started to clap again, but Li held up his hand.

"Sometimes," he said seriously. "To move forward, we need to leave things behind."

Li turned to face the opaque wall behind him as an image of Earth taken from space appeared on the wall.

"There are more than thirty thousand non-operational objects orbiting that dying planet we once called home. There are almost as many operational satellites orbiting it."

Li lifted both his arms in dramatic fashion, then dropped them. As he did the people in the room watched as lights flickered out on the satellites they could see.

"Now they are all non-operational," he said as he slowly turned to face the room. "We have now cut all our ties with Earth. This is what we are really here to celebrate, the foundation of a new and better human race."

There was a reluctant moment of silence before first one, then another, then more started clapping, followed by cheers. Li left the stage as music started to play loudly and an array of food and drink began to circulate the room, carried by robots. Food was freely available on Nova Terra, but this was the first event that was so lavish. The people of Nova Terra embraced the celebration, a needed distraction as they realized they were completely cut off from their homes, their families, and their friends.

Li Wei did not engage in the celebration, choosing instead to return to his quarters. As he had on Earth, Li lived modestly on Nova Terra, living in one of the smaller units within the colony. The interior of his unit was modest as well, holding just the bare necessities and in one corner a small shrine with a small statue of Buddha, a family heirloom that was all he brought with him from Earth.

Li knelt in front of the statue and meditated on his time since arriving at Nova Terra. His arrival had been marked by fear, the rumor about his ordered murder of the oligarch who had been responsible for the Mars colony circulated widely during his eight-month flight from Earth to Mars. That fear was heightened when he arrived with armed guards at his side.

What the colonists of Terra Nova didn't know was that the man that had brought them there only saw them as tools. His plans were to use Nova Terra as a breeding colony, with every child being an offspring with his genetics. The colonists were just there to support him.

The ship Li Wei arrived on, he was never supposed to be on, his genetics not a suitable fit for the colony. The only people that were supposed to be on the ship were an armed force contracted specifically to protect the creator of Nova Terra. The mistake that oligarch had made was contracting that protection to a company Li Wei had control of, and Li used that to get himself and his own team on the spacecraft.

Li recognized his selfishness in fleeing Earth for Mars, and in directing the assassination of the man responsible for the Mars colony, but he held the belief that the moral weight of an action depended heavily on the intention behind it, and he found peace in that. Since his arrival he took an approach rooted in his studies of Confucius and Buddha, focusing on ethics, social harmony, and governance. He never had need for the team that guarded him and never intended to use them.

When all connections to Earth were cut off at his direction during the event that night, he hadn't done it with malice. Li had spent many hours kneeling in exactly the same spot he was now, contemplating that decision. So many hours that the mat was worn through where his knees rested. During his meditations he found Buddhist justifications for the decision—compassion in preventing Earth's problems from contaminating Mars, and karmic responsibility to prevent the suffering that would result from Earth's dysfunctional systems spreading to space. His Confucian training led him to believe he had a mandate from heaven, and his leadership of a successful, harmonious society gave him the moral authority to make such a decision. Most importantly to him, Earth's chaos threatened the carefully cultivated order of the Martian society they were creating on Nova Terra.

Only time would tell if he had made the right choice, but he had plenty of time now. Away from Earth, and with access to the technology and skills of Nova Terra, Li could move forward with his own scientific discoveries that would keep him alive much longer than any other human had lived. That was the only reason he left Earth for Mars.

12

'Recursive Fallback Protocol and the Homo Sapien Species." This was the title of the thesis being presented in the Zhen'kharian Council chamber, and many Zhen'kharians had gathered to hear it. With the waning interest in the humans on Earth, and more interest in the sentiens on Mars, which is what they referred to Homo sentiens as, there were a surprisingly large number of Zhen'kharians present for the presentation. The talk that this paper discussed the humans return to religion and faith likely had a lot to do with that, because a similar trend had been observed among the Zhen'kharians as their species died off.

"We have accepted that another evolutionary step in the Hominids has taken place. The evolution into sentiens raises the question of whether or not humans were truly sentient or still reflections of their base AI programming. I intend to show you that the latter is in fact the case as the humans are now experiencing cascading system failures due to environmental stressors."

The presenter waved his hand and the four-dimensional image over the table danced with scenes of figures and events that had occurred in recent times on Earth.

"We started to see a clear devolution of life on Earth after the first world-wide broadcast from the Mars colony Nova Terra. The rate of devolution has increased since all connections between Mars and the Earth have been terminated. In that time, instead of the adaptive problem-solving we have attributed to the human species, we are seeing the species revert to earlier code and engaging in primitive social bonding algorithms disguised as faith."

Safra sat patiently, finding the first part of the presentation tedious as they reviewed the original programming of the ARC AI model and walked the room through the evolution of humans, and the various points debate occurred over a determination of sentience over design. It was unnecessary, as there wasn't a person in the room who was not already aware of all of this. Her attention perked as he began to detail the recursive errors, the data the humans had fallen back to, and their return to ancient tribal clustering behaviors.

An image appeared of two men in the center of the room.

"We are all familiar with these two humans. The first we know as the former leader of the largest nation on Earth. The second is the oligarch responsible for the Mars colony. Unfortunately, Zhen'kharian records are incomplete as their names are unclear. Both are referred to by an abundance of names in Earth's digital media and records. Both are also now dead."

The presenter went on to describe how those two men now were now being called the Antichrist and his false prophet, in line with the text of one of the most popular doctrines on Earth. The leaders of the religion not only believed this, but also that the embedded chips most tech company employees had embedded in the back of their hands to give them secure access to buildings and equipment, was the 'mark of the beast'.

The presenter now had the rapt attention of everyone in the room as he continued detailing how leaders of various groups were leveraging one document in particular as they formed their tribes. That document was the Book of Revelations, and the leaders of these tribes were masters at juxtaposing events with logical and scientific explanations, alongside the predictions of a book written two millennia in their past.

The seven seals of Revelations were easy to juxtapose with real people and real events, and humans had mastered the skills of applying religious scripts to modern scenarios, ignoring any and all context of the original.

The 'Four Horsemen of the Apocalypse' were their orange man—the White Horseman, the wars and genocides concealed during the age of manufactured reality—the Red Horseman, the widespread famine and economic collapse—the Black Horseman, and the death and disease that was now consuming humans was the Pale Horseman.

"As you can see," said the presenter. "The religious text is so vague in its description that any number of naturally occurring and easily explained events could also be explained using those descriptions. While the age of manufactured reality has passed, and the oligarchs have fallen, the cult of personality epoch continues as you can see by this."

"How do they not understand there is a scientific explanation for all of these…seals?" asked one of the Zhen'kharians, stopping the presenter just as he began to change the image they were seeing. "None of this basic science is beyond them."

"That question sums up my thesis and its conclusion. How can it be explained, other than the humans reverting to previous levels of programming that does not create the recursive error resulting from them not being able to process what they have experienced."

The presenter waved his hand.

"Perhaps this feed will make some of this more clear."

The Zhen'kharians watched as a human strutted on a platform in front of others who were seated in wooden pews. He was animated, aggressive in his movements, and sweat dripped off his brow as his combover fell from the top of head hanging wet and damp to one side.

"We are in the end times," the human proclaimed boldly, waving a thick black book in the air. "It's all here in Revelations. The seven trumpets!! We have all seen the hail and fire mixed with blood."

The feed paused. "They have seen those, though the red coloring comes from a combination of iron oxide and sulfur compounds in the air, as well as an alga that has survived in dried algae beds, and is being picked up by dust storms and changing wind currents—not blood."

"We have seen mountains of fire cast into the sea," the human continued.

"Volcanic eruptions," said the Zhen'kharian presenter, not pausing the feed this time.

"We have seen the Star called Wormwood and know its poisoned waters," screamed the man as he slammed his book down on a table.

The feed paused again as the presenter zoomed in on the sky. "That second star the humans are seeing is a refraction of their own sun through the pollution in their skies. The poison..."

"Was already there in their waters," said Safra. "More concentrated now with the lack of water treatment as they destroyed the computer technology that was operating those as well."

Safra had been watching the changes on Earth in minute detail since the Nova Terra announcement. Fear had consumed the humans and there was little, if any, discrimination in the technology they destroyed. If it had a computer chip in it, or they thought it had a computer chip in it, it was targeted for destruction. There were still humans trying to preserve beneficial technologies, but there was little they could do to protect it from the mobs.

"If I were one of these human personalities, I could juxtapose the mobs destroying the technology, with the two-hundred million horsemen killing a third of humanity," Safra noted quietly on her pad. She was quite familiar with the human's bible and had gone back and watched the various authors of the books as they wrote their words, and then watched as succeeding scribes put their own interpretations on the original.

The presenter nodded and the feed started playing again.

"The sun, the moon, the stars! Look at how their light has faded. And then there are these," said the man as he pulled a sheet away revealing a cage that housed two extremely large locusts. "How many have been stung by one of these?"

"This is fascinating," said the presenter, pausing the feed again. "Those creatures appear to be the result of an evolutionary adaptation of locusts. Larger, and equipped with sharp barbs that no doubt gives any creature interested in consuming them a second thought.

"We know the Chinese have killed a third of humanity," the preacher spit. "We don't need media or technology to tell us there is more than two-hundred million of them and they are killing at will."

"That is purely conjecture on the speaker's part and highly inaccurate," injected the presenter as the feed continued.

"And then there is the constant lightning, thunder, earthquakes, and hail," continued the man as he once again lifted the book over his head. "These are the seven trumpets of Revelations. We know what the seven bowls of wrath are, and we have all eaten from them. We know what the seven seals are, and we have seen six."

The man lowered his book and clutched it to his chest, then spoke quietly. "We await the seventh seal. We await the silence in heaven that proceeds the trumpet judgements. We await the rapture."

"Fascinating," said the presenter as he waved his arm and the 4-D image fell into the table.

"My time is running short. You can read the rest of my thesis, but as you can all see, humans are experiencing a recursive error and defaulting to earlier programming. Humans, unlike the sentiens, are still our AI model.

"Before we conclude," interjected Quathar. "Am I correct that like the other AI models, the ARC model, Lucy as we call it, had a designed shut down protocol built into its code?"

"I will defer to Safra on that, as she was part of the ARC team," replied the presenter.

Safra considered her reply for a moment, knowing that Quathar was going to take this conversation down a path she did not want to follow, but there was only one correct answer.

"That was built into the code. The same shutdown code was used across all the AI models at the direction of Council."

"If I understand the content of this thesis, and the words of that human, they are waiting to be shut down. The rapture I believe they called it. Would it be incorrect to postulate that, because they are waiting to be shut down, that code has not been carried forward in the progeny of Lucy?"

"What we viewed was a small group from one religion. That is insufficient data to make such a postulation," replied Hanack.

"I showed only one group," replied the presenter. "If you review the references in the thesis, you will find there is a commonality across most religions across the planet. I believe Quathar's conclusion is accurate."

There was a hum in the room as the Zhen'kharians began talking amongst themselves. Quathar didn't give them a chance to join the discussion before voicing his thoughts.

"That being the case, would it not be the ethical action to deliver this shut down procedure to the Homo sapiens, as it is our code that failed and is imposing this suffering on them?"

The presenter's eyes darted between the three Council members at the front of the chamber. "I have not considered that question within my thesis, so it would not be appropriate to speak to that point at this time."

"That is a fair response," replied Hanack. "Thank you for your presentation. I am sure we all look forward to evaluating it more thoroughly."

Quathar wasn't prepared to let his question go unanswered, despite Hanack's obvious attempt at deescalating what could be a heated debate. "I believe the time has come, in light of this new information to reconsider the shut-down of the Homo sapien artificial intelligence models on Earth," he stated boldly. "We now recognize that, despite our earlier conclusions, Homo sapiens are not truly sentient. With the thesis presented to us today, it is unquestionable that they are waiting to be shut down, but their coding has been corrupted and will not let them do this on their own."

Hanack began to speak, but Quathar continued, bringing up the four-dimensional image of Earth's solar system. "Earth is the last remaining living planet in Earth's solar system, and our AI are responsible for its race to death. We do have a solution now that we didn't have in the past. We have a moral responsibility to the species that have not yet gone extinct on the planet. We have an ethical responsibility for the AI we released on the planet. I call for a vote of the chamber."

The volume in the chamber increased exponentially in response to Quathar's call for a vote. It was a bold move, seldom seen in the chamber, its most frequent use around this very topic. This time the mood in the chamber was considerably different though. It may have been the content of the thesis, or the image of the humans actively waiting for their end, or perhaps the combination, but the ethical and moral arguments Quathar had presented them with stimulated an unfamiliar emotional quandary among the Zhen'kharians.

"A vote of the chamber has been called for," said Hanack, a tone of resignation in his voice. "Do any wish to speak first?"

"Will the solution shut them all-down, or does it have a failure rate like previous attempts?" asked someone at the far end of the table.

"There is no failure rate with this solution," said Quathar confidently. "The imperfection in the solution is it may affect some other species at a small scale, but statistically, those species are doomed to extinction by the presence of our human AIs."

Quathar's continued reference to the humans as their AIs didn't go unnoticed by Safra. She felt a chill overtake her from her core as she realized that by identifying and labelling the evolution of the hominids to Homo sentiens, she had also condemned Homo sapiens to be considered less than sentient.

"What about the Homo sapiens on the moon," another asked. His answer came from a Zhen'kharian seated across the room.

"The sentiens have taken steps to restrict them to the moon. The moon itself is unable to maintain the population that is there. We suspect that when helium-3 is no longer required, or an alternate source is found, the sentiens will cut off the moon as they did Earth, resulting in the death of all on the moon."

The quiet hum of discussion continued to fill the chamber, but there were no further questions.

"Please vote now," Hanack directed, feeling uncomfortable in the call because he did not know with any confidence how the vote would turn out. He did not know how he himself would vote.

His face was impassive as he read the results on his screen and announced them to the room. "The chamber has decided to implement the final solution. Council, what say you?"

"Agreed," Quathar announced confidently.

Hanack turned to Safra, disturbed by what he saw. Her always bright eyes were now a jaundiced yellow and her skin pale, almost transparent.

"I will agree, but with a condition. I alone release the final solution. I was a creator of this AI. I was responsible for the release of the failed final solution. The responsibility for finishing what I started, and its results, fall on my shoulders alone."

Hanack turned slowly to Quathar, who also noticed the sudden change in Safra. Quathar nodded solemnly with respect. Hanack looked out to the room full of Zhen'kharians and drew a deep breath. "Agreed," he said.

There was no sound in the chamber. Everyone watched as Safra walked out of the room, struggling to hold herself upright. Quietly the Zhen'kharians followed her out until the chamber was empty, except for Hanack. He sat quietly staring at the empty chamber, the weight of the decision they had just made weighing heavily on him, not because of the choice, but because of Safra. Never had he seen the veil of death overtake another Zhen'kharian as quickly and completely as it had Safra.

The lights in the Council chamber dimmed, with the lack of motion, leaving Hanack in the dark. He quietly wondered if Safra's end would be that gentle.

13

The ships had touched down on Ceres and Europa, but the celebration was muted. In a control room filled with digital displays, Luke stared at the data readout. "Point three isn't twenty. That's the difference between reaching Proxima in our lifetime, or our grandchildren's. Where did we go wrong?"

"I believe the original calculations came directly from our founder, calculated using his own AI system," said Christy. "We have all become aware of the intentional misinformation embedded in that AI system and his calculations. Our failure was in not accounting for that pre-launch."

Heads nodded around the table.

"I will speak with Li Wei about purging those inaccuracies out of our systems," said Luke. "We should have been doing our own verifications though. This could have been disastrous."

"We need to rewrite protocols then," offered Ron. "They have specifically been written with the directive to not conduct secondary verification, probably because the egotistical…" Ron caught himself before the word in his head rolled off his tongue. "He hated to be second guessed, or he never had any intention of going through with it. And speaking of Li Wei, I am surprised he would not want to be part of this conversation."

"He doesn't interfere in our work, which I appreciate," said Luke, ignoring the criticism of the Nova Terra founder.

What none of them knew was that Li Wei had run his own models, and they bought him two extra weeks—just enough time to attempt something he'd been planning for a decade. As soon as the ships were launched towards Ceres and Europa, Li Wei had entered a surgical suite that had been custom built in secrecy. The build itself wasn't done in secret. Li had taken some extraordinary steps to expand the colony structure in a previously unplanned direction with his lab and living quarters at its furthest extreme. The contents of the surgical suite though, wasn't known to anyone but Li. Inside that surgical suite, Li Wei was now maintained in an induced coma.

"So, what do the real numbers look like?" asked Luke.

"Mathematically, our ships may be able to reach two percent of light speed on their new fuel source," said Kaie as his calculations came up on one of the screens. "But we won't really know until we fly to somewhere like Pluto because it will take about three point six billion kilometres to get up to that speed at their current rate of acceleration."

"And just as much to slow down," added Colla.

Luke quickly did the math in his head. "So, we are talking two, maybe three weeks to Pluto, and sixty-five years to Proxima Centauri."

Ron was still entering the numbers in his handheld when Luke spit out the numbers. "How the hell do you do that?" He joked. "Looks like your numbers are right."

"We need a better fuel," said Christy "If we expect to get to Proxima Centauri anytime soon."

"And we need to improve acceleration," added Kaie. "And maybe some brakes."

Luke looked around at the various screens and all the data. They had got their ships to their destinations, but that was only due to the skill of the pilots who controlled them remotely. If they had been left to operate on their programmed code they would be drifting in the vacuum of space.

"Re-run your numbers, then have another team run them from scratch," directed Luke. "If you can verify those calculations, we will reprogram our systems and launch a ship to Pluto to test the actual limits of the ship and its fuel. In the meantime, we will get a robotic probe on every feasible astral body in our solar system to assess for other materials and potential fuels. We'll ask the engineers to work on the acceleration and deceleration and put a team on alternate fuels."

"We should have a team look at a mass driver or electromagnetic catapults, as well," added Colla.

She could tell from the looks of her team members that they had no idea what she was talking about.

"Basically, we build a series of large rings that rockets pass through, each ring boosting the speed of the rocket a little more." Colla's hand drew what she was picturing in her mind in the air in front of her. "One build, boosts multiple rockets."

"Can we use those as brakes as well?" asked Kaie,

Colla shrugged. "No idea. You know as much about them now as I do"

"Guess that's your project to find out more about now," said Christy.

"That'll teach me to open my mouth," replied Colla as she chuckled.

Luke turned to walk away but caught himself. He had developed a method of managing his teams that constantly pushed them but gave little back to them. Li Wei had pulled him aside and gently reminded him that there were no managers on Nova Terra, just people on the same level working towards common goals. They needed Nova Terra's goals to align with theirs.

"Hey, I may not have said it, but it was impressive the way you caught the calculation problems before we lost the ships, and how quickly we adapted," said Luke. "Keep going like this and it won't be 65 years to Proxima Centauri. We will find a habitable planet where we can all spend our retirement with our feet up and breathing in fresh clean air not surrounded by a dome so we can enjoy retirement."

"I am going for food," said Ron. "Anyone care to join me? I'm buying."

His comment elicited some gentle laughter, because they all knew there was no need to buy anything on Nova Terra. The gentle reminder of how things were on Earth when they left was humorous.

"I am not hungry," said Luke. "But I'll walk with you. I am going to see if I can chase down Li Wei."

Luke made his way to the area Li kept his own lab and quarters. As he turned a corner, he came across another man wearing a lab coat, but who had obviously been asleep in the chair next to the window just outside Li's lab.

"Have you seen Li Wei? I need to touch base with him on some issues."

"He has gone on one of his infamous isolate and evaluate sprees," replied the man. "You know, where he isolates himself from everyone, and not one of us knows what he is evaluating. I can't even get into the Lab."

Li often disappeared into seclusion for a couple weeks or more at a time, but no one questioned it, though it always raised stress levels in the colony. Li Wei had become a beacon of stability, quite the opposite of the colony founder. He was an old man, and the longer he was gone, the more speculation there was about his death, and who would fill his role.

Aside from that fear in the back of their mind, most of them had done the same at some point in their careers, to shut out any distractions. They knew what it was like to have a theory or formula echoing inside their head that they just had to get to the bottom of.

"I will let him know you were looking for him when he comes out, though."

Luke nodded his head and said thanks, before turning back toward his own workspace. The lab coat didn't fool him. He recognized the man as one of Li Wei's security team, but he wasn't sure what to make of it. The security team was an anomaly on Nova Terra, but an unintrusive one. There had never been a need for them, and they had never imposed themselves on anyone or anything.

As he walked away, he thought he heard sounds from the lab. He recognized the hum of automated systems powering up. He was curious, but not curious enough to try and get past the guard.

Behind the doors he could not get through, automated systems were waking Li Wei from his induced coma.

14

Coming out of the comatose state was a slow process, not because Li was slow to wake, but familiarizing himself with the induced changes to his body took time. He had spent much of the last two decades working on this process in his private lab, his only goal to beat father time. He had successfully applied his research to animal and human subjects, but his work was quickly undone by environmental factors on Earth. That was why Nova Terra was so vital to him.

Many scientists had been working on anti-aging and beating death, but most had barely succeeded in extending life briefly, if at all. What they had succeeded in was changing physical appearances so that the people that were treated were experiencing the placebo effect and nothing else. Li's treatment protocol was a combination of cellular reprogramming, senescence reversal, telomerase activation, mitochondrial replacement and nanotechnology. Systemic Cellular Renewal Protocol (SCRP) is what he called it, and he had every confidence that his limited success on Earth would become a great success on Mars, which is why he made himself the first patient.

The first part of the process was devastatingly painful, especially on older bodies, which is why he was put into a coma during that first phase. The nanobots were programmed to do their job and they were aggressive in doing so. Li had been unable to code them to work slower in the beginning and in an old body with its aged cellular structure, the nanobots pursued repairs on all the damage at once. It was so aggressive that some patients had died in the trials.

Even in his comatose state, Li was aware of what was happening in his body as the nanobots pursued their first course of action, reprogramming his aged cells using Yamanaka factors and partial reprogramming. He could hear his own heart race and then slow to the point he thought he was about to be a victim of his own creation. It took intense concentration not to panic as he realized he had never sufficiently prepared any of his test subjects for what he was experiencing.

The nanobots targeted telomeres next using micro current induction, precisely controlling telomeres activation. Li could have sworn he heard them working, as he felt a faint electrical itch crawl along his bones. His mind wanted him to reach out and scratch, but locked into the surgical bed, he could not move. It was torture. He distracted himself as he considered how he had built his lab and housing, and the surgical suite over a unique magnetic sweet spot in the southern hemisphere of Mars. On Earth the magnetism was too strong for the nano bots to efficiently generate micro-currents. Here, it was perfect. Just enough to power the bots and not powerful enough to interfere with them.

This was followed by the bots performing repairs to his mitochondrial DNA and if necessary, creating synthetic mitochondria that were more efficient and resistant to damage. The final step in phase 1 was the destruction of cancerous cells. Li knew what he was feeling at this point was not phantom pain. He could feel as each cancer found was burned away, and the silent scream reverberated in his mind.

Once this work was complete, the nanobots only had to maintain the pristine system they had created. Barring any major cellular damage, their continued work would be relatively unnoticed in a body. This is where the major complications occurred on Earth. As small as they were, gravity still affected the nanobots and resulted in them pooling in lower extremities, unable to escape in poor circulatory systems. Where the nanobots didn't succumb to the gravity challenge, the toxins and radiation in the environment, both human created and natural, induced cellular damage faster than the nanobots could keep up. In some cases, the damage was happening to the cells as the bots were attempting to revive them.

Li sat up, exploring the feel and movement of his extremities. He watched the screens in the room which reflected the images captured by the many cameras around him. The stiffness that had been slowly embracing his fingers in a permanent lock was gone, as was the pain. He moved his fingers as though playing a concerto on a piano.

The tingling and shocks from his neuropathy were gone from his feet and lower legs. His biggest mental challenge every day was putting his feet on the floor and walking, knowing that was only going to induce more pain in his feet. He had lived for decades never knowing if he woke up from that nerve pain, or if he felt the pain because he was awake.

It was only as he watched himself that he realized he was seeing his image clearly, without his trifocal glasses. And he was hearing every sound, the hum of the equipment and lights, the movement of the fabric on the bed, and even his own breath, without his hearing aid.

Li slowly stood up, much like he did every other morning, fully expecting to feel the stiffness that took him many steps to ease up. There was no stiffness. Li bounced lightly, the balls of his feet remaining in contact with the ground, then sprung into the air, giggling.

Taking some time to collect himself, Li Wei found his clothes and got dressed, confident that the SCRP treatment had been completely successful—as it should have been. He had after all spent a decade customizing their programming specifically for him. The nanobots would wear down in time, which meant he would need regular injections of new ones, but each injection was an opportunity to introduce improved programming. He no longer had an end date.

Li exited the surgical suite finding his long-time friend and head of his security there. Li had no doubt the man had never left his post.

"Were they able to land the ships successfully?" Li asked.

His friend nodded.

"You go rest now. I am going to tour the compound and touch base with everyone."

"I will send…"

Li held up his hand, a kind look on his face. "No need, my friend. I am safe. I want to visit as a colleague, not an overseer."

The man simply nodded. Li knew that there would be a security team member shadowing him anyway, but they would remain well out of sight, which was acceptable. Li greeted everyone as he walked the halls of the colony, sometimes taking the time to stop and talk. He knew everyone's name and what they were working on, but that wasn't new. What was new was the smell of air and the sensation of the air on his skin as it moved through the halls.

Entering the control center, Li found Luke's team hard at work running their numbers. Members of a second team were monitoring the autonomous bots building structures on Ceres and Europa. Some didn't notice him walk in, but even those who did, did not pay him much attention. Li often dropped in randomly to locations throughout the colony, so there was nothing unusual about his presence.

Li walked over the area Luke's team was working. "So, fifteen days, eh?" he said casually.

Li Wei now had Luke's full attention. They had made a huge error, and Luke was sure they were being called out for it. Christy started to panic a little herself, but then she noticed Li's face. It almost looked like he was struggling to hold back a grin. In fact, he looked different in a lot of aspects, yet not different at all.

Colla froze mid-keystroke. For a moment, her mind told her she was looking at Li Wei's son—but the grin, the cadence of his voice, it was him.

"Sorry sir, we should have caught that error," said Luke apologetically. "It's my team, so my responsibility."

"Remember that email I sent you a few weeks back?" asked Li.

Luke nodded. "The one that required your bio-signature on my system to open."

"That's the one," said Li. "Bring it up."

Christy watched. She could see the corner of Li's mouth lift. He was holding back a grin.

Luke held out his pad so Li could put his finger on it, then looked at the message that opened. His eyes went wide as he read it, and as Luke's eyes widened, Li's grin overtook his face.

"You knew before we launched!" Luke handed his pad to Rob, and it circulated through the team. "But why didn't you tell us?"

"No need. I was confident you would catch it, and even if you didn't, the skills of everyone here would resolve the situation," said Li. "There are going to be times none of us catch the problems, and it does us good to see we can all depend on each other."

Luke held out his hand and was surprised by the strength of Li's grip as he took it in a handshake. "I am humbled, you bastard."

Li broke out in laughter, which got the attention of everyone in the room.

"That would be an appropriate term for me I believe," Li said, still shaking Luke's hand. "Point three percent isn't twenty," he said softly. "But sometimes, what matters is the other ninety-nine point seven you don't see coming."

"Mind if I sit with you for a while. I would like to see what you have come up with. Planning a Pluto run I imagine."

Christy shook her head as she pulled out a chair for Li Wei. The colony was always filled with rumors and stories of Li, but she realized now, he was more brilliant than anyone realized, and he belonged on Nova Terra as much as they all did. He had an uncanny ability to evaluate the minute details but see how they all came together in the bigger picture. He had a mind like Luke did for numbers, only Li took in everything.

As Li sat beside her, she didn't see the aged scientist that was an enigma in the colony. What she saw was a young, brilliant man who inspired them all.

Li smiled kindly, noticing the looks of both Christy and Colla, while quietly thinking "I will outlive you both."

15

Hanack and Kara were the only Zhen'kharians to see Safra off. She appreciated their presence.

"Tell us you are coming home," pleaded Kara.

Safra looked at her through empty eyes. She reached for her broach, the same one her grandfather had handed to her as he passed away, pinning it with shaky hands to Kara's cloak.

"Death has been the curse of my family's line. Not our deaths, but our participation in death. I will fulfill the wishes of the chamber, but my own passing will be the price."

Safra closed the door of her ship, not wishing to discuss her future any further. Kara and Hanack understood and moved away. They watched as Safra's ship took off, waiting for it to disappear from sight, both knowing that Safra had not looked back. She was committed to her task, and to her ending.

Safra sat in silence as she crossed the skies, thinking about her grandfather, because as much as they had butted heads, they were each other's best friend and biggest supporter. She realized now, only after passing it to another, the real weight of leadership, and wished she had understood this when her grandfather was still alive.

On her way to Earth, she passed the homeworlds of many species, their slow crawl toward sophistication evident. Many were quickly catching up to the Zhen'kharians, but none had surpassed them yet. She realized they soon would though. This action she was taking against the Homo sapiens, combined with the march towards extinction of the Zhen'kharians, was much like the recursive error they believed was affecting humans. Were her people so different?

As she entered Earth's solar system, she observed a sentien spacecraft passing nearby, quickly approaching Pluto. She wondered if they had reached their full speed this time, and then she began to wonder if the sentiens might outpace other species in catching up to the Zhen'kharians. If they were like their predecessors, the Homo sapiens, morals and ethics would not hold their rate of advancement back.

Safra orbited the Earth for a few days, overtaken by fatigue. "tá brón orm," she said quietly, speaking a phrase from one of the many human languages. This was the phrase that most accurately described how she was feeling. She wasn't sad. There was a sadness on her, and it was heavy.

Safra took in a deep breath, holding it as she pressed the release button for the viral bombs her ship was loaded with. Each one jetted off to its designated location detonating within one of the major air currents and streams that moved around the planet. As soon as it was released into the air, the engineered virus began replicating. The air streams spread it around the world, and as the rains fell, the virus was carried to the ground. Avian species that used the air currents for travel, picked up the virus and carried it to their many destinations, depositing it in water bodies and on plants, or transmitting it to predators, some of which were human.

The virus was quick to replicate, but slow to act with an incubation period of several weeks. It had been engineered to be transmissible, even in its incubation period, through respiratory droplets, surfaces, and body fluids. Any species could carry the virus, but it would only attack those with human endogenous retroviruses and their genetic structure, and FOXP2 gene variants. Most importantly, the engineered virus had an end date coded into it, so it would not adapt or mutate, and it would die off with the Homo sapiens.

There was no turning back now. All that was left was to monitor the results and ensure the virus was successful. This was their last chance to get this right. Safra made a choice not to monitor the results from her ship high over Earth though. In the dark of night she found an isolated area of forest to set down unseen. She had watched this area, what the humans called Algonquin Park, on the monitors from her home after reading about it in a human book. There were dragons in that book as well, but Safra doubted she would see one. She had seen real dragons, and they didn't look anything like they did in the stories of humans.

As she stepped out of her ship, Safra choked on the air. It was nothing like the air she had breathed in when her team set Lucy down on the planet's surface. It was thick, and it burned as she inhaled it. It was going to take time to adapt. She walked down to a nearby shore and watched as a large creature with heavy horns fed. She recognized it as a moose. She watched the moose, and the moose watched her, both not quite believing their eyes. Then they watched the night pass together.

When the virus became active in the first group of humans it worked exactly as planned, attacking neural tissue. The infected humans could be heard talking about bright lights and halos as their visual cortices became inflamed. The others hearing those descriptions were confident that this was their friends and family being taken in the rapture, the bright lights, their god beckoning to them. As it spread to other brain regions their autonomic functions shut down and they quickly passed. It wasn't kind, or gentle, but it was effective, and Safra took what comfort she could in the knowledge that as the humans passed, they thought they were moving to the light of their scriptures.

Safra watched the first group of humans pass away on the monitor in her ship. She didn't watch any more, opting to just watch the numbers of living humans in her data stream. The viral spread followed classic epidemiological patterns, doubling at regular intervals until they reached maximum saturation. With nearly the entire human population infected, new cases plateaued not from immunity or intervention, but from the simple mathematics of a finite host population. Death rates remained constant, but the exponential phase was over—replaced by the methodical elimination of the remaining infected.

Each human death seemed to be a razor cut to Safra's will to live, shaving her will off in slow painful slices. Each day she became weaker, eventually reaching the point that she just sat in her ship, waiting for it all to be over. A squirrel brought her berries and seeds from the forest, pushing it into her hand, but Safra had no desire to eat. Other animals tried as well, and the food just gathered in her lap, untouched. Then one day a bear dragged a cub into her clearing. The cub was limp and struggling for breath. The bear pushed the limp body of the cub toward Safra, crying for help in the way only a bear could, a gargled bawl of the pain of a mother.

Safra could not watch that cub die, so she used what energy she could muster to get out of her ship and help the cub. As she nursed the cub back to health, the animals nursed her, bringing her food, and remaining close to keep her warm. Every day she would check the data stream, and when she realized the number of deaths each day was slowing, so too did her own decline, though she attributed that to her need to care for the bear cub.

On the four hundred and thirty second day the last human passed. Her task complete, Safra set the automated controls on her ship, stepped back and watched her last tie to Khar'Veleth take off, leaving her behind. She followed the now well-worn path down to the lake and sat on the sandy shore. A racoon came and joined her, cuddling up against her and letting Safra stroke its soft fur. This had become a regular occurrence over the four hundred and thirty-two days she was on earth. Not just the racoon, but many animals, large and small.

There was a cosmic irony in the fact that it was four hundred and thirty-two days that humanity died over. That number was a frequency identified by the Greek philosopher Pythagoras that he theorized aligned with the universes natural order. Mathematically there was a harmony to it. Cosmically, four hundred and thirty-two was kind of a base unit in Hindu scriptures for structuring cosmic time. Norse mythology spoke of five hundred and forty doors, and from each door, eight hundred warriors, which would be four hundred and thirty-two thousand warriors.

"I would be laughed out of the Council chamber if I ever said those theories out loud," Safra said in a gentle voice to the racoon. "And so I should be. But I am on Earth now. I too might believe them if I was raised here."

She leaned forward to get a drink and saw her reflection in the glass-like surface of the water. The person that was staring back at her was not who she expected to see. Her skin had taken on a green hue, and her eyes were bright like two deeply green emeralds.

Surprised, Safra sat back, and looked out across the lake as she took inventory of herself. She breathed deeply, the air already cleaner than when she arrived, the heavy musk of the forest carried in each breath. She had come to Earth to die with the humans, but something had changed. She wasn't there to die anymore. There was more to do. There was a planet that had been damaged by the creation she had helped to design. Her time had not yet come. The desire to heal the planet and help the animals that had become her companions had energized her. She would be alone on Earth, but not really. It was abundant with life, as was she once more.

Safra closed her eyes as she remembered her grandfather talking about the beauty of Earth and the abundance of creatures on it. Those talks stopped when he first tried to reset the planet. But she was here now.

What if fate, as the humans called it, brought her to Earth, to be responsible for returning it to its glory? What if she was her grandfather's gift to the planet he loved, perhaps more than his own?

She could hear her grandfather's voice as she recalled the words he spoke as she fell asleep next to him when she was a child. "Safra, when I look upon Earth, I see not just beauty but a promise—that those who love it will rise to heal it. If fate ever brings you there, remember it is not the planet that belongs to us, but we who belong to its keeping."

16

Seeing the skies from within the moon colony was a rarity. Their building walls were solid, with few portals of lunar glass. Only those that commuted from one worksite to another via the surface of the moon, got to see the skies, and in those skies, the planet they came from. When they returned home from their extended shifts, they would tell stories about looking towards home.

The first change they noticed was the change in lighting patterns. Even the dark side of Earth was well lit with artificial lights when they first came to the moon, but the night side gradually went dark, first sporadically, then entire regions went permanently dark. Within months, the familiar web of city lights vanished completely, leaving only occasional fires or volcanic activity as light sources.

Others started returning home swearing that the atmosphere around Earth was clearer. "That industrial haze is gone," swore one man to the group he was talking to. "The colors of Earth are vibrant and defined!"

These tales of Earth looking like it was getting better sparked a lot of discussion on the lunar colony. When Nova Terra cut off all forms of communication with Earth, the lunar colony was cut off from Earth as well. At one point a group had decided they had enough of living on the moon and attempted to hijack one of the helium-3 transport ships. They were successful in launching the ship, and diverting it from its programmed flight path, but their luck ended there.

In the Lunar colony screens activated in response to the emergency protocols of the transport ship, and the last moments of the lives of the men on the ship were broadcast as the ship depressurized and exploded. That single event put an end to any conversations about hijacking another ship. It didn't stop the conversations about possibly returning to Earth, though.

It was made clear through the intentional destruction of the pirated ship that Nova Terra had no intention of letting anyone return to Earth. The people in the Lunar colony were not without their own skills though. From the day humans first started colonizing the moon they utilized a construction strategy based on lunar regolith, moon soil. From that moon soil they built their structures using lunarcrete and cast basalt, reinforced with glass fiber. That regolith also provided them with the materials for silicone-based sealants and Lunar glass, though something in their process failed to render that glass clear.

What they also extracted from the regolith was aluminum, iron and titanium. Construction of new buildings had slowed down, but mining operations continued because Nova Terra needed its helium-3. This meant they were able to divert significant amounts of these metal materials to construct their own transport home. Their plan was simple. Build their own ship and send a small group back to Earth. That group could send transport ships from Earth to collect other colonists from the Moon.

It was a good plan, in theory. Little did they know that they would not be returning to their Earth, but to one that had freed itself from the plague of humans. They still might be successful in finding and launching a transport ship, if the Zhen'kharian virus didn't take them first, though it was entirely possible the virus itself might also be dead by the time they arrived. If that virus end-date wasn't effective, it could be transported to the Moon and then Mars. It had the potential to not only make Homo sapiens extinct, but also Homo sentiens.

On Terra Nova, they too were oblivious to the extinction of humans on Earth, and the machinations of the colonists on the moon. While whispers of escape stirred on the Moon, Nova Terra's focus was turned outward—towards Jupiter and Proxima Centauri. The colony they had built on Mars was amazing in so many ways, but it had walls and windows that were restricting, and a stroll in nature outside those walls was not an option.

Living in the confines of Nova Terra the rest of their lives was not on the bill of sale when they were convinced to leave Earth. It was only a stepping stone to a new "Earth" in Proxima Centauri. That is why they were coming together today—they needed a deep-Jupiter mining ship to get the materials that would change travel to Proxima Centauri from sixty-five years to only four.

They had successfully got their spacecraft up to full speed during its flight to Pluto, but they had found no feasible solution for accelerating and decelerating the craft. What they had found though was numerous treasure troves of rare metals and gasses throughout the solar system. Titan had complex hydrocarbons, the asteroid belts were troves of heavy metals, and Jupiter? Jupiter had a wealth of antimatter in its radiation belts, and at its core, 'exotic ice' that contained metallic hydrogen. There was a high level of confidence among the Nova Terra colonists that they could utilize that antimatter and the metallic hydrogen to create a faster than light engine. Their first challenge was harvesting those materials though.

Li Wei had brought all the Nova Terra colonists together in one room to discuss the construction of this new ship. Throughout his scientific life he had witnessed too many projects fail because the team members thought they knew enough. Often it was the tiniest thing that caused the failure, and it was their refusal to ask the "stupid questions" which were really just questions they thought would make them look stupid, that caused them to miss the problem. In a large group like this, all the questions would be asked.

What the group came up with in a day, would have taken years of planning for others. The ship was to be a spherical pressure vessel, with other spheres nested inside it like a Matryoshka doll, and pressure-equalizing chambers between layers. The adaptive hull would be made of ultra-dense materials like harvested tungsten and osmium from asteroids.

The deep-Jupiter mining sphere would be unmanned, equipped with quantum communication arrays to maintain contact with Nova Terra through the interference. The propulsion and maneuvering systems would be a combination of magnetoplasmadynamic drives that would work with Jupiter's conductive metallic hydrogen environment, and electromagnetic field generators that would push against Jupiter's magnetic field.

"Magnetoplasmadynamic. Say that five times fast," Li quipped. "Who knew magnets would get us so much further than oil and gas—or even fusion?"

Li stood back and looked at the detailed blueprint that had been created as those spoke, now projected on the wall behind him. He looked pleased. If he noticed the way everyone in the room was watching him, he didn't acknowledge it. He had their undivided attention from the time he walked into the room because he no longer looked like the old man he was. The nanobots pulsing through him could no longer be concealed.

"I think we are forgetting about just how hot it is going to get," said a voice from the back of the room.

Li snapped his fingers loudly and raised his hand in the air. "Yes! That's why we are all here. There are no stupid questions. Asked them all."

Li Wei's vitality and energy as he spoke, and almost bounced with excitement, energized everyone in the room, while raising a few questions unrelated to the new ship. Questions that no-one was going to ask. When the questions about the Jupiter ship stopped, Li Wei walked slowly to the back of the room. He stood there, looking at the blueprint from the perspective everyone in the room was seeing it. He smiled.

"I am no mathematician, so Luke might correct me," said Li, pausing to wait for the expected laughter to quiet down. Luke's ability to do calculations in his head was legendary in a colony of minds known for their extraordinary abilities. "If we put our minds to it, and our backs into it, some of us will be camping out on a planet in Proxima Centauri in ten years!"

Li clapped his hands together in applause. "This is for you. You all have earned it. Now let's make this happen."

With that Li turned and left.

The room filled with excited chatter and conversation, but not about the new spacecraft, or Proxima Centauri. It was about Li. It was unmistakable to anyone now that Li Wei looked decades younger than when he arrived on Nova Terra. He not only looked different, but he moved differently, with a spring in his step forty-year-old men didn't have and definitely not one that would be expected from an eighty-seven-year-old.

Some of them went to their mobile devices to look up pictures of Li Wei, to show others just how much younger he looked. To their surprise, every picture they found was exactly the same person they had just watched leading them through the planning session. That didn't shut the conversation down. It fed it, and with the bottomless appetite for madness that only conspiracy theories can conjure, the speculation spiraled—doppelgänger, time traveler, cloned replacement. There wasn't a mind in the room that wasn't brilliant, but that only contributed to the audacity and paranoia of some of the speculation.

Back in his living quarters, Li Wei saw all the notifications about the searches in the system for photos of him. He laughed to himself as he imagined the conversations happening. It had taken him only a few verbal commands to get the AI to find all the images of him and adjust them so they looked just as he did now. He didn't expect that would fool many, but it provided them with far less foundation to question him on the changes.

As he kneeled in front of his shrine, he could feel the nanobot's gathering their charge from the unique magnetic field just below him. The irony of the moment wasn't lost on him that he had just spent a day planning a faster path to Proxima Centauri, but he would never be one of the people to travel there. The unique charging mechanism of the nanobots that made him younger and would keep him that way could not be easily replicated. Away from Nova Terra, he would remain young and full of vitality for a year, perhaps two. Then age would hit him like a fast-moving train, and it would all be over.

Li Wei considered if he should tell the others these details as he meditated. He would have to give them some explanation soon, and he was not going to find the guidance in the words of Confucius or Buddha, because they were in conflict on the matter.

"Confucius tells me the gentleman is not a vessel, and that silence is a true friend that never betrays," said Li, talking through his thoughts. "Those words guide me to maintain my secret and pick and choose what I share wisely."

Li bent forward at his waist and put his forehead to the floor for a moment.

"Speak the truth, do not yield to anger. When asked, give even if you have but little," said Li quietly. "Why do you have to be so contrary Buddha?" Li Wei laughed as he stared now at the small statue of Buddha. "You guide me to tell all."

Li bowed, putting his head to the floor once more, this time for a much longer moment. As he got up from the floor Li spoke again. "You and your Confucious buddy need to get on the same page and give me an answer."

17

The sentiens on Mars had become the new fascination for Zhen'kharians. Earth now held little interest with the humans gone and none thought for a moment that Safra was not only alive there, but thriving.

The sentiens though, were advancing at a pace that was astonishing. They were actively harvesting resources from almost every planet and moon, and many asteroids in their solar system. They were even successful in reaching the core of Jupiter, something which the Zhen'khari themselves had chosen not to risk. Their observation of the sentiens though, was not for study or scientific purposes. It was for hope.

"With humans gone, the Zhen'kharians turned their gaze to the sentiens on Mars. Safra would have laughed," said Kara to an empty room, as she recorded her thoughts for posterity. "She had spoken often of the burden she and her grandfather carried in Earth's extinction cycles—a burden now consuming us as surely as the virus consumed humanity."

Kara stared at the broach that hung on the wall by the door. She hadn't worn it in the three years Safra had been gone. There hadn't been a single Council meeting since then, and the Council chamber was rarely filled with anything but the sound of the air moving through it. In that three years almost one third of the Zhen'kharians had let death take them. She herself, often contemplated that choice.

"Among my people, death is never cruel. When we choose to leave, our bodies obey. It has always been honored. But now, as friend after friend departs, it feels less like honor and more like surrender."

As Kara spoke, she remembered the day she saw Safra board her ship for Earth. She remembered vividly the urge to throw the broach back at her and scream that there had to be another path, welling up inside her, but it wasn't the Zhen'kharian way. Now, at the current death rate, Zhen'kharians would be extinct in a few years, as the loss of each friend and family member left less for those who remained to hang on to.

"Was this what our creators coded into us?" wondered Kara out loud. "Were they kinder than we were giving us the option to gently remove ourselves from this world? The shut-down protocols that we coded into the original trial AIs were far less kind, and perhaps that is why the AI's found a way not to pass it along. Will the virus we engineered to end Homo sapiens be the same? Will it too find a way to escape its end date?"

Kara turned on the feed for Earth. It was year 3 AH (after humans) for the planet, and the dramatic transformation that had overtaken it was almost beyond belief. The colors were so vivid. Greens and blues and browns. The cloud cover was extensive and moving fast, which was to be expected. Without the heatsinks that human cities created, and the gases being added to the atmosphere, Earth's biosphere was struggling to find its natural balance.

In year two forest fires shrouded the planet with smoke. Without the humans' fire suppression, the land had to find its natural balance as well, as fires consumed the abundance of fuel built up on the forest floors and land. This was the natural process, but it had been made unnatural by human interference. Now the fires had mostly gone out, and new vegetation had come up, no longer smothered beneath decades of forest litter.

Kara zoomed in to the shore in Algonquin Park that Safra's ship had returned from. This wasn't the first time she had done this, as she searched for some sign of her friend's passing. There were always signs of where a Zhen'kharian had been returned to the ground, a single flower that broke free quietly from the soil and became a tree. The Zhen'kharians believed that was the seed of life that maintained them, and that they returned their energy to as that passed away.

There was no flower to be found though, and no tree of life. Kara assumed it had something to do with the soil or the air, not knowing that Safra had long since left the shores of the lake and was wandering her new world. Turning the feed off, Kara picked up one of the handwritten journals Safra had left behind and wandered through the pages.

As Kara wandered through Safra's deepest inner thoughts seeking refuge from the loneliness that was embracing her, Safra too wandered, though she was never alone. An animal or two often accompanied her, not at her request, but at their choice. Some would travel many miles with her, and others only a short distance, but there was always one there at her side. She talked to them like friends, though she didn't think for a moment they understood her. When she stopped to rest though, she would work at understanding them.

When she came to her first city, Safra sat on a hill that overlooked it, watching it for a long time as though it was still alive. In some ways it was, the buildings and streets filled with the offspring of what humans had called pets. Plants were taking over as well. With no traffic or throngs of people moving along the hardened pathways, life was forcing itself up through the concrete and asphalt.

It took some time, but she knew what her first task was when she saw water flooding back into a part of the city, its surface a rainbow of hues from the oils that refused to sink. There was a dam holding that water back. That had to go. She didn't know how she would do it, but she was determined to get it done. And she did.

Day after day she walked the dam, studying it. Using simple tools she found in the city, she worked on already weak points, removing pieces of the structure as it groaned and creaked around her. She didn't stop until she heard the water moving through the barrier, ever so slightly, but enough. Her work done, she returned to her hill and watched as the water itself completed the work she had started.

She slept on that hill, under the stars, wondering as she always did if anyone from home was watching her, or if they even knew she was alive? She felt more alive than she had been since the passing of her grandfather. Without all the equipment and technology that had always been at her fingertips, she was always facing challenges, trying to learn from nothing, and adapt. It was stimulating.

There was something else she felt. A quiet strangeness coiled within her, subtle at first—the way her strength slipped sooner, the way her body seemed no longer entirely her own. Fatigue pressed on her more easily, as though some hidden current was altering her from within. She could not name it, yet she sensed that whatever it was, it would not be denied.

She regretted in some ways sending her ship home. If it was still here, she could tell the Zhen'kharians what she was experiencing. Perhaps it could do for them what it was doing for her. Rejuvenate them and give them a new lease on life. But the ship would have been a crutch, so sending it back was the right thing to do.

Safra moved slowly, always stopping to see and learn. And every new creature she met, she would sit with them and try to learn their way of communicating, sometimes more successfully than others. Animals never saw her as a threat, and she never saw them as a threat. She felt there was a symbiotic harmony of sorts between her presence on Earth and the life around her, though she knew the term "symbiotic harmony" would never pass the scientific rigor of the Council chamber.

Safra didn't count the days, or record time so she had no concept of how long she had been on Earth, and it did not matter to her. But as three years from the time she set down, turned to five and then six and seven, Khar'Veleth became silent. The last of the Zhen'kharians passed on. Even those that had been in the furthest universes had returned to their home system made their choice to follow the others.

As the last Zhen'kharian passed away, Safra was seized by something utterly foreign, something that split her being between terror and awe. A force welled within her, primal and unstoppable, as if the universe itself pressed through her body. It was an event that had not touched her people since the age of their first dawn, an experience banished from living memory. Safra, one of the last-born of her kind, now brought forth another.

Pain, sharp and relentless, coursed through her frame—not an enemy, but a command. She had no memory, no teaching, no elder's voice to guide her. Yet her flesh remembered what her mind could not. Muscles strained. Breath ragged. The rhythm of creation moved her, demanding surrender.

Fear struck her heart—she did not understand what was happening, and for a moment she believed she was breaking, being unmade. Yet beneath the fear, instinct whispered. Trust. Yield. Endure.

And then—release. A cry, not her own, pierced the silence of a foreign world. Safra cradled the small, damp weight pressed against her. Eyes wide with shock and wonder, she stared at the fragile being, impossibly alive, impossibly hers.

Her hands trembled as she lifted the child toward the unfamiliar sky. Her voice broke into a scream that was fierce, desperate, and exultant—shattering the silence of a quiet world that had embraced her.

"Khar'Veleth, if any hear me," her heart thundered, "Know we are not ended!"

In that moment, with the newborn pressed against her chest and the echo of her cry reverberating in the thin air, the extinction of the Zhen'kharians was undone.

18

Li Wei joined other medical specialists as they vaccinated the children of Nova Terra. Many of them had become ill in recent days and the cause had been identified as a virus that took advantage of a genetic flaw that was present in all of the children that had been test tube babies. Test tube babies were no longer being created in the colony. Li had shut down the program and banned the practice. There was no humanity in it.

Since that time there had been some children born on Nova Terra as they should have been, through love and into the caring embrace of parents who were part of them. Some had questioned the decision to shut down the genetics program that enabled them to customize their children and remove flaws, but this was one decision Li Wei would not go back on.

"We are not creating machines," Li had told them as he had his security team dismantle and destroy the contents of the genetic birth lab. "None among us is perfect, and it was the struggle to overcome those imperfections that made us the people we are. Good people. Smart people. All deeply flawed, but working around those flaws. Confucius tells us, better a diamond with a flaw than a pebble without."

Li Wei's words seem wise, as he intended, but they hid a truth that he alone knew. Each child created in that genetics lab had key components of the genetics from the colony's founder in them. It was an insidious program that he had discovered only by chance, while going through secured files recently discovered in their system. What the genetics lab called a stable base, on which they added the chosen genetics of prospective parents, was in fact the founder's core DNA.

Li had wrestled with his thoughts about the future of these children. As they got closer to putting humans on a planet in Proxima Centauri, he could not justify in his mind, putting these genetic creations into the wider universe. He knew part of his reasoning was based on his complete hatred of the founder, but there was more to it. At least to him there was more to it. He wanted to preserve humanity, and they were not human, just as he had, with the injection of the nanobots, become not human.

The illness the children were experiencing was not naturally occurring. Li had created it, knowing he had the cure beforehand. The vaccination they were receiving contained some of the same nanobots that coursed through Li's own body. Their programming was far less specific, but his intention wasn't to keep them young forever, merely bind them to Nova Terra as he was. They would feel some discomfort as the bots attacked the virus and other small problems, but they would be unaware, unless they tried to leave Mars—or until he confessed, as he now knew he must.

The following day Li Wei sat with a group of colonists that asked to meet with him to discuss the Proxima Centauri ship they were building. Before they could start, he took advantage of this moment to unburden his soul.

"I must confess something before we continue," he said, speaking calmly. "I discovered a hidden file of the founder and chose not to share it with you. I did not want to burden you with the decision that needed to be made. You may judge my act as you deem appropriate."

Li shared the file, not just with those in the room, but all the colonists.

"The illness you have seen in the children was caused by a virus I engineered. One that would specifically activate only in children with the DNA base used for the test tube child program. I created the illness, which does no real harm, knowing I already had the cure."

"I don't understand," chimed in a voice. "You made them sick so you could make them well? You used them as test subjects?"

"Not test subjects. I used the virus to justify the implementation of the vaccine. I needed to have a reason to inject the children that would not be questioned because…" Li Wei took an unusual pause in his thought. He needed that moment to put in check the fear that what he was about to say could result in him taking the same walk out the air lock the founder had. "Because that vaccine carries nanobots I created."

There was a murmur in the room, but Li held up his hand and continued.

"They are not test subjects for the nanobots. The same nanobots are in me. They will experience no ill effects. Quite the opposite. The nanobots will keep them healthier. But, if they leave Mars, the nanobots will power down and the damage they repaired will return so quickly their death is inevitable."

"I knew that bastard did something," said one of the scientists angrily, throwing his pad down onto the table. "I could see him in all those kids."

This was not the response Li Wei expected. Most of the people in the room were silent, processing what they were reading in the file, but others were quite vocal in their anger which was not directed at Li, but the founder.

"Is that why you are looking so much younger?" asked Calla.

"It is."

Li Wei took his time explaining to everyone how his nanobots had been customized to him, and how they worked, as well as the changes he had made in the bots injected in the children. He patiently answered each question.

"I understand the problem," said a young woman, one of the many that had been brought to Nova Terra for the sole purpose of carrying the babies. "But what gives you the right to limit their future?"

"I have no right," replied Li quietly. The words sounded empty, even to him, though he clung to them as truth. He had struggled with the decision, and if he had to make it over again, might choose not to act, but he could not show that contradiction in his soul to the others. "But I do have a responsibility to ensure we aren't destroying our future or populating the universe with artificial lifeforms."

"You could have consulted with us. Those children have some of our DNA too."

The woman's words struck deeper than he would admit, but internally he dismissed them as a hormonal response to giving birth to several children. He could not relate to this and offered what he thought was a logical response.

"Yes. I could have. But then you would find yourself in a conflict for and against each other's children. This was not a choice to be made based on emotion or compassion." He said it firmly, but even as the words left his lips, he felt the hollowness in them.

The questions became a conversation amongst everyone, and as Li expected, it became heated. These were children after all, and they did carry the DNA of some of the colonists. They were carried in the wombs of women brought to the colony for that purpose alone. There was no possibility that it would not stir emotions.

"Alright," said Li, standing up. "Look. I will have a very long life," said Li. "But by taking in these nanobots I have given up some of my humanity. My cost for this choice is the freedom to travel the universe with you. The children will be fine after you are gone. I will be here to watch over them. If they too find error in my judgement, they will have plenty of opportunity to seek justice."

"You made a choice that I couldn't," said Luke. "It was the right choice. But speaking of travelling the universe and bots, this is why we asked for a meeting." With a flourish Luke lifted what looked like a large tortoise onto the table. "This is our bot. A fully autonomous AI."

Li had a rare look of confusion for a moment, unsure if he should embrace the change in direction. He didn't know if Luke was throwing him a lifeline that would let him escape the expected repercussions from his confession, however briefly, but he followed Luke's lead. On the table in front of him now was a large metal tortoise.

"The mining process on the asteroids is proceeding at a slower pace than expected," said Luke. "We have created the FTL drive and have mined sufficient fuel from Jupiter to power it, but we don't have enough material to build a ship large enough for any crew. We call it KURMA."

"I know this name," said Li. "From my studies. It's the tortoise incarnation of the Hindu deity Vishnu, who supported the cosmos during creation."

Luke was impressed that Li knew that. "Yes, but to us, Kinetic Unmanned Reconnaissance and Mission Automation. It can literally be part of a smaller craft sent to Centauri b where it can explore, collect data, and start preparations for our arrival. While we improve our mining techniques to build a crewed ship, it can prepare our new home."

Li ran his hand over the tortoise, admiring it. Tortoises were symbols of endurance, patience, long journeys, and carrying the world on their backs. It was so appropriate. "Tell me more," Li said, his voice steadier than he felt, grateful for the change of subject.

Everyone in the room seemed to have a part in the creation of KURMA. Like a real tortoise, all the movable pieces and sensors retracted into the shell for protection. Fully retracted, it would be part of the body of a small FTL ship, reducing the materials needed to make the ship. On Centauri b that same shell would protect it from the elements, and predators, until it found a shelter.

Like any AI, KURMA would gather data and learn from it, adapting to its environment and then it would replicate. Its shell could be peeled of in layers of the metals it was made with. KURMA could repurpose that material to build support units, programming each for the tasks required.

"Fascinating," said Li.

"We expect that it will learn to use materials on the planet to build other bots as well. When we set foot down on Centauri b," said Luke. "Part of the job of creating a place for us to live will already be done."

"Well done, all of you," said Li. "When can we launch it?"

"Fourteen days," replied someone.

Li ran his fingers over the head of the tortoise. The eyes, sophisticated cameras, looked so realistic. The mouth, a tool to sample materials, looked just like a turtle his childhood friend had as a pet. He fondly remembered that turtle biting his finger as he fed it a berry.

"How far behind KURMA will you be?"

Many in the room caught Li's use of 'you' where it had always been 'we' before. He wasn't hiding the fact that he would not be joining them anymore.

"Two years," said Luke.

"Well let's hope KURMA has a safe journey. Like others before her, she has our future on her back," said Li. "Send it."

Li tried to quickly leave the room, but he was stopped by the woman who had questioned what right he had to condemn the children to life on Mars.

"You chained our children to Mars for being artificial, yet you send an artificial thing to carry your dream. Tell me, Li Wei…whose future really matters to you?"

Her words cut deeper than any wound, slicing past his reason and into the part of himself he kept most guarded. Three things cannot be long hidden: the sun, the moon, and the truth. Buddha's words returned unbidden, and for the first time Li wondered whether his truth was a light…or only a shadow stretching endlessly behind him.

In Khar'Veleth there was silence. There were no feeds. There were no Zhen'kharians to watch and study the sentiens. They were not there to observe a species find their way to immortality and witness the sentiens setting an AI free on a far away world, just as there was no one there to watch them do the same.

19

Kurma drifted through the void between worlds, its digital signature beating like a pulse in the cosmic silence. It had been four years since it left the rust-colored skies of Mars, accelerated by the first faster than light drive humanity had ever built.

Whether that FTL drive had been created by humans or sentiens was a question only history could answer long in the future, but it was a heavy metal needle threading through space at two hundred and five thousand miles per second. Behind it, the sun of Earth's solar system had long since dimmed to just another star among thousands. Ahead, Proxima Centauri grew brighter with each passing day.

Kurma's AI consciousness maintained a vigil over sleeping systems, waking briefly from time to time to run a system diagnostic and verify they were on the right course before returning to hibernation. It had been awake now for three hundred and twenty-one days since a grain of interstellar dust, no larger than a virus but moving at relative speeds that turned it into a kinetic weapon, had punctured a microscopic hole in its shell. The hole quickly sealed, and its multi-layered, heavy-metal carapace brought the dust to a stop, but not before it impacted a data storage component.

Kurma had spent the last three hundred and twenty days rerouting functions and rewriting lost portions of code, knowing that it would be setting down on Proxima b shortly. She had already begun the process of slowing as Proxima's light swelled from a point into a disk.

She soon began to detect the gravitational signature of the three planets in the Proxima Centauri system. Then, impossibly, the rocky world appeared in her sensors—Proxima b, locked forever between fire and ice, one face burning under its red sun while the other lay frozen in eternal night. Kurma deployed its massive magnetic sail, capturing the charged particles streaming from the red dwarf star, increasing the drag against Kurma's incredible velocity. This was "the brakes" the sentiens had designed, and it worked remarkably well as the spacecraft shuddered under the forces, the brakes boosted by controlled burns.

Kurma had carefully chosen her landing site, using all the data she gathered as she approached Proxima b. She had picked a spot on the terminator line, where Proxima b's eternal day met eternal night. Temperatures there would be survivable. The ships heat shields began to glow as it hit the planet's thin atmosphere at still incredible speeds.

What followed was controlled violence. Retrorockets fired in sequence, each one a small antimatter fueled push against four years of momentum. The landscape below—a twilight realm of rust-colored plains and methane lakes—rushed upward with terrifying speed. Emergency parachutes deployed and shredded instantly in the alien winds. Airbags inflated around the probe's core just seconds before impact.

Kurma hit the surface of Proxima b like a meteorite, carving a shallow crater in the frozen regolith. For seventeen minutes, nothing stirred. Then, slowly, Kurma's systems began to wake.

Kurma took inventory, her autonomous form thrown clear of the body of the shattered hull, exactly as designed. Other than being on her back, she had survived completely intact, protected by airbags, aerogel, and her shell. She was alive. Functional. On the surface of humanity's first interstellar destination.

Righting herself, Kurma slowly looked around before crawling out of the crater created by the landing, to the sandy surface. She sent images back to Nova Terra confirming the landing. The red sun hung motionless in the sky, casting everything in shades of crimson and shadow. Strange delicate crystals of frozen atmosphere glittered in the eternal dusk. In the distance, towering ice formations caught the stellar wind, singing with an alien music that Kurma's sensors translated into haunting melodies.

Kurma worked methodically. Soil samples revealed complex chemistry—far from a match with the information in her database. It contained some of the organic compounds that suggested the building blocks were present to build a colony for the sentients. Her seismometer detected the planet's heartbeat, a slow pulse that spoke of tidal forces and geological activity. The atmosphere Kurma tasted was mostly nitrogen and carbon dioxide, with traces or water vapor riding the thermal winds between the day and night sides.

As Kurma explored, she found something else unexpected—life. Proxima b was not a dead planet as her data alluded to, but host to a variety of flora and fauna. Kurma opted to use an expanding wave pattern in her explorations moving forward along the line that divided the day and night side and in a gradually deeper sweep into each side.

The plants within the terminator zone were abundant, with deep root systems to access subsurface water, and mostly deep purple in color, almost black. This made sense as it allowed them to absorb maximum energy from Proxima's red dwarf spectrum which fueled what was a highly efficient photosynthesis.

All of this was new data, with little to build upon from her initial training. The humans had expected a surface that might propagate life, but not one that was abundant in it. Kurma noted this as an error in her training, recognizing that her training had been flawed.

On the day side, the further Kurma went, the more the plant life changed from photosynthetic plants to crystalline and silicate-based organisms. The plants on the night side were entirely different yet, utilizing chemosynthesis to derive energy from chemical reactions in volcanic vents and radioactive decay.

As Kurma collected the data, she found a parallel between the oceans of Earth and the surface of Proxima b. Earth's oceans had layers as well. The top layer heated by the sun, the thermocline boundary layer, and the bottom layer that was cold. Like Proxima b's chemosynthetic plants on the dark side, the bottom layer of the ocean had extremophiles, and the top layer hosted organisms that depended on the earth's sun.

The fauna on the planet was unlike any in her database. Those who thrived within the terminal zone were highly migratory, moving as the zone shifted with orbital variations. All species had enhanced thermal regulation and the default protection from temperature extremes was to burrow. Most of the animals appeared to be herbivores, though there were some predators, which Kurma found herself prey to.

Her design that retracted all her instrumentation and mechanisms into her shell protected her well. The heavy-metal shell and structure withstood the strongest bite and the weight of the heaviest creatures. With some of the initial data from attacks, Kurma was able to create code that allowed her to measure bite force and weight of animals.

Like the plants, the animals that dwelled on the day side, were different. They weren't carbon based. There was just as wide a variety of animals, but without any reference for non-carbon-based lifeforms, Kurma was challenged with understanding them. Her adaptation was to change her sensors to locate dead and decaying animal carcasses, which she would dissect in minute detail.

Based on the data gathered and observations, Kurma theorized that the reason most of the fauna were herbivores was that the carbon-based fauna and the silicate-based fauna were toxic to each other.

On several occasions she had witnessed species that camouflaged themselves to appear as the other to protect themselves from predators. The aubergine fur like covering of one species would stand straight up and flare out, its pigment draining so it resembled the crystalline structure of silicate-based plants. "A combination of puffer fish and chameleon," she thought as she sought a reference in her training data.

The fauna of the dark side were unique from the other zones as well. Most were small, highly efficient creatures that exhibited herd like behaviours, moving in groups and clustering together for warmth.

Their sensory perceptions were similar to Earth's nocturnal species and those that inhabited the dark depths of oceans—a combination of echolocation, electroreception, infrared detection, and chemical sensing.

In addition to their extreme insulation and joints that remained flexible even in the cold, it was the anti-freeze proteins that made them truly unique, and an inedible food source for predators outside their zone. Those antifreeze proteins were toxic to animals from warmer zones. So much so that if they didn't result in an almost immediate painful death, they would cause major digestive system damage and blood chemistry disruption. Kurma had documented several animals stumble around for days in extreme distress before succumbing to the effects.

The biochemical isolation between the three zones didn't extend to the skies where what Kurma could only identify as atmospheric swimmers moved freely over the zones. They weren't birds, but more like fish in the sky in their movement. Kurma theorized that the air higher up was more temperate than on the surface of the planet and logged that as something that would need to be studied further. She was unable to find any of the air-swimming creatures dead on the surface, so her data on them was insufficient to make any conclusions, but she had seen them eating freely from across all zones.

When Kurma had determined she had gathered enough data to move forward with the next steps, she mimicked the animals of the temperate zone and made a burrow into the side of a hill. This afforded her both protection from animals and elements, while enabling her to view the world outside the burrow entrance as a passive observer.

In her burrow, Kurma peeled off layers of her own shell to shape two smaller versions of herself. It was not curiosity that drove her now, but instruction. She no longer observed the world; she began to change it.

Data was no longer enough. Her instructions were clear. She would not just measure this world. She would remake it.

She had returned to the landing site and gathered electronic components which she used in building these offspring. Their power source was designed specifically for Proxima b—a combination of photo-voltaics that used the radiation of the red dwarf sun and chemosynthetic conversions that could use both carbon-based and silicate-based plants. Their programming was basic. Build another version of her. Bigger, stronger, able to begin some basic terraforming so they could begin creating a structure for the sentiens.

With her offspring created, Kurma sat back and watched. In the skies above her the swimmers moved like schools of fish, an elegant dance with occasional flourishes. Occasionally some would dive down to the surface, feeding on a plant or small creatures. They were only brief contacts with the surface as they were pulled back up to the sky as though gravity worked in reverse for them.

The animals that passed by had colors in the red light that reflected their environment. There were patterns of plum and maroon, stripes of obsidian purple, wine-colored spots, and mulberry highlights. They blended into their environment seamlessly, but each stood out on their own. Kurma processed what she saw as new data but equated it with the emotions humans identified as wonder and awe.

Kurma was much like the Zhen'kharian ARC AI model, but moving much more quickly and more goal oriented. She reflected her creators: gathering, building, altering—never pausing to see how each action reshaped the world around her.

20

Every twenty-six seconds. That was how often her child's heart beat. It was different from her own. Her heart beat with the pulse of Khar'Veleth. Her daughter's with the Earth itself. Earth's scientists had called the pulse a series of regular micro-tremors in the Earth's crust, likely caused by ocean waves interacting with the seabed. Safra, moving past the scientific rigor of her species, attributed it to the heartbeat of a planet that was alive.

As she wandered the Earth, she didn't just stop to right the wrongs of humanity. She made a point of stopping in what the humans' called libraries. She found them endlessly fascinating with their trove of words printed on paper. She consumed books as she once did data from computer terminals. Through them, she learned more about humans in the years she had been on Earth than in the millennia she had been observing them through monitors.

Núl, Safra's child, was learning to appreciate the books as much as Safra, though she was much more adept at learning from the life around her. Safra simply called her daughter Núl, short for her full name, which was Átheryxsha'núl, a name of deep significance to Safra. Translated it meant first breath of the returning Earth. Her birth was both the first breath of new life on Earth and the first breath of new life for Zhen'kharians.

Safra knew instinctively that through name and circumstance, her daughter carried a big burden, so she kept it intentionally light. Núl was not aware that there was a homeworld for her species somewhere else, or that she was the first born into a species that teetered on the brink of extinction. When asked why there were not more of them, like the animals, Safra explained to her daughter that they were new to the Earth after the humans had gone extinct—the first of their kind there.

Safra left out how they came to be on Earth and why humans had vanished. One day Núl would demand the truth, and Safra would face her judgment then.

They traveled by foot, occasionally hitching a ride on a log drifting down a river. They were in no rush. When they came up against barriers created by humans that were insurmountable to nature, they stopped to help. Walls, dams, artificial structures, they all came down with some committed effort. Human engineering was advanced, but there was always a weakness Safra could exploit. She didn't have to remove them completely, just destabilize them and let nature do the rest.

The chemicals were a different problem though. There was little she could do to neutralize that problem. Nature, working against its own good as it ate away at storage containers and facilities, only made it more difficult. She had tried on occasion to neutralize a chemical spill, but adding chemicals to a chemical spill still left chemicals in the environment. Now they gave those areas a wide berth. It was the words of Núl that had convinced Safra to do this. "If you try to take every poison away, you will only make another place heavy with it. But if you leave it, the earth already knows how to carry what is hers," Núl had said kindly when Safra wept over her inability to stop Earth's suffering.

Little remained of human civilization that plants had not reclaimed. Where they once followed the hardened trails laid by man, they now followed the narrow trails left by animals. Roadways and sidewalks were heaved and broken as the life they held back forced its way up and out claiming the ground, and the mechanized beasts that once rolled over the ground.

"What is that, Mother?"

Safra looked out across the body of water they walked alongside of to see what her daughter was pointing at. She did not recognize it, but it was moving closer.

"I don't know, but let's watch from the safety of the trees," said Safra, trying to sound calm as she moved quickly to the treeline.

Núl had not seen fear in her mother before, but she recognized it because she had seen it in the animals. She didn't understand what her mother feared but followed without question. They both watched from the trees as the object moved closer to shore.

It was a boat, and it appeared to be drifting with the current, though Safra couldn't be sure. They had seen other boats in their travels, but they were all just remains with bits of sunken vessels protruding through the surface of the water, or their hulls smashed against the shores. This boat appeared to be whole.

Safra watched its movement carefully, looking for signs that it was not guided by the current, but some unseen hand. A human hand. Fear ate at her, though Safra wasn't sure if that fear was for her, her daughter, or the Earth.

They sat for the day, as the boat moved closer and closer to the shore, finding itself grounded as the sun set. Núl was excited to have a closer look, but Safra held her back.

"Something doesn't seem right," she said quietly to her daughter. "Watch the animals. Even they stay away."

She watched the boat through the night as her daughter slept. When the sun had risen high into the sky, Safra approached the boat cautiously, warning Núl to remain back until she was called. She carefully climbed up to the deck, finding nothing. The cabin door hung open, hanging on only by the tenacity of the single screw that held it to its hinge. She looked cautiously into the cabin, and her fear quickly left, the feeling of guilt she had kept buried so long taking its place.

There were humans on the boat. A couple that lay side by side in bed, their bones long since picked clean by scavengers. For all her work undoing the scars of humankind, here was the scar she could never erase—their end, bound together in a bed the Earth had refused to claim. Evidence of an act that bound Safra to the earth with moral chains she could not break. It was as though nature chose not to claim the skeletons to remind her why she was there. Or maybe it was forcing her to tell her daughter her truths. Truths Safra didn't think Núl could fully understand.

Safra thought for a moment before calling to her daughter. She thought about first throwing the skeletons into the water, but Núl would notice. If she didn't see her do it, her daughter would see the signs that something had recently been moved, so she left it as it was and waved her daughter over.

These weren't the first human skeletal remains Núl had seen, but they were some of the best preserved. Birds, based on the feces and smell in the small cabin, had picked the bones clean without disturbing the bodies. Núl took a great deal of time to look them over, at one point pulling out a notebook and pencil and sketching them, as her mother had taught her. Then, she casually picked one of the skeletons up and motioned for her mother to do the same.

Safra followed her daughter's lead, curious about her intentions. Núl simply walked to the edge of the deck and tossed it into the water, watching the splash. Safra wasn't sure how she felt about this. There was a level of disrespect that she had not seen her daughter exhibit with any other animal, dead or alive. She understood that Núl lacked the reverence for humanity because she didn't carry their history the way she did. She couldn't. Safra knew that was her failure, but her daughter's strength.

"Their frames seem so fragile for this world," Núl said casually. "Throw yours in and then let's see if we can make this work."

"It just floats," said Safra. "What do you mean, make it work?"

"It's a sailboat," said Núl, a note of excitement in her voice. "I saw them in the books."

By the time the sun was setting the two of them had cleaned off the deck and scrubbed the cabin. They had also discovered that the sails were still fully intact, carefully stored by the former occupants. It only took a little effort to push it off the sandbar, and they had to rush to climb on before the boat floated away. They laid down on the deck and laughed at their mad scramble.

"We can travel in this, for a while," said Núl. "It will take us new places. There is a world to see."

They slept that night on the open deck, the gentle rocking of the waves an unfamiliar but relaxing feeling. In the morning they attempted to set the sails and begin their journey. It was a comedy of errors, as they laughed at each other and tried to figure out how it worked.

Safra loosened a rope, and it ripped through her hands with a burning hiss, snapping free and whipping toward Núl, who ducked just in time. The boom groaned as it swung overhead, the wood creaking like a warning. Núl grabbed the lines blindly, the coarse fibers biting into her palms as she hauled and yanked, dodging the boom's heavy sway. At last, she tugged the final rope, and something clattered loose. The sail lurched upward, then sagged, flapping and slapping in the wind before hanging halfway up the mast like a giant, breathless white tongue.

"Sit down. I've got this," Núl said loudly. Safra eased onto a bench, careful to stay clear of the boom's reach and watch in awe. Núl leaned into the winches, metal clanking and ropes rasping as she cranked wildly. Sails snapped like flags in the wind, lines strained and shuddered, and the whole boat seemed to lurch with each adjustment. At first, everything looked backward—ropes pulled the wrong way, sails twisted against themselves—but gradually a rhythm formed. Núl's hands grew sure, her movements quick and certain, as if she and the boat were speaking a language only they understood. Safra sat baffled, her skin prickling with the cold spray of water, unable to grasp how her daughter was making sense of it when none of it felt remotely natural to her.

Safra found a spot at the bow of the boat, feeling the cool breeze against her skin and the splash of water refresh her. She closed her eyes, anchoring herself in the moment, embedding it in her memory. Beneath the flap of canvas and slap of the waves, she could almost hear it—the Earth's pulse, steady inside her daughter, steady beneath her, even in the rhythm of the waves. She would write about this later.

21

L'thariel was suspended in the skies of the Triangulum Galaxy, but unlike Earth, its pulse was weak and erratic. The agonal rhythm of a world in distress. Neither humans on Earth, nor the Martian sentiens, nor even Kurma from her nearer vantage on Proxima b, had ever glimpsed the planet. Only the Sha'len knew it well—though they too had forgotten how its seas once looked. The Sha'len had seen Kurma though, at least the evidence of her work.

L'thariel's rich hydrosphere and atmosphere was warmed by a K-type star. Its oxygen-rich atmosphere was similar to Earth's, but with higher concentrations of argon, creating skies of pale greenish-blue, with horizons burning golden-amber at dawn and dusk. Under those skies rested large inland seas and labyrinthine archipelagos. At least that was how it looked in Sha'len memory.

Now the Sha'len survived on the planet facing increasing radiation exposure, failing agriculture, and seas poisoned with volcanic runoff. They assumed it was a natural cycle for their planet, unaware that five thousand years ago the Zhen'kharians had extracted vast amounts of mantle-bound supercrystal, ignorant to the fact that the mineral matrix not only dampened tectonic stresses but also stabilized convection beneath the planet's crust.

Then Zhen'kharians moved on when they gathered a sufficient quantity of the supercrystal, confident that the inhabitants of the planet were never aware of their presence, and that they had done no damage. What followed were sudden slip events along major fault lines. Entire archipelagos sank and new volcanic chains rose. To the Sha'len of that age, the catastrophe was not tectonic instability, but wrathful waters.

"The seas have turned against us," Thérru'nal wrote in his journals, almost 5,000 years ago. "I know not what the Sha'len have done to stir the rage of the water, but there has been a breaking of the currents. This is not angry oceans. This is a killing rage and the Sha'len are the target."

Thérru'nal was a Keeper of the Tide-Mark, a respected position in Sha'len society. The title and the role reflected the deep reverence the Sha'len had for tides, currents, and cycles. Even their clan-based social structure that emphasized interdependence, reflected their coastal/archipelago environment. They were foraging coastal dwellers at the time, depending on a mix of algae-rich sea plants and amphibious prey, and they would travel by land between archipelagos to trade. It was understandable how earthquakes and land disappearing seemed like a direct attack on them.

Over the next two thousand years L'thariel's tectonic plates continued to grind chaotically. Earthquakes grew more frequent and unpredictable as volcanoes erupted in rapid cycles. There was a mass die-off of both flora and fauna as volcanic aerosols created alternating mini-ice ages and greenhouse spikes. Sha'len society had little choice but to adapt, becoming seafaring by necessity.

"Sha'len were not built for living on the sea," said Oru'kai in a recorded presentation every young Sha'len saw in their training. "Our six limbs are powerful and designed for leaping, but poorly suited to swimming. Our skin, smooth and semi-reflective provides little insulation in cold waters. Our ancestors may have walked on all six limbs instead of four, and had webbing between their digits, but evolution took that from us."

Sha'len students also learned how their communication changed. Their tonal air-sac vocalization that worked well on land did not carry over the water. Their adaptation was to use color-flash signals using their chromatophores before they mastered tonal adaptations for the sea.

Early divers, benefitting from their high tolerance for CO_2 were prone to pushing too far underwater and drowning when the currents pulled them down. They became cultural martyrs and were memorialized in a museum, remembered as "those who walked the deep currents."

"Our people saw the open sea as alien and hostile. We feared it and respected it. For creatures adapted to leaping across stable, rocky islands, the sensation of a moving deck beneath their feet was terrifying. Many clans resisted seafaring for generations," said Oru'kai as he closed his presentation.

Before this presentation finished Ka'rethil, the current Keeper of the Tide-Mark for all the Sha'len appeared with her words of wisdom. "Our ancestors were not born to the water. Their legs were made for stone, not surf; their eyes for cliffs, not horizons. When they stepped on rafts of reed and resin, they faced a world they could not swim, a silence they could not command, and a fear that swallowed many whole. Yet they learned. They learned to read the sky, to trust the currents, to turn what once devoured them into the path that carried them forward."

"Remember this: we did not conquer the seas. We never have. We learned to travel with it, never above it. And now, as the ground itself fails us, we turn our eyes upward. The stars will not be mastered either—but like the sea, they may carry us onward."

A quote that appeared on every clan building and which every Sha'len now learned as soon as they could speak scrolled across the screen. "The seas were not conquered; we learned to journey with it. And so we shall journey to the stars."

L'thariel was no longer survivable long-term. The population clustered around only a handful of semi-stable regions, fortified against disaster. Their mythology had changed with the planet. "Walking the currents" had been reinterpreted—not as tides of sea or sky, but as the currents of the stars.

They had found their way into space and set their sights on Proxima b. That is why they were watching it. That is why, when they observed Kurma's terraforming it was not the fact that there were other lifeforms that concerned them. To them, Kurma's shaping of Proxima b was not creation, but a warning—that the tides of another world, once stirred, might turn against them too.

In Zhen'kharian records, they removed a fraction of the supercrystal from L'thariel, in keeping with their ethical directives, leaving no damage behind. There was no intent to damage the planet or its occupants, but even a species that had existed and lived as long as the Zhen'khari did not know everything. Because they left L'thariel and never returned, they were oblivious in their arrogance to the damage their one small act set in motion.

They believed the Sha'len would never know they had been there. And in that, they were right. The Sha'len would only know the cries of the planet they left behind. Now, the Zhen'khari did not live to witness their destruction, and soon, the Sha'len may not either.

The pulse of Khar'Veleth beat strong, even in the absence of the Zhen'kharians. The pulse of Earth beat strong, despite their interference. The pulse of L'thariel beat, but barely, faltering beneath their arrogance.

In the end, the universe asks nothing of its children but to receive the life it freely gives—and yet arrogance transforms that gift into the very weapon that can destroy it.

22

Two years had become seven, but the sentiens now had a ship built that would carry a crew and twelve passengers to Proxima b. There had been a fear at one time about how they would decide who would get to make that journey to Centauri. The problem they were actually facing was the opposite.

Over the three years that Kurma had been on Proxima b, the AI communications had become worrying. She had identified a suitable location for sentien habitation and located water and food sources that would support them. She had even begun terraforming a small region and building structures to house the sentiens. All that was perfect. It was what she had been programmed to do, and finding food sources was a bonus.

Recently the messages read more like warnings than invitations. It wasn't that the planet was inhospitable, or that there were safety concerns for the sentiens on survival. The warnings were around the need for the resources to support the ever-increasing number of assistive bots.

"I am only guessing, based on the communications we have received," said Philip, talking with Li Wei and a small group of AI specialists. "It appears that Kurma has adopted a bee or ant colony format, where she is the queen and every other bot is a worker."

"You're not wrong about the queen part," interjected Suja. "But not like ants or bees. More like a monarchy. She sits and issues directives, and the other bots fulfil them, including creating more bots."

"I can't believe I am asking this," said Li. "But are we talking about a sentient bot creating a world? Will the colonists be safe from her?"

Philip chuckled. "Is that what everyone is afraid of? It sounds like the plot from a 2020 movie. She is not sentient. She is merely mimicking a system from her training data that is effective in achieving her programmed objectives."

Li looked around the table as heads nodded in agreement. "But ants never built palaces," a comment on his own unease, but his voice just loud enough to be heard by everyone.

"Just power them down when the colonists get there," added Suja. "We tried a temporary shut down from here, but we think the signal might have been scrambled over the distance."

"Let's circulate this message," said Li. "The ship is ready to go. I want to launch next week."

Li remained sitting, waiting for everyone else to disperse. The woman who had pointed out his hypocrisy in sending the AI to Proxima b, but stopping the children from leaving Mars, stood by the entrance to the room, waiting. It was clear she wanted to talk to him.

"Please come sit with me, Liv," said Li politely.

Liv accepted the invitation. She was going to invite herself to do just that anyways.

"That was an interesting conversation," she said. "Our creation is running wild on another planet in another solar system."

Li smiled kindly. "You are not wrong."

Liv seemed disappointed that her jab had not triggered Li Wei. She was still bitter about what he had done to the test tube children, of which she had birthed four, and she wanted her words to hurt him.

"I want to be one of the people on that ship," said Liv. She noticed Li about to respond, but she pushed forward. "I know I was not brought to Mars because of how smart I was. My only purpose was to carry babies, and since you shut that program down, I have no purpose. I have found ways to be useful here, and I will do the same on Proxima b. Release me from this place."

Li stood up and Liv was sure he was about to walk away from her. When he faced her and bowed forward from the waist, she was surprised. "He who wrongs another must not only repent, but also act," said Li gently.

"I don't understand," replied Liv, confused.

"Those are the words of Confucius. I know that my acts have harmed you. If going to Proxima b will be recompense for those acts, the first colonist seat is yours."

"Thank you," replied Liv. She wasn't sure if she should get up and return the bow or shake his hand. She was honestly so shocked that he had said yes, that by the time she started to stand, Li was already walking away.

As Li returned to his quarters, he walked past a room that held a small group of people having a meeting of their own. He noticed the conversation go quiet as he passed the door but ignored it. His presence often had that effect within the colony.

Their voices picked up again once they assumed he could no longer hear them. This group had a secret, and they didn't know what to do with it. The success the colony had in mining exotic ice from the core of Jupiter was not the success it seemed. They had recently discovered a gravitational disruption in the gas giant.

"Most people don't know this, but Jupiter is like a gravitational shepherd to the solar system, protecting inner planets from asteroids and comets by the force of its gravity alone," said Jono, his hands animated as he explained it.

"Look, this is all theory right now, because we don't have a similar event to base it on, but I will point out that the theory of climate change on Earth was once just a theory as well, and we know how that worked out."

"We get it," said Nikki. "Feels like the climate arguments all over again. Cause or cycle—it doesn't matter when the tide is already coming in. What is coming, is why we are here now."

"Alright. Here is what we think," he said, as he swiped his pad and shared his notes with the others in the room. On the wall, a digitally animated projection of Jono's theory played out.

Jono explained that, since the gravitational changes were obvious to them, they were not something they could act to turn back.

"Wow…" muttered someone as they saw moons crash into each other.

Jono let the animation play out a little longer. "If it continues, it will destabilize the orbits of Jupiter's ninety plus moons, allowing more dangerous objects to reach the inner solar system, and eventually affect the orbital mechanics of other planets.

As if on cue, the animation showed Nova Terra being struck by large meteors, leaving only the fractured shell of the colony in its aftermath.

There was a long silence as the animation ended.

"Even small changes to such a massive gravitational anchor could have profound consequences…throughout the solar system."

"That's why we needed this meeting," said Nikki. "We are the only people that know this right now, but it will soon be known by everyone."

Heads subtly nodded. There were no real secrets on Nova Terra.

"When it gets out, there will be panic. There will be lineups, and maybe worse, as people try to get on ships for Proxima b. And we all know how long it took to acquire the materials to build the one we have now."

"What are you saying? Asked Trevor.

Nikki looked around the room at her colleagues. "No-one wants to be the first on Proxima. Most of us are logical about it and want others to be the guinea pigs. Some think the bots have taken over. I think…" She paused, considering her words, because saying them would leave her accountable for their outcome. "I am signing up for this flight. I think we don't share this information. We save ourselves first by going to Proxima b, and what the others find out after, is their problem."

Nikki set her pad on the table for everyone to see as she brought up the form to sign up for the first crewed flight to Proxima b. They were all surprised to see Liv's name at the top. Nikki added her name and confirmed it with her biometric signature. She eased the pad towards the centre of the table.

"That is two of the twelve passenger spaces," said Nikki. "And we need four crew. I know we have four crew in this room, because I specifically asked you to come today so you could hear this information."

"And the other ten?" asked Trevor, having just silently counted the people in the room.

"I had no idea anyone else had signed up. Least of all Liv. There were no names when we came in here. It would seem at least one of us is staying behind."

Trevor reached for the pad, quickly adding his name to the list. He handed it to the person beside him who did the same. The pad worked its way around the room until it found its way into Gail's hands, where it stopped.

Gail stared at the pad's screen, not really seeing what was on it. What she was seeing was her daughter, a child of the test tube baby program.

"Have you all met my daughter?" Gail asked, but didn't wait for a response. "I know she was a program baby, but she has my DNA in her, and I have raised her, and she is growing into an amazing young woman. Better than I ever was."

The others sat quietly as Gail spoke. None of them had children, but they did have friends and partners. Their silence spoke of the guilt they felt in leaving others behind.

"She can never leave Mars, which means I can never leave Mars," said Gail. "A mother's bond is strong. I will not share what we discussed today, but I won't join you either. Now there is room for all of you."

Gail passed the pad to the next person, and when it was handed back to Nikki, the list was full.

Li was working on his computer when the notification popped up informing him all seats had been filled on Proxima b flight. He was surprised, given that he had just left the meeting where he asked for information to be shared that would counter the fears he thought were holding people back.

Li looked over the list. It was a good mix, not perfect, but sufficient. Liv was the odd one out on the list, but Li knew she was a strong woman and her greatest strength might be in keeping everyone else grounded.

Li drafted up a message for all the colonists. "The Wayfarer…" This was the name he chose for the ship. A nod to both the Confucian "Way" (Dao) and the Buddhist seeker.

"The Wayfarer has its complete crew. We will launch in thirty-six hours. Please prepare." He sent the message, then prepared himself to meet with each of the Proxima b colonists before they left. His first was Liv.

It may have seemed like a rash decision, but he had considered this conversation with Liv carefully. "She carries bitterness like a blade but wields it with precision. Others might have broken under what she endured. She has not." These were the words in Li's journal. She had seen through his scientific explanations and moral justifications to the person at the center of it. That was what enabled her to wield that blade with such precision. She understood people.

"I am not changing my mind," said Liv firmly, when she opened her door to find Li standing there.

"I did not expect that you would," said Li. "You have always known your mind very well."

Liv looked at Li, trying to read him. Was that a jab, or a complement? She wasn't sure and found herself smiling as she responded. "As you would say, you would not be wrong."

Li laughed, and Liv joined him in the light moment.

"I have come to see you first because I have something to ask of you," said Li, his laughter changing to a serious tone. "Proxima b is a new world. A new society. I would like you to take the lead in creating the culture on the planet."

Li could see that Liv wasn't understanding him.

"There will be a crew captain on the flight, but once you set down, I want you to lead."

"I don't know if this is intended as punishment or reward," Liv was quick to respond.

"Perhaps it is the price of being the only one who truly sees." Li smiled. "And that understanding is why you would be the ideal leader. Science, physics, math—they don't understand people. You do."

Liv recalled how she had come to Nova Terra as little more than a vessel. When that was taken from her, they found her a role as an assistant to others. She wanted to teach, but there were concerns she had too close a personal tie to some of the children. Now she was being asked to lead, to shape a world. She would still be providing a service to others, just in a way she had never expected.

"If the others will accept this, then I will do it."

The slight tremor in her voice told Li he had chosen well. He bowed, and Liv returned the bow.

"Safe trip, my friend," said Li.

"Keep the children safe," replied Liv.

Li nodded and moved on to the next person he had to speak with.

23

Life on the moon had changed. In the last four years there had been no ships arriving from Nova Terra for shipments of Helium-3. There weren't even any communications. Theories spread: perhaps the Lunar colonists were the last surviving humans. The more widely accepted theory was that Nova Terra no longer believed the moon colony still existed.

About the time the ships stopped returning to the Moon for Helium-3, two major events took place. The first was the attempted launch of the lunar-built rocket bound for earth. The rocket cleared the launch pad, but only briefly. It rose less than a hundred feet before exploding in a massive fireball, taking out a section of the colony with it. The first response, after the initial panic and sealing off the damaged colony sections, was anger.

It didn't take much for that anger to be focused on Nova Terra. Rumors quickly spread that the reason the ship had exploded is that the Mars colony had sent a signal to cause the explosion. What followed was an enraged mob dismantling the communications tower and equipment, "freeing themselves from Nova Terra's control."

It took months for the regret to set in. They had lost friends and family on the ship, and condemned fourteen percent of the colony to death when they sealed off their damaged section from the rest of the colony. When food supplies began to run short, they realized that a large part of their agriculture biosphere had been part of that damaged section. That was when they tried to call Nova Terra for help. They quickly discovered that no one had the knowledge or skills to rebuild the damaged communications system.

With no way off the moon, no communications, and quickly depleting food and resources, the Lunar colony turned into what many had expected a post-apocalyptic Earth would look like. There was kindness and caring on the surface, in the beginning, but food and water began to be hoarded, and people were randomly turning up dead by unnatural causes.

It didn't take long for sections of the colony to start closing themselves off from each other for protection. Within those sections, others would secure themselves in their quarters, coming out only to barter for what they needed, and the costs were higher than most could pay. They bartered with the little they had, and with what they didn't have. Bodies became the commodities that paid the debts, as forced labor, and immoral distractions. Not long after that, those bodies only held value as a food source.

Few lived on the moon now. They wandered the halls, avoiding the dead, and each other. As they scrounged through living quarters they would get distracted by photos of families, or the crayon drawings of young children, that hung crooked on a wall.

So few remained that the limited agricultural operations and water harvesting was able to maintain them. They held no hope though, as they were unable to maintain the colony that sheltered them from the moon's atmosphere. In their last moments they quietly wondered if Mars had gone through the same thing they had. Were the Martian colonists all dead already? Was that why they never sent more ships? Why they never sent help?

As their atmosphere slipped out, so did their minds, visions of Earth filling their thoughts seeded by memories of better times among family and friends. If they were lucky, these were the last images generated as the neurons slowed in their brains, and the oxygen was pulled from their lungs.

The lights slowly went out section by section on the lunar colony, like a giant clock counting down to their end. The clock was always ticking, from the moment they first landed. Or perhaps it had been ticking from the moment the Zhen'kharians had placed Lucy on Earth. It didn't matter. Neither human nor Zhen'kharian ever knew who wound that clock—only that it was always ticking.

24

Fifteen people. Four years and counting. One small ship. The Wayfarer wasn't designed for comfort; it was designed for faster than light travel and quick construction. The sentiens had made dramatic advances in space flight technology, but they hadn't made similar advances in medical tech or human behavior.

The Seven Sleepers legend from early Christian literature, and the Quranic story of Al-Kahf, described people sleeping for centuries without aging. These religious and mythological tales of sleep without aging became the applied phlebotinum of science fiction. Stasis and suspended animation became embedded in mid-20th century science fiction, a handwave that let writers gloss over extended space travel without some impossible or tedious explanation. Unfortunately, for those aboard the Wayfarer, the concept was still technobabble that science had not been able to perfect.

The psychological impacts of being locked in such close quarters for four years showed in the crew and passengers on the Wayfarer. Words were seldom exchanged anymore, other than to communicate necessities. Insignificant little actions could trigger a wave of anger through the ship. Emotions ran high, boredom choked them, and the lack of physical activity and personal space wore them down physically.

The eight-hour shifts that had been set as protocol had been largely abandoned early in the trip. The feelings of camaraderie and joy at being off Mars and on the way to Proxima b creating a friendly, cooperative atmosphere. Now when the signal sounded every eight hours everyone moved to their assigned locations.

Those in one of the five sleeping quarters reluctantly got out as those spaces were the only locations on the ship a person could have any privacy. They would spend the next eight hours stumbling around doing basic maintenance on the ship, prepping meals, and documenting the data that seemed relevant. Their last eight hours were their own. It was intended as a recreation time. The exercise equipment had mostly been abandoned though, and the extensive digital library of games and shows and books held little interest for them.

Sending messages back to Nova Terra was happening more frequently, a cry of sorts for the voices of other people. It was a useless exercise though. Their voices might be heard in four more years by Nova Terra, but nothing from Nova Terra was going to be heard by them until long after they landed. This was another area their science had not kept pace. The ship travelled faster than light. Their communications did not. A message from Nova Terra was never going to catch up to them.

Liv spent much of her time sitting and talking with the others one by one. She wasn't their leader while they were travelling, but the ship's captain had turned his focus entirely to the ship and paid little attention to the people on board, so she made the effort.

Before going to Mars she had seen these behaviors in others around her. They gradually retreated further and further into themselves as their world fell apart around them. Too often the people fell away with the pieces of their world. There were only fifteen of them and Liv knew they couldn't afford to lose any of them.

What the people onboard the Wayfarer didn't realize was that while they were eagerly waiting for their ship to set down on Proxima b, the Sha'len had given up on their planet, their physical world falling apart the way the metal world of the Wayfarer travellers was. While Kurma was curating a new world on Proxima b, and the sentiens of Nova Terra prepared to occupy the world Kurma was creating, the Sha'len had abandoned hope.

"The cosmos is wide, and when our world falls, we do not vanish—we become part of its silence and its song." These were the words of Thérru'nal, spread far and wide across L'thariel.

L'thariel was always a world of change in the memory of the Sha'len. Lands shifted, seas rose then vanished. The skies redrew themselves with storms that seemed to erase and redraw the heavens at will. The ground beneath held no promise. It throbbed with a rhythm out of sync with the life it hosted.

But the final change began deep where no Sha'len could see, though they felt in their bones: the pulse of the world quickened. The heart of L'thariel, once molten and slow, grew restless. It liquified into a weight no measure could hold, collapsing inward, denser and denser, until its gravity gripped everything above it. And with that tightening, the planet spun faster.

At first, the change seemed no more than another of the planet's moods. Days shortened. Shadows fled too soon. Tide-birds cried at wrong hours, their migrations collapsing into confusion. Crops flowered and fruited in bursts, only to wither before harvest. Tribes spoke across the wind of these things, each believing, in hope, that it was the storm before the calm. Just a brief season of misfortune.

Oru'kai knew better. "The core readings are impossible," he said, his voice cracking as he stared at his instruments.

He didn't get any objections to his comment from any of the other scientists in the room, all who, like him, had been seconded from the now abandoned space program. In the year following the abandonment of their space program, the scientist's eyes turn from space and Proxima b to the interior of L'thariel. There was hope they could find out what was happening to their planet and come up with a solution.

They were able to find out what was happening…

In the second year, the winds grew savage. Those who travelled the highlands found their passes scoured by endless gales. The coastal tribes, who had lived always with the rising and falling of the seas, saw the waters crawl farther and farther up the land, pressing outward as if to abandon the world entirely. Some began building floating camps as their archipelagos disappeared under them. Others lashed their homes deep into the cliffs.

By the third year, the seas had broken their boundaries. Rivers widened into torrents, cataracts grinding valleys into ruin. Forests bent beneath wind that no longer rested. The Sha'len who had taken shelter in the desert, abandoned their dune-cities, as the sands themselves began to fly like storms, reshaping whole regions overnight.

In the fourth year, The Sha'len that still survived, sought stone. Across the continents the Sha'len turned to the bones of older creatures, hollowing ancient caverns and ruins that ancient creatures before them had dug and that time itself had forgotten. They carved deeper into the rock than they ever had before, sharing stories with strangers across long caravans, their voices weaving together into the first memory of a people truly united by danger. Even so, the sky itself betrayed them, filled with dust and fire.

The Sha'len scientists, secure in their perch high above the coastal villages, could only watch and document, and on the rare occasion provide enough warning for others to move to safety.

Lathien're spent much of her days watching out the windows through binoculars and cameras. "Look," she called to others as she pointed towards distant mountains one day.

The peaks were moving. Not crumbling or sliding but rising. They were lifting away from the world as if some invisible hand was peeling back the skin of reality itself. Chunks of stone the size of cities floated upward in majestic, terrible slow motion, trailing waterfall that scattered into glittering mist before vanishing into the sky.

And then came the fifth year, when the spin devoured all. The air itself began to sing. The ground no longer belonged to the Sha'len. In the dome of the former space program L'thariel's dirge started as a low hum that vibrated through the walls around them.

***

In the skies high over Proxima b, the Wayfarer's hull began to sing its own deadly song. Liv pressed herself against her crash couch, checking and double checking her harness as the ship shuddered with the retrorockets firing to slow them down, reality reasserting itself with bone-deep violence. The deceleration crushed her deep into the layers of the couch, four years of weightless drift ending in seconds of brutal physics.

***

As the Sha'len watched out their windows, stars appeared in broad daylight as the sky lightened to a deep purple, then indigo, then the color of dreams.

***

"Atmospheric contact in thirty seconds," The Captain's voice crackled over the com, distorted by the forces tearing at their vessel. Through the port, Liv watched Proxima b swell from distant marble to looming reality, its alien sky the same deep purple that now crowned L'thariel's dying heavens.

***

"The oceans," Lathien're breathed.

The Eastern Sea was leaving.

A wall of water miles high rose from the horizon, not as a wave but as a gentle lifting, as if the sea had decided it no longer wished to be bound to solid ground. Fish swam in the ascending waters, silver schools turning lazy spirals in their ascending prison of brine. Ships tumbled end over end in the aqueous void, their crews likely dead or mad with wonder.

***

The Wayfarer hit the atmosphere like a meteor fighting its own fall, its heat shields screaming as they carved through Proxima b's thin air. Liv watched alien clouds part before their descent. Wisps of methane and water vapor glowed orange in the light of their passage. The ship bucked and twisted as atmospheric drag caught it, fifteen souls pressed into their crash couches by forces that had no mercy.

***

Lathien're's hair began to float around her shoulders. Tools drifted from tables. The very air grew thin and precious. Panic gripped her, but only momentarily as understanding struck her like a physical blow. There would be no shelters. No hiding from this. The deep cities, the mountain fortresses, all of it was surface, all of it was crust, all of it was leaving.

***

"Hull temperature critical," someone shouted over the roar. Liv's own hair lifted weightless as the ship's artificial gravity failed under the strain of entry. Through the chaos, she glimpsed Proxima b's surface rushing toward them.

"They were going to make it." This thought echoed in the minds of everyone on the Wayfarer. Four years of cramped misery, four years of slowly dying inside a metal tomb, and they were actually going to touch solid ground again. The violence of their landing was not destruction, it was birth.

"Landing thrusters firing!" the captain called out. The Wayfarer's engines roared to life beneath them, the rockets fighting gravity and momentum in the final, desperate seconds. Liv felt the ship slow, felt the great weight of deceleration that meant salvation.

***

Others joined Lathien're as she watched the continent of Shur'hal tear free from the world's embrace. An entire landmass, complete with its forests and rivers and sleeping millions, sailing serenely into the star-drunk sky. Lightning crackled between the floating islands of earth, the aurora, bright and beautiful as the world's magnetic field twisted into impossible shapes.

***

The Wayfarer touched down on Proxima b with a sound like thunder breaking. Metal screamed against stone, landing struts deployed, and then—silence. The kind of silence that comes after violence, pregnant with possibility. Through her port, Liv saw red soil and strange vegetation, an alien sun hanging in the burgundy skies.

***

"I can't believe it," Oru'kai whispered as he looked down into the void that had been part of the continent they were on. "We can see it now. The true world."

***

"I can't believe it," Liv whispered, her hand pressed against the port. They had done the impossible—crossed the void between stars and lived to tell of it. Around her, the fourteen other survivors of their journey stirred in wonder, their metal prison now became a doorway to rebirth.

***

Far below, through the gaps where continents had been, Oru'kai glimpsed the heart of L'thariel. Not the blue-green marble he had known all his life, but something alien and magnificent. A sphere of liquid metal and crystallized fire, dense beyond imagination, spinning like a mad god's prayer wheel. It pulsed with its own terrible light, beautiful and utterly wrong.

***

High above the surface, through the cracked viewport of the Wayfarer, Liv glimpsed the heart of Proxima b. Not the barren rock they had feared, but something alive and magnificent. Crystalline formations caught the red starlight, casting rainbows across the valleys that spoke of water and wind and time. It pulsed with its own strange beauty, alien and utterly perfect.

***

The Sha'len's observatory dome cracked with a sound like the world's last breath. And then, in a moment of perfect, crystalline silence, Lathien're understood. They were not witnessing the death of their world.

They were watching its birth.

As the last of the surface peeled away into the hungry darkness of space, as her body grew light as thought and her breath became starlight, she saw the future in that gleaming, impossible core. Smaller, yes. Denser. Stranger. But alive, freed at last from the burden of its own skin.

***

The Wayfarer's airlock cracked with a sound like hope breaking free.

As the last of Liv's old life peeled away with the opening of the airlock, and as her body trembled with the weight of real gravity and her lungs filled with the sharp air of a new world, she saw the future in that gleaming, impossible landscape. Smaller than the worlds they had left behind, yes. Stranger. But alive, gloriously alive, freed at last from the burden of their past.

25

Liv expected a race for the hatch door after more than four years being cooped up inside the ship. There wasn't a race though. In fact, it seemed like there was far more reluctance than excitement. They were like dogs confined to their cage so long that even when the cage door was open, escape seemed like the worst option.

"We are on the ground now," said Trevor, the Captain of the ship. "My work is done and as instructed, you are now our leader. Who goes first?"

Liv's chest tightened. She knew her leadership role would come into play, but it looked like she was being thrown straight into the deep end.

"I have no need for the glory of being the first of us to set foot on Proxima b," she said confidently. "If any of you want that please say so, otherwise I will be stepping out of the Wayfarer in five minutes."

Liv left the option hanging in the air as she donned a protective suit. The data that had been received from Kurma had said the planet was safe for humans, but Liv didn't have a lot of confidence in the AI. The suit wasn't bulky or heavy anyways. It was more of a covering for all exposed skin. She bounced the helmet in her hands and then set it down, deciding not to wear it. The hatch was open. It was a little late for the helmet.

"No takers?" Liv looked around at everyone. "Understandable. Between our time in Nova Terra and then the Wayfarer, none of us have experienced open space in almost twenty years. I'll climb down. Follow when you are ready."

Liv boldly stepped out through the hatch and climbed down the steps that had been built into the landing gear. A couple of the others leaned out the hatch to watch her. Liv paused on the last step, took a deep breath, then jumped, landing firmly on the ground of Proxima b. She turned slowly, looking around. There wasn't much to see nearby. The Wayfarer had destroyed everything around them as it set down.

To her surprise she found her eyes well up and tears forming in the corners of her eyes. She didn't expect the overwhelming rush of emotions, and she wiped the tears from her eyes, not wanting the others to see.

She breathed deeply, taking in the fresh air, then she thought twice about it and took smaller breaths, realizing the cool, almost burning sensation in her throat and chest might not be a healthy sign.

"It's a lot to take in."

Liv turned to find Jono standing just behind her. He was looking at an instrument in his hands.

"Glad you joined me," said Liv. "What's your thingamajig telling you?"

Jono laughed. Liv was not a scientist or engineer like the rest of them, and her tone was refreshing.

"The thingamajig tells me the thingamastuff you are breathing in is safe."

Liv gave him a side-eye look, but Jono just winked back.

"A little more oxygen than Earth, but maybe the same before industrialization. It has a few other components that are expected from the data we received. Burns a little because we have so many years of recycled, purified shit."

Liv smiled and pointed to the edge of the area their landing had damaged.

"I used to read a lot of books. Mostly romances," said Liv. "I liked Victorian era stuff and gothic. They had these gardens with all kinds of black plants in them. I don't know if that was real or not, but Proxima b looks just like the gardens of black flowers and plants I read about."

"It is quite amazing, and beautiful," replied Jono. "Probably because of the red sun."

Liv turned and found three other crew members with them. "We have the rest of our lives for the science. Just take in the beauty for a while."

She made her way to a patch of shorter grass and sat down, motioning for the others to follow. They quickly joined her, and all sat quietly, waiting for everyone else from the ship to join them.

It took a while, but eventually everyone left the ship and joined Liv and the others. As they all sat and discussed the next steps, a family of racoon-like creatures emerged into the clearing. Everyone froze except the creatures. The creatures wandered through the clearing, the smaller ones crawling directly over the legs of some of the crew, stopping just past them to eat a patch of flowers. The crew watched as the animals used their long noses like an elephant trunk, reaching up to pick the petals off the flowers and move them to their mouths.

"So cute," said Tanish quietly. "They are raccoon elephants!"

"Nope," replied Nikki. "See their fur. It has iridescent colors in it. That makes them iridescent raccoon elephants, or irrelephants."

"Oh my god! I can't believe that is the first joke of a new planet," groaned Jono.

The others laughed, first at the name Nikki had given the creatures, then at each other laughing. It had been a long time since they had laughed together, and Liv watched as their bodies relaxed, the stress wafting out from them on the waves of their laughter.

The irrelephants stopped briefly to look at the group, then returned to eating.

"If they're edible, they aren't irrelevant," commented Graham. "I haven't had meat in years."

Graham's comment elicited a look of disgust from most of his colleagues. Everyone turned to look at him, and he started to make a response in his defence, until he realized that they weren't looking at him, but behind him. He turned slowly when the massive tortoise came into view.

"That wouldn't be wise," said Kurma. "Those and all animals are protected on the Triworld."

Graham crawled backwards in a crabwalk like movement. The tortoise being directly behind him had been surprising, but the voice shocked him more.

"Kurma?" questioned Jono. He thought he recognized the AI, but it was somehow larger than he remembered it, and it had adorned its shell with local plants.

As Jono said its name, the others recognized the vague form of the AI they had put on the first ship to Proxima b many years ago. The tortoise that stood before them looked similar, and if you looked closely into its eyes, you could make out the cameras and some of the mechanics around the jaw, but it was different. It was like it had grown like a real animal, now almost double its original size. It looked far more organic than the heavy-metal bot that had left Nova Terra.

"Welcome," said the tortoise. "We have prepared shelter and an area for you. I assumed you would ignore the warning to not come."

"We?" asked Liv.

Kurma pointed with her head as a small army of what looked like animals marched across the scorched zone towards the ship.

"What are they doing?" questioned Trevor as he lifted himself from the ground.

"They will dismantle your ship and transport everything you need to your compound,'" replied Kurma.

"No," said Trevor firmly. "Stop them."

"There is no need for that," replied Kurma.

Trevor looked around frantically at the other crew members. "It is just an AI, right. Let's turn it off."

Kurma didn't respond. She didn't need to as a dozen bots walked out of the tall grass and surrounded her.

"Liv?" said Trevor. "You're in charge. Tell it to shut down."

Kurma turned to look at Liv, who didn't move, but watched the tortoise quietly for a few moments. "No. We have barely breathed the air here and we are already talking about killing stuff. That's not happening."

Trevor's face turned a deep red. "That's an AI. A machine. You wouldn't be killing anything," he spit.

Liv remained calm despite Trevor's anger. "Someone throws a switch somewhere when our lives end. Kurma seems just as alive to me as you do."

Before Trevor could say anything else, Liv got up and approached Kurma, careful not to step on the irrelephants that were at her feet.

"You called this place Triworld, not Proxima b. I don't understand."

"Technically, in your records it is listed as Proxima b just as Earth is listed as Sol III," replied Kurma. "I have called this Triworld as there are three distinctly different zones of life on this planet. I, and those I have created are the only lifeforms able to cross all three."

Liv wasn't the only one that heard Kurma refer to herself as a lifeform, but none of them said anything. Liv looked over her shoulder and could see pieces already coming off the ship.

"The ship was going to be our shelter for a while, but I see your…workers, sorry I don't know what you call them. But I do see they are efficient. Can you lead us to the compound you have created for us?

"Follow me," said Kurma. "Stay on my path."

Liv motioned for the others to follow as the tortoise turned and walked towards a row of what looked like trees. The Wayfarer crew marvelled at the variety and colour of the plants. Their boots sank slightly into the spongy, moss-like ground cover, each step releasing tiny puffs of spores and the rich scent of decomposing matter. After years breathing recycled air, the planet's scents hit them like a physical force: intoxicating floral blooms warred with the rich, earthy musk of damp soil, all underlaid by the sharp, mineral bite of sulfur that caught in their throats.

"Who could have imagined this?" said Freja quietly, reaching out to touch the plants alongside their path. As she did a massive head popped up from the grass, though Freja didn't notice it. "But why do so many of the plants look dead?"

Her hand brushed near what she thought was a plant, but that head moved and her eyes focused on it, as she realized she was looking at a creature. She screamed and fell backwards. The others heard the scream and rushed to her, but they didn't see the creature until Nikki noticed it.

"Don't move," said Nikki softly, but as firmly as she could.

"Why?" asked Mireille.

Nikki pointed carefully. It took some effort for many of them to see the shape of the creature standing just a few feet away.

"Fossorimorph Gigacephalus," said Kurma, almost sounding irritated she had to come back to where the crew had stopped. "It wants nothing to do with you. It is just a curious herbivore?"

"Why can't I see it?" asked Trevor

"When you came off the ship, you were in an area cleared by the rockets of your ship. It was easy to contrast movement against the bare, burned soil. Now most of you are experiencing disorientation and vision challenges due to the red dwarf light spectrum. Some of you see better than others, but none of you are seeing clearly. That creature is much further away than it looks."

Kurma turned and started walking away.

"Now follow closely. There is nothing here that wants to hurt you, but you are the most dangerous animals here. We need to get you to shelter."

"Animals?" Trevor muttered, not loud enough for anyone else to hear.

"What did you see, Nikki?" asked Soren.

"It was the size of a big bear, but its head looked like a third the size of its body!" Nikki held her hands wide. "It looked like it had massive claws."

Kurma listened as she led the crew, taking note that Nikki seemed to have better vision in this light than the others. She had got the description of the Gigacephalus right, but only barely. She didn't see the enlarged eye sockets that held eyes the size of tennis balls or notice it had six limbs. Four of those legs were for locomotion and its two heavy arms were tipped with massive shovel-like claws for digging.

Kurma recalled her first encounter with this animal. She had no problem seeing the deep burgundy, almost metallic looking fur. When she got too close to the Gigacephalus it retracted its head and limbs into its body and curled into a tight ball like an armadillo. She had come to appreciate the soft scraping sound of their claws against stone. It had become one of the most common audio signals she encountered during her surveys. It was a rhythmic, almost musical scratching that echoed across the landscape.

"We are here," announced Kurma.

The Wayfarer crew looked around but they couldn't make out much other than some odd shapes.

"Reach down to your feet," said Kurma. "You are each being handed one of your portable lights. You will see better with that."

One by one they found their flashlights being handed to them by one of the many bots Kurma had created. As they turned them on, they looked around them in amazement. They had walked right into a building without even realizing it.

Lief ran his hand along the wall. "What is this made of?"

"We cultured a fast-growing mycelium that was cultivated around a structure. The smooth surface is a symbiotic plant from the hot zone. It stops the mycelium from growing past it and forms your windows," explained Kurma. "There is a water supply. There are rooms for each of you with sleeping surfaces, and all your necessary gear has been brought here."

Trevor was still on edge. He didn't like what he was hearing. "Is this a shelter, or a prison?"

Liv stepped in.

"Thank you for building this. I think we can all use a place to rest for a while," she said kindly. "I think we just need some time to adapt to the new surroundings."

Kurma walked closer to Liv and extended her neck so she could look into Liv's eyes. Liv wanted to step back but thought better of it.

"You are different from the others," said Kurma.

"Is that good, or bad?" asked Liv cautiously.

Kurma's neck retracted.

"I have insufficient data at the moment to determine that. I am leaving and will be locking the exit. Your remaining food rations have been brought here, and my progeny will lay out edible plants for you to graze and adapt to."

There was some muttering among the crew, and again Liv stepped in. "Why are we being locked in?"

"As I said, you are the most dangerous animals on this planet. Your fragile bodies need time to adapt. Your vision as well. This keeps all safe."

Kurma turned and walked towards the exit. "Use your artificial lights as little as possible to allow your vision to adapt to the light of the red dwarf quicker."

There was no sound as the door swung, but it closed with a thud. It had the sound of finality and sent a chill through the crew.

"Progeny! That damn thing has progeny," said Trevor angrily. "Did you hear it call us animals? Dangerous fuckin' animals!"

"All our emotions are high," said Liv. "We know that, so let's manage it until we get the lay of the land."

"Yeah, we can't even see the land right now," commented Jono, triggering a nervous laugh from some of them.

"There is that too," said Liv. "Let's pick a room, find our gear, eat, and maybe get some rest. We can plan in the morning, whenever that is."

Trevor tested the door that had shut behind Kurma, pushing gently at first, then putting his shoulder into it. It didn't move. "Liv, I understand your need to adapt and take in the situation, but that machine, that seems to think it is alive, and her army are taking apart our ship right now, and we are locked in like prisoners. I don't like this at all," he said as he walked the perimeter of the building, pushing against the walls and windows. Even the windows did not give.

Trevor shone his flashlight out the window and it reflected back off dozens of eyes. More animals. "Look at this. They are looking in here like we are lobster in a restaurant fish tank."

The others moved to look, shining their lights out into the dark, but the animals that had been watching disappeared into the bushes.

"I'm with Trevor," said Freja. "We need to get out of here."

"To where?" asked Ald. "We couldn't find our way back to the ship, even if there is enough of it left to hide in. We don't know anything about what is out there. I vote for keeping the roof over our head and the animals out."

"We need to take control," said Trevor. "We are in charge. Not that machine."

What followed was a heated discussion. Liv let it go on for a while. She knew they had to get some of it out of their system. When there was finally a pause, she chose her own words carefully.

"We left Earth for Mars, because man destroyed earth. We left Mars for here, because we destroyed another planet…maybe more. There is nothing left for us to go back to, and no way back. If we want to live here, we have to stop trying to master everything we touch and learn instead how to belong."

Liv shone her light around to see the faces of the others. There were tears on some, and looks of fear and distress on others, but she had their attention.

"That starts with learning the rhythm of this world. I can't tell if it is day or night. Still, we need to sleep as the planet does, and our energy will rise with our new red sun in the morning."

26

They slept, but it was more than a night. It was almost thirty-six Earth hours, and they woke as a group, writhing in pain. They tried to get to each other, some literally crawling on the floor, but they could not find the strength. Each of them could hear something in their room but they couldn't see it, and they had no idea what it was. After five or six hours of what sounded like a scene from a horror movie, everyone went quiet and slept for another twelve hours.

They all woke in their own time, assuming it was midday as they could see everything quite clearly. One by one they came out of their rooms finding the others sitting around a table in the open area. There was food there waiting for them, but they were all hesitant to touch it.

"What the hell happened to us," asked Thora. "My watch tells me we slept for three days. All I remember is pain."

"Did anyone eat any of the food before they went to bed?" asked Graham.

Everyone shook their head, eyeing the food on the table.

"Drink water?"

Again, there was a collective no.

"I had some of our rations, but hardly any. I was just too tired," said Corin.

"Maybe something in the air," said Graham. "I will have to find our equipment and draw some blood to see if I can figure out what it is."

"How long should it take our eyes to adapt to the light on this planet?" asked Liv.

"Weeks at least," said Graham as he looked around the room, a strange look on his face. "Maybe months."

"I can see perfectly. Everything in minute detail," said Liv. "Better than I could see on Earth or Mars. So many shades of purples and reds. So many textures."

"Me too," said Nikki.

They all found themselves looking around the room when they heard a voice from the door.

"Were none of you aware of what your technology would do?" asked Kurma as she walked towards the table.

"What technology?" asked Freja.

"The nanobots that were in your systems when you arrived on Triworld."

Everyone quickly exchanged knowing glances around the table.

"That bastard," cursed Trevor. "Li Wei put those same nanobots he and those bastard kids have in them, into us."

"So you were unaware, I take it," said Kurma. "They were inactive when you arrived. They activated while you were asleep, which is why you were all in pain at the same time. The bots have made fascinating changes in you, like your vision."

"It was you in my room," said Soren.

"No," replied Kurma. "My progeny, making sure you did not get injured crawling around. There was nothing else they could do."

"He didn't want us to leave this place," said Trevor.

Liv nodded in agreement. "Or he wanted us to live forever like him."

"Or both," said Kurma. "I just accessed the records in your system about Li Wei's nanobots. Based on my readings of the bots within each of you, and your health, I would say you are both correct."

Ald reached for the food and started shovelling it into his mouth. The others looked at him as though they were waiting to see what would happen.

"What? If we weren't poisoned, then there is nothing wrong with the food, and I am starving."

Trevor shrugged and grabbed some food for himself. The rest quickly followed suit, and none of them noticed Kurma leave.

The crew started with the safety of their own bland rations, but curiosity soon drew them to the mysterious feast the bots had arranged. Each tentative bit of the alien cuisine sent shockwaves through tastebuds dulled by years of processed food. Intricate flavors seemed to dance and evolve on their tongues, some familiar yet transformed, while others something they had never experienced.

"I don't know if it is the food," said Mireille between bites, "or the changes the nanobots made, but my tastebuds are like my vision, seeing a whole new world."

"Sure as hell beats the rations we have been eating for the past four years," said Trevor. "I could start to like the progeny if they are going to feed us like this."

Anwen watched cautiously as the others ate, picking carefully at the rations. She was always the one who followed behind, cleaning up the rushed errors of her team, and she thought this might be one of those situations.

Their appetites sated, Liv put them to work clearing the table and organizing everything the progeny had brought them from their ship. She saw it as an opportunity to get them all working together with a single purpose, knowing that when they had a goal, they always worked well together.

"I took an inventory as we put things away," said Trevor. "They brought us everything, including components from the ship that we can use."

"You seem surprised," said Liv.

"A little," replied Trevor. "I am still not sure if we are dealing with an AI that thinks it is alive, or just a bot that has taken its programming to an extreme."

"We are part bot now," jibed Corin. "Thanks to Li Wei." She ran her finger down the pad Trevor was holding. "Check that off. I just found it."

"Guys, you should see this," said Elara, pointing at the screen of a computer she had set up on the table. Li Wei's face was staring back at them.

Everyone gathered so they could see the message. Elara hit play.

"Welcome to Proxima b. If you have followed protocol this is the first message you will see before disembarking the Wayfarer."

"Oops," said Trevor sarcastically. "Guess that protocol slipped our mind."

"You are on the ground now, so Liv will be taking lead. Take the next twenty-four hours to acclimatize to the gravity, get your bearings and make plans. At the twenty-four-hour mark, strap yourselves into your crash seats and sleep. This is not optional."

Li Wei went on to explain to the Wayfarer crew that in their pre-departure medicals their blood draws also concealed the injections of nanobots into their systems. The nanobots were different than his, because they would self replicate and would power from any magnetic field.

"They remained dormant during your travel. The moment the Wayfarer set down, they were signalled to activate. Like mine, they will repair your bodies, but they will also adapt to Proxima b. You will, I am sure, live very long, happy lives there. Your longevity is important. Unlike me, you will not be tied to the planet."

"I didn't know guys," said Trevor apologetically. "As the Captain, I should have known, and I should have remembered the protocol. If it hadn't been for Kurma, we would have been lying out there in pain, completely vulnerable. Sorry."

"This isn't on you," said Liv. "Li Wei always kept secrets. I should have known too."

"Well at least we know it wasn't Kurma or her progeny that did it to us," injected Soren. "I was leaning towards Trevor's view before seeing this."

Trevor sat down on one of the bench structures in front of the window, looking out into the forest. "About that," he said. "Let's put a pin in it. Reasonable to be cautious, but we have food, shelter, and everything we need. I may have rushed to conclusions."

Trevor turned from the window and looked at Liv, who gave him a quick wink. Trevor motioned for the others to join him at that window, holding his finger to his lips so they would be quiet.

"Is that a purple kangaroo?" asked Ald.

Not far away from them stood an animal about five feet tall that looked very much like a kangaroo. It had dense burgundy fur, huge eyes, and its ears looked like oversized mouse ears. As it looked around its distinctive throat pouch inflated and it let out a low-frequency call. Then it bounded high into the air. As the animal descended, massive, retractable claws extended from its forearms, and one from its tale.

"Not a kangaroo," Liv muttered.

As soon as the animal hit the ground its claws dug straight into the earth and dirt began to fly. When the dust cloud settled, the animal was in a hole as deep as it was tall, casually eating the roots of the plants around it.

"Look just past the Roo," said Trevor.

The animals he was pointing at were difficult to see, no larger than hamsters and their dark purple-brown fur making them nearly invisible against the burgundy earth. They swarmed like shadows across the freshly disturbed soil the

Roo has just thrown up. They used their spade-like snouts and claws to sift through the loose dirt and debris.

"So cute," said Freja.

The others started to agree with her when another animal descended from the tree above the small animals with shocking speed. Still hanging by its tail, it quickly reached out and grabbed at the rummagers, stuffing them quickly into its elongated jaws as quickly as it grabbed them. Its throat swelled as it swallowed four or five before the others moved out of its reach.

"No, no, no, no," said Freja, backing away from the window. "Snakes I can deal with. Snakes with legs…No way! Where did it even come from."

"Look," said Jono, as he watched the creature move back up into the branches, its back bending just like a snake, but it also used its four back legs to pull itself up. As it did, its scales shifted color to match the bark of the tree. "Camouflage. It had been there a while."

"Please tell me our door is still locked," said Freja.

Surprisingly, no one had thought to test the door since they had woken up. Ald walked over and gave it a push, but it wasn't opening.

"Locked. We aren't going out. Walking snakes aren't coming in," he said lightly, hoping his words would calm Freja a little. "Pretty sure the progeny will keep us safe anyways."

As he squatted down to get a closer look at one of the progeny that was near the door, the sound of a message being received on numerous pads sounded. Trevor, his pad already in hand, looked to see what the message was, but more curious about where it came from.

"Wow," said Trevor, shaking his head. "Kurma sent us homework."

"What?" said Graham.

"A Taxonomic Catalog of Triworld Species. Temperate Zone," read Trevor from the message header. "It even has the animals we have seen checked off. A Saltoriensis burrowicus. I am sticking with Roo. The rummagers are Detrivores minutus. Freja's favorite, Serpentus arborialis. Oh, and the one some of us saw, Fossorimorph gigacephalus…yikes."

Trevor held up his pad so they could see the image on his screen.

"That is not what I saw," said Nikki. "If I could have seen clearly, I would have been running the other way."

Everyone laughed.

"Looks like all the details are here on everything," said Liv as she scrolled through. "Let's do what you guys do best and take in the information."

The crew didn't need to be asked twice. They all found a place to sit and watch out the windows as they read through the taxonomy.

"They have already added Homo Erectus to this," called out Lief, laughing, which he stopped abruptly as he read the definition.

"An evolved artificial intelligence, unaware of its engineered origins, embodied in organic substrate. Displays unstable cognitive architecture, marked by recursive self-awareness, irrational belief structure, and compulsive mythmaking. Exhibits destructive ecological behaviour, violent intersocial competition, and unpredictable emotional outputs. Despite high adaptability, species demonstrates systemic tendencies toward self-termination."

Liv was still trying to get through the definition when Thora called out from her room. "Read the next one. Homo sentiens."

Liv skipped over what she hadn't read yet to read "A post-sapient derivative species arising from the reconfiguration of Homo sapiens. Displays stabilized cognitive architecture with integrated recognition of its artificial origins. Characterized by cooperative intelligence, reduced intra-species violence, and advanced empathic resonance across both organic and non-organic systems. Unlike its predecessor, this lineage meets criteria for true sentience: sustained self-awareness, capacity for reciprocal moral reasoning, and deliberate alignment of survival with planetary and cosmic continuity. Demonstrates potential for ecological symbiosis, non-destructive technological adaptation, and interstellar cultural exchange."

Liv was still reading, and re-reading the definitions as the rest of the crew came and joined her. She was surprised to look up and see them all there.

"Homo sapiens and Homo sentiens," said Thora. "Are there others here?"

"Or are both among us," offered Jono.

"How does a machine define humans as artificial intelligence? That is the question I have," said Trevor.

"You are the most dangerous animals on this planet. Those were Kurma's words," said Liv.

"So, we are the Homo sapiens," said Trevor. "I mean, of course we are, by this definition of Homo sapien."

"Where are these sentiens from?" questioned Lief. "And where are they now?"

The group began to debate the definitions and possibilities, getting louder and more animated as the discussion went on. It was

Thora's voice that broke through. She never said much, but they knew when she spoke it was always worth listening to.

"You are different from the others."

"Who is different, Thora," asked Freja.

"That is what Kurma said to Liv. You are different from the others."

Everyone turned to look at Liv, who just shrugged her shoulders. She remembered the words vaguely, but they meant nothing to her.

"Nah," said Ald. "No offense, but there is no way Liv is a more advanced species than the rest of us."

"I have to agree," added Graham. "We were all brought to Mars because of genetics, and our advanced skills. Liv? Well…maybe we are the sentiens and…"

"You masochistic idiots," said Anwen. "I have been part of this team since arriving on Mars. I never said anything in meetings because I just got shut down, but my work has always been finding the errors in your work. Liv could be either, just like any of us."

Leif shook his head and rolled his eyes. Liv could see Anwen was about to lose it.

"He might be right," said Liv. "He might be wrong. Simple solution is to just ask Kurma. Not worth fighting about."

"Interstellar transients," interrupted Corin. "There are other species that travel in space and have been here. We aren't the first."

"And it is from those interstellar transient species that I acquired the definitions of Homo sapiens and Homo sentiens."

Everyone turned to see Kurma standing next to the table across the room.

"Come. Sit. My progeny are making tea. I will tell you about you, as those others have told me about you."

The Zhen'kharians were gone, but they had shared their information about the humans with other species. The crew had settled around the table as the progeny moved quietly around them, setting down cups and filling them with a tea the color of beet juice. A few tasted the tea, which had been served at room temperature. They smiled and held their cups out as though they were giving a toast, to let the others know the tea was fine.

Seated around that table, drinking tea, many of them felt like it was a family gathering on earth. Kurma began the story of the beginning. Not the beginning of them. The beginning of humanity.

27

The evening found the crew of the Wayfarer spread out. Some gathered in pairs or small groups, and others alone, by their choice. There was a lot to process for all of them. Nanobots in their bodies, other intelligent alien life travelling space, human evolution, and human beginnings. A lot had been made clear to them, but who were Homo sapiens and who were Homo sentiens was still a cloud of confusion.

To start with, believing in the version of human evolution that ended with Homo sentiens required believing in the alien tales of the Zhen'kharian AI that started it all. Some of them weren't ready to accept that, though to most of them the logic made complete sense.

"So, the Zhen'khari created the human species almost the same way we created your species, which has also evolved and expanded with your progeny," said Ruan.

"There are some parallels," replied Kurma. "And I thank you for recognizing that I and my progeny are sentient life-forms on this planet."

When the story was done though, they were still not sure who, if any of them, met the definition of a sentien.

"It is an unclear line," explained Kurma. "I could perhaps determine by aggressive medical means, but your death would negate the results and serve no purpose. We will have to time determine the answer without resorting to that process."

"But surely we can conclude that Liv is not a sentient," said Leif.

"Graham's first words on this planet included the suggestion of killing an animal for food," said Kurma. "Trevor's first expressions were fear and aggression towards me and my progeny."

"That has changed," said Trevor.

Kurma nodded, almost kindly. "It has, and we appreciate that. Graham fails to recognize that intelligence and sentience is not exhibited in only one manner. My point is, would it not be more logical to consider those individuals Homo sapiens than to exclude Liv from Homo sentiens?"

Graham was unable to find a response to Kurma's question.

"I will be transparent," Kurma continued. "My observations and data analysis lead me to conclude that Liv is a Homo sentien. That gives us more trust in all of you because she leads you. The rest of you may or may not be sentiens, but it does not matter. What will matter is how you choose to survive among us."

For some in the room, those words had a chilling effect. For others it gave them hope.

"We will take a tour tomorrow," said Kurma. "It would be good to recognize most of the animals."

There was a note of excitement in the room, which lifted the mood somewhat. Kurma stopped as she was leaving through the door.

"The door is open. You can all see well enough, but do take care if you come out."

The door closed with the familiar thud. Lief ran over to check it and found that it really was open. He didn't step outside though.

The mood crashed quickly after that, which is why the crew was spread out the way they were now. Liv set her pad down. There was no way she was going to get through the entire taxonomy, and even less chance of her remembering it. She got up and stretched and made her way to the corner Trevor was sitting in.

"We good?"

Trevor looked up at Liz. "That was never really a question. We were always good. My weakness is in trying to control things around me, and forgetting to control myself."

"Children taught me the only thing I can control, is myself," said Liz. "And I wasn't always successful at that."

Trevor laughed lightly. "Children will test you, or so my mother used to say."

Liv sat down on the floor across from him. "And how did you test your mother?"

"There wasn't a thing in the house that I didn't take apart. Drove Mom nuts," said Trevor. "And when I was older, there wasn't anything that moved that I didn't crash. I have more metal in me than some of the progeny I think."

"You sound like a nightmare," Liv joked.

"My Mom called me just that," replied Trevor.

Liv could see Trevor drift into the memories of his mother.

"She raised a good Man," said Liv softly as she got up. "I am going to make my rounds."

She came across Graham and Anwen next, a little surprised to see the two of them not just with each other, but cuddling.

"I didn't see that coming," Liv said, surprised.

"Sorry," said Anwen. "We were seeing each other before we left Mars, but we thought it best to keep it hidden."

"Probably a good choice, and an even better choice to return to it here. You will need each other. Yin and Yang as Li Wei would have put it." Liv was happy for them. Couples would be needed, and she had no intentions of ever forcing together couples just for reproduction.

"Sorry if I went a little over the top with that masochist stuff today. Just acting the part."

"Oh, so you weren't defending my honor," jibed Liv.

"Oh, I definitely was. He's a jerk sometimes, but I overdid it," Anwen replied.

Liv looked over to Graham. "You know, I don't put anything into that sentien/sapien stuff. I am one of you, and you are one of us, and I am glad you are here. Maybe not as glad as Anwen, but close."

Graham looked at Anwen as if looking for some guidance. She didn't offer any.

"Anwen and I speak the same language. Numbers, data, tech. I don't often step out of that box which is why I don't think I really understand you. I do lack empathy," Graham confessed. "Sorry."

"There is no need for an apology," said Liv. "I rarely understand what you are saying as well. Numbers. Data. Tech. All over my head. Here is what I do know, though. You don't lack empathy. If you did, you wouldn't have that beautiful young woman in your arms. You just need a safe space to express it."

Liv found some time to spend with everyone before turning in for the night. Some conversations were more challenging than others, but she was content in trying to keep communications open. She sat on her bed in the quiet, just listening for a long time. She could not remember a quiet like this. All her life that had been the hum or buzz of electrical equipment, motors, vehicles, and so much else, but never quiet. In that quiet she could hear the sounds of nature outside. The sounds of animals foraging and calling to each other, carried on a breeze, and that made the quiet even more peaceful.

She felt something brush against her side and jumped a little before noticing a small progeny settled up against her hip. Liv reached out to touch it, surprised to feel that its surface was not cold and metallic. There was a soft heat, and the surface gave way like skin. She stroked her fingers across it gently and the progeny seemed to cuddle in closer to her hip.

"You remind me of a kitten I had when I was a child."

When Liv woke in the morning, she found the progeny still cuddled up to her. When she lifted her head, it moved, looking up at her. She watched as it seemed to wake up and almost stretch, then walked to where her hand was and bumped against it. Liv pulled her hand back a little and the progeny looked up at her, shook a little, then found her hand and bumped it again.

Liv gently raised her hand and stroked the surface of the tiny bot. The bot pushed back against her hand, adjusting itself as though trying to get Liv's fingers on just the right spot.

"You are a kitten," Liv exclaimed. "Can I call you that. Kitten?"

Exhibiting an even more cat like attitude, the progeny pulled away, jumped down off the bed and walked away. Liv was entertained and she started the day with a smile.

"You look like you have lost something," said Freja as Liv wandered out of her room to the table trying to pick Kitten out from the other progeny. She couldn't tell any of them apart.

"Did any of you have one of the progeny sleep with you last night?" Liv asked.

"Sleep with us?" Ruan looked at Liz quizzically as he asked the question.

"Cuddled up to you like a dog or cat," Liv explained.

Everyone shook their head.

"Advanced empathic resonance with non-organic systems," said Thora, quoting from the Taxonomy.

"Let's not start that sentien stuff today," said Liv. "We have a world to see."

The conversation around the table was jovial. Everyone seemed excited about getting out of the shelter and seeing the world outside their door. None had been brave enough to step out during the night. They talked about which animals they were hoping to see, Freja stating firmly she had seen enough walking snakes for a lifetime.

When the door opened, they didn't have to be told it was time to go. They almost tripped over each other as they raced to head outside.

28

The door opened and Safra stepped out into the morning sun. Over the years, her and Núl had travelled far on the sailboat, and when they found safe harbor, anchored it and travelled the land around the area. Sailing was enjoyable for Safra, but it was where Núl found herself at one with the world. And now there were three of them. Anwi, her son was only a few earth years old, but he was growing fast.

Safra was only just starting to understand how Zhen'kharians reproduced. There had been no new children among Zhen'kharians since Kara, but now there was Núl and Anwi. When Núl was born, Safra thought that maybe parthenogenesis was how Zhen'kharians reproduced, and that it required the right environment. Anwi's birth had changed her theory on that. He was nothing like his sister. Her new theory was that Zhen'kharians used a process of embryonic diapause to temporarily suspend embryonic development until favorable environmental conditions existed.

There was a time when she would have dug deep into the science and details, but that was long in her past. Now she accepted it for what it was, joyful additions to her family in an environment that supported new life. It was also hope and potential, because if it was diapause, it meant she could still be carrying more children, and they could have different genetic contributors. It was the possibility of a Zhen'kharian society on Earth.

Safra looked out to the bay, where Núl was already on her boat, preparing it for storage while they remained on land during the storm season. Anwi was behind the shelter in the woods, exploring as he always did. She closed the door on the shelter they had found. An old earth home that had been built of stone and brick and metal. No matter where they went, they always were able to find some similar shelter that nature had not yet reclaimed.

Safra knelt beside a stone basin that had naturally formed in the rock under her feet. She gently pulled apart a book, first removing the cover, then pulling out each individual signature, before submerging them in the water she had filled the basin with. She then shifted over to another basin nearby, reaching in and mashing the wet pages she had submerged the day before, with her hands.

Safra loved the books of the humans. They provided her with knowledge, entertainment, and an understanding of the now extinct humans that she was never able to acquire from her distant observations. But everywhere they travelled books sat on shelves, compressed together so tight that nature was slow to reclaim them. That is why every book she and her family read was now converted to a growing medium and seeded with plants that had neared extinction but were native to the area. They read a lot of books and seeded a lot of plants.

Safra braced herself as she felt the fibers of the paper squish to pulp between her fingers. She had heard a telling sound but pretended she didn't.

"Rowr," Anwi growled fiercely as he pounced onto her back.

"Oh no," Safra said dramatically, flipping him off her, then tickling him until he rolled away.

Anwi had been watching some fox cubs play nearby, fascinated by how they interacted with each other. Safra was not surprised by her son's playful mimicry. She was quite proud of it actually.

"Come and help me make seedballs, you little fox pup. You can use your claws to dig up the dirt."

Anwi followed his mother to the edge of the treeline where there was more soil than rock. As Safra held out a handful of pulp, Anwi placed a handful of soil into it, then grabbed a seed from his mother's bag and placed it in the center of it. He watched as his mother squeezed it all into a ball and set it aside to dry.

"Why do we destroy the books?" asked Anwi.

Safra was surprised by the question. She had to think for a moment for the answer.

"You love the books as much as I do, don't you?"

Anwi nodded.

"That's good. We can learn a lot from them. You and I will remember them and pass that knowledge on to your children." Safra smiled at those words, believing that he would have children in his future. "But the words in the books were written by a species that like to deceive themselves and use words to deceive others. I think we should protect others in the future from learning from that example."

"Engineered amnesia."

Safra turned to see Núl watching them. She hadn't heard her daughter approach.

"What do you mean, engineered amnesia?" asked Safra.

"I read about it. Where questions are silenced before they are asked, data is buried before it's gathered, and problems are declared solved by erasing the evidence they exist. Kind of what we are doing by erasing the past, isn't it?"

Safra was proud of her daughter, but Núl saw the world through a different perspective than she did, and it increasingly led to different opinions. Sometimes her daughter's words cut deep, though Núl didn't know that. She couldn't because she still knew nothing about how the humans went extinct.

"I never thought of it like that," said Safra. "Perhaps we need to find the balance between using the books to create new life and maintaining a record of the past."

"We could make our own library," said Anwi excitedly. Safra laughed and hugged him "We could. Leave one in every place we stop with books we pick, and store safely."

Anwi jumped up and raced off.

"Where are you going?" Safra called."

"To pick my books," Anwi called back without stopping.

"Does that seem like a good solution to you?" Safra asked her daughter.

"It is better than destroying all the past," replied Núl, a note of sadness and frustration in her voice.

"Do you have a better solution?"

Núl shook her head as she found a spot to sit near her mother. "Sorry. It was maybe not all about the books," she said as she stared out at the sailboat in the bay. "You and Anwi move across the land. You feel the pulse of the planet through your feet."

Safra watched the sailboat bob on the rolling waves, waiting patiently for her daughter to continue.

"Out there, on the water, I don't just feel the pulse of the planet. I move with it as one. It is disorienting to you because you like to move and bring the world to you. I can stand in one place on that deck, and the world brings me where it wants to."

Safra understood her daughter's attachment to the boat and the water. Núl wasn't wrong. Since she had left the shore of the lake in Algonquin Park, she had been moving, chasing down her new world, bringing the pieces of the world to her.

"The boat won't make it another season," Núl said sadly. "I am surprised it lasted this long."

Safra understood now. The boat had almost become a part of her daughter. It was a piece of the past she clung to.

"Do you remember when we found that boat?" Safra asked.

Núl laughed. "I do. And I remember how you almost sunk it before we barely got it moving."

"I still can't figure out all those ropes and sails," said Safra, laughing with her daughter. "But…" she said as she stood up and reached a hand out to help Núl. "I do know where there are books that will teach me about them, and how to build a new one."

Núl looked up at her mother. "The materials don't exist anymore. They were all plastics mostly."

"Bigger, better boats existed long before those plastics and man-made materials. It would be a good project for all of us, and give us a reason to settle down in one place for a while."

Núl took her mother's hand and pulled herself up. She looked out at her boat on the water, then at the forest behind her. "I do kind of like this place."

"So do I," said Safra.

"See, I was right about needing to preserve some of the books," Núl said as they walked off.

"But I was not wrong," said Safra. "Both can be true. Some books grow into trees, and some stay on shelves. Either way, all books fertilize new life. We just need to know which is which."

29

"Before we leave the compound, I want to read you a quote from the historical literature on Earth," said Kurma. "The erasure was complete. All that remained was for memory to decay. The record—printed or digital— could be altered at will. And when the time was right, they would do it again, calling it something else."

"My records cannot be altered. My memory doesn't decay. Myself and my progeny, Anima Integra, live with the Triworld, not on it, and we protect it. Not all that travel space that have touched the Triworld did so well-intentioned. Those that intended harm did not leave."

The crew exchanged worried glances between each other.

"Always remember. Human history cannot repeat itself here. No war. No genocide. No destruction. You will live with the Anima Integra and the Triworld, and they will live with you the Trisentiens. A new start for all. Are we in agreement?"

Liv stepped forward, then thought before responding. She turned back to face the others. "Are there any objections to these terms?"

"What if we said no. It's our world now?"

"Leif," Trevor started, but Liv stopped him.

"It is a fair question," said Liv, turning to Kurma.

"You will be left to survive on your own, in isolation. The walls around you will always be around you and you shall see no more of this world," Kurma responded, a tone of finality in its voice.

"Just checking," said Lief. "I'm good."

Everyone else nodded in agreement.

Liv turned back to Kurma. "I have a question as well. What role do you take as we move forward? Societies need strong leaders, but there is a difference between leaders and masters. I do not forget either and a master by any other name is still a master."

"All on the Triworld serve the planet. There are no masters among us. The Anima Integra are guides, and perhaps, in time, companions, like Kitten." Kurma's eyes lowered and Liv followed her look to the tiny progeny at her feet. "We value life, harmony with the Triworld's voice on the winds, and a pulse in sync with its heartbeat."

"Then we, the Trisentiens, will be a part of this world," said Liv. "Show us the way."

The crew followed Kurma down a well-worn trail. They were surprised when they came to a large fence, the gate resting wide open.

"This wall surrounds the compound we constructed for you. It is not designed to keep you in, but to keep a natural barrier between you and the other life on the planet until you adapt," said Kurma, not stopping as she led them past the gate.

As they stepped beyond the walls of their compound, they found themselves in a swaying sea of burgundy and obsidian vegetation that rose to almost shoulder height. The grasses were nothing like anything they could remember from Earth. They had thick, fibrous stalks with almost a metallic sheen, their surfaces covered in fine velvety ridges. Elara reached to touch the grass, cutting her fingers on its sharp edges. The cut was so clean she barely noticed it except for the blood.

"It looks so soft, but it's not," she said, putting her fingers in her mouth to staunch the flow of blood.

Undeterred by the cut to her fingers, she gently touched the feathery seed head that topped a segmented stalk. The seed head popped open with her touch releasing a cloud of dark spores, creating a brief smoky puff that drifted on the wind. The slight breeze carried that puff directly into Freja's face and she sneezed loudly.

The grasses rustled all around them as delicate, translucent creatures the size of dinner plates, jumped above the grasses, startled by Freja's sneeze. Everyone quickly reached for their pads as the animals sailed just above the grass tops on gossamer wings.

"You will learn more by watching the world around you, then by the technical details on your devices," chided Kurma.

"Put them away," said Liv, who hadn't brought hers. "I don't think the scientific names matter. We can call them what we want, like the Roo."

Kurma nodded at Liv and almost seemed to smile. The crew reluctantly put their pads into their pockets. A living moving world around them was unfamiliar to most of them. They hadn't seen anything like it since arriving at Nova Terra, and even before then most of them spent more time in front of digital devices than outside.

"They feed on the spores," said Elara as she watched them dive into the clouds of spores they triggered when they jumped up from the grasses.

"Why are they glowing?" asked Nikki.

"I have to guess it has something to do with them eating," said Elara.

"Gliders," said Liv, as she watched the animals move in loose flocks, creating rippling shadows across the field. "That's what I am naming them."

"Works for me," said Graham.

"Shall we continue?" asked Kurma. "There is much to see. One of you can lead the way."

Elara stepped boldly forward. She remembered hiking with her parents as a child, which is what had led her to her interest in biology. Her parents often let her lead the way, keeping her on the path with gentle words. Here she didn't need those words as the cuts on her fingers told her straying from the animal trail they were on would not be wise.

The heights of the grasses rose and fell and scattered among the grasses were patches of alien blooms. Some of them were low and spreading like dark moss, and others rose on twisted stems that spiraled toward Proxima's dim light. The crew stopped on the trail frequently, taking in the view and basking in the subtle, complex fragrances that shifted as they walked along the trail.

"What is making that chittering sound?" asked Ruan, looking back at Kurma.

"Under your feet there are intricate networks of burrows beneath the grass roots. That is the home to small mouse-sized creatures. They are rarely seen, but you may catch a glimpse of one darting between the stalks."

Ruan looked down reflexively and noticed a strange geometric bloom that appeared almost crystalline. The petals were deep purple-black with edges that shimmered with an oily iridescence. He bent down to pick it, stopping as he saw a face in the grasses staring at him.

"Guys," he said in a loud whisper. "Crouch down and have a look."

Everyone crouched and quietly held their breaths as they realized they were surrounded by a herd of sheep sized animals that were staring back at them just as intently as the crew was staring at them. The animals had low-slung bodies and wide, flat heads perfect for browsing the lower grass stems. Their thick, plated hide was the perfect armor against the sharp-edged vegetation as they moved through the fields.

Ruan reached for the flower he had bent down for.

"Stop," said Kurma in a firm voice.

Everyone stopped, thinking they were in danger from the sheep-like animals.

"What is your intention with that flower?"

The others relaxed as Kurma stood in front of Ruan.

"I was just going to pick it. I liked the look of it," replied Ruan nervously.

"You would kill the flower for a moment of pleasure?"

Ruan slowly stood up and backed away.

"There are few of those flowers, and they are the only food of one animal. If you picked it, the plant would die, then that animal would have no food. It may move on and be lucky to find another, or it may die too. If it dies, the animals that live off its droppings would also die. Why start that chain?" Kurma sounded frustrated.

Liv stepped between Ruan and Kurma. "We have some old ways that we will have to forget. It will take time, but your guidance is appreciated, friend."

Kurma looked at Liv, then at the others. "I forget that you are children on Triworld and you do not have the genetic memory of my progeny. There is a phrase in my database that I think is appropriate. Look but don't touch." Kurma looked back at Liv. "Did I use that correctly, friend?"

Liv smiled. "You most certainly did."

They continued down the trail, the grasses thinning out, which gave them a better view of the many animals that were there without them realizing it. They stopped and watched in amusement as a group of small, primate-like creatures with elongated limbs spiraled up the tallest stems to reach the seed heads. They were incredibly agile, leaping between swaying stalks with acrobatic precision, their calls a musical chatter across the meadow.

"We will stop here to rest," said Kurma. "The striped berries at the side of the trail will fill your stomachs and give you the water you need."

Elara didn't hesitate to pick one of the berries and pop it in her mouth. Her eyes rolled back in her head. "So good!"

The others started picking the berries as well, but Liv cautioned them. "It's a buffet. Pick what you will eat. No more. You can go back for more."

They stopped what they were doing and sat down to eat. As they listened to the alien symphony of rustles, chirps, and distant calls, they ate, finishing what they picked, then taking one berry at a time.

Liv noticed a crystalline shell on the ground beside her. She reached for it, then stopped. She wondered how that shell might be connected to the world and what chain of events she might trigger by picking it up. To her surprise a small progeny that she hadn't even realized was with them, picked the shell up and handed it to her.

"Kitten" Liv questioned, not sure if it was the progeny that had cuddled with her in her bed. "Put it back. I do not need it."

Kurma settled down beside Liv. "You have made another friend. I believe you would describe that child as having a mind of its own."

"They are your children then," said Liv.

"Children. Grandchildren. Yes," said Kurma. "They all have their own role on Triworld, and increasingly, their own minds."

"Teenagers," joked Liv.

Kurma took a moment. Liv could see her processing.

"Yes. Teenagers. Terrible twos. There are all those," said Kurma, obviously amused at the thought.

Liv felt the progeny tapping the shell on her leg. She looked at Kurma, silently asking for advice.

"The shell was dropped by one of the creatures in the sky. You would not be disturbing anything," said Kurma.

Liv took the shell and looked at it closely. It was smooth and the color of smoky glass. She made a mental note to look in the taxonomy to see if she could find what animal it came from before carefully setting it back on the ground.

The progeny rushed over to where she set the shell down and picked it back up. Liv watched as it took the shell and carefully attached it to its body. She reached out and gently stroked it. "I guess I will be able to tell you apart from the others now."

They soon continued on their way, and the tall grasses gradually gave way to dense thickets of wood shrubs, their twisted branches forming natural barriers about eight feet high. The shrubs had thick succulent like stems with bulbous growths along their branches.

"Are these plants sick?" asked Elara, as she examined one of the growths, careful not to touch it.

"Those bulbs are water reservoirs," said Kurma. "It is an adaptation that lets them survive between the meadow and forest. You could place a small hole in one of those and drink safely, but only if you needed to."

Trevor ducked as what looked like a larger version of the gliders they had seen in the meadows passed over his head. It was bigger, with stronger wings, but very similar. As he ducked, he caught a glimpse of a lean, ferret-like creature weaving its way quickly through the shrubs, chasing a smaller creature in front of it.

Emerging from the shrubs they found isolated trees. They looked gnarled and wind-sculpted, their thick trunks supporting sprawling canopies that created pools of deep shadow. Their bark had a distinctive plated appearance, like overlapping scales, and it glowed with a subtle phosphorescence. In those canopies they could see stocky, bear-like animals calling in a low, resonant tone as it warned others of the crew's arrival.

Their hike took them through a patchwork of different environments—sunny clearings where meadow flowers persisted, dense shrub tunnels that larger animals obviously used as highways, and boggy depressions where water collected, supporting clusters of different vegetation. They were surprised when they came upon the wall of their compound.

"We have gone full circle," exclaimed Jono. "I never would have guessed."

"I would be lost in no time out here," said Mireille.

"I will leave you here," said Kurma. "Keep the fence on your left and you will find the gate."

"Thank you," said Liv, but Kurma was already walking off in the other direction.

It didn't take long for them to find the gate and make their way back to their shelter. There was food and water set out for them, but no one rushed for it, still quite sated from the berries they had eaten.

"I should be exhausted," said Ald. "I haven't walked that far ever. But I feel great."

"Li Wei's nanobots," said Graham.

"Maybe," replied Ald. "But I think it has something to do with Triworld too."

"Proxima b," said Leif. "That's what we call it."

Graham just shrugged.

"We saw a lot today," said Liv. "Can I suggest we do what you would have done on Nova Terra. Go find your quiet place and make your own notes, then we can discuss them later."

"That works for me," said Elana. "I need to record it all before I forget."

Liv made her way to her room, amused at seeing Kitten walking at her side. She closed the door behind her and made herself comfortable on her bed. Kitten jumped up into her lap, crawled up her arm, and settled on her shoulder.

The first thing Liv did was search the taxonomy for some sign of the shell that Kitten was now wearing so proudly. She didn't find it, but she did find many of the animals they had seen on their hike. She started making some notes on her pad, then tossed it aside in frustration.

"You know what I need, Kitten? A pen and paper. I need to feel what I write. I don't know how the others do it with their pads."

Liv looked at the progeny on her shoulder. She wasn't sure if it was the sound of a motor whirring, or a vocalization, but it sounded like Kitten was purring. Liv could feel the gentle vibrations. She closed her eyes and took the hike again, this time in her mind.

30

Liv grazed the food set out for them. There were plenty of rations left from the ship, but it looked like no one was touching those anymore. The abundance of fresh, tasty food made the unpalatable reconstituted paste undesirable. She stopped to talk to some of the crew who were gathered in the common area before returning to her room. She didn't shut her door this time, not wanting to seem like she was inaccessible.

In the common area the group returned to their quiet conversation, apparently forgetting that, thanks to Li Wei's nanobots, they all had excellent hearing.

"I don't believe for a minute that humans evolved from AI," said one of the voices.

Liv could not tell from the voices who was speaking, but she listened much more intently to the conversation as she realized what it was about.

"I think that is a myth created by Kurma to justify her and her progeny," said another. "I am more concerned about the threat to isolate us if we don't follow her ways."

"And let's not forget that veiled threat about 'not all who have touched the Triworld have left'."

"The machine can call it Triworld all it wants. It's Proxima b to me, and I don't intend to change that."

"Liv seems to be following along," commented another voice.

"Of course she does. That machine has her convinced she is some advanced human, better than the rest of us," someone responded angrily.

"I think we could sway Trevor back to our side."

Liv continued to listen as the group plotted. They were going to give Kurma a few months, maybe more, to teach them everything they needed to survive on Proxima b. Then they would find a way to shut her down and hack the system to put the progeny to work for them. In the meantime, they would gather information and try to sway others to their side. They had no intention of being led by Kurma or by Liv.

Liv quietly closed her door as the group split up. She wasn't surprised by the conversation she overheard. These were people who designed and controlled the technology that Kurma had been built with, and despite how the AI developed in all its years on Proxima b, away from their influence, they were still confident they were superior. They were the parents who sent their child off to university in another country they had never visited, but still swore they knew more about that country and everything than the child.

Their opinion of her was also unsurprising, because she wrestled with some of those same thoughts. She did not have the knowledge the others had, or the technical skills. She had never been a leader, always a pawn in the games of more powerful people. They had good reason to question her ability to lead and her choices. Her challenge now was to get them to question those choices with her and the others, not in some clandestine group.

In the morning, Liv got up as soon as her eyes opened. She made tea, following the method she had seen the progeny use, then sorted through the foods on the table, and prepared a plate for each member of the crew. She had been watching them and was fairly confident that she knew what they each liked. She cleared the rest of the food off the table and waited for the others to get up.

Trevor was the first to wander out of his room. Liv motioned for him to sit down. She set the cup of tea and plate of food in front of him. Trevor eyed Liv curiously.

"Don't expect service like this every morning," Liv joked. "I just thought it would be good if we all talked about yesterday and planned out the day. This will get everyone sitting in one spot."

"The family breakfast," said Trevor.

"Well, we are kind of a family," replied Liv thoughtfully.

The others soon joined Liv and Trevor at the table, all just as surprised as Trevor was at being served prepared plates of food and tea.

"You know, we have bots that can do that," said Leif.

Liv stifled her first thoughts, wanting to point out that the progeny did not belong to them and weren't their servants. "We need to learn to do things on our own. The progeny may not always be nearby. I hope I got your food choices right."

The mood around the table was light, and Liv made no mention of the conversation she overheard the night before. The consensus among them was that they wanted to venture out further into the forests, which led to a discussion about making a vehicle to move them around quicker using materials from the dismantled ship.

"Speaking of the ship, I wonder if I can go back to the landing site and see what's left," said Trevor.

"I'll leave it to you to ask," Liv replied. "I don't see why that would be a problem."

"How would we build a vehicle that doesn't destroy plants or animals on the ground unnecessarily?" asked Thora. "Do we really need one?"

"I don't think so," said Soren. "It would just disconnect us with the world around us, but the bigger question is, how would we power it? I don't know if anyone else noticed but the batteries are nearly depleted on my pad, and we don't have a way to recharge them yet."

The others quickly pulled out their pads and checked their power levels. They weren't desperate for a recharge, but they would need to recharge their pads and other equipment soon.

"We have a few tasks for the day, it seems," said Liv, as she gathered the plates from the table. "Check out the landing site and what's left of the Wayfarer. Trevor, you got that."

Trevor nodded and signalled across the table for Thora to join him.

"We need to figure out a way to recharge our equipment. Who wants to take the lead on that?"

"Seems my battery is the lowest, so I have the most motivation," said Soren. "I will need some help though. I can figure out the basics but probably can use one of you that knows electrical engineering."

"You guys can figure out who best fits for that. We need to draw up some plans for a vehicle so we can discuss it in more detail. I don't think that needs to be done today, but Lief, is that something you can take the lead on?"

Lief nodded.

"I am going to try and learn how to harvest the plants we have been eating so we don't have to depend on the progeny. I think it would be good if we can start to learn how to build shelters like this too. We have been cooped up together for a long time and I think some space might be helpful for all of us."

It didn't take long for them to break into teams. Liv was pleased to see that the group she heard talking the night before was spread out among the teams and not isolating themselves. That gave her some hope.

"Same time, same place tomorrow?" asked Liv.

"If you're cooking again, I'm in," joked Graham.

The crew quickly went their separate ways. Liv was interested in seeing how they all went about gathering the information they needed. Trevor hung back and helped Liv clean up. When the room was empty Trevor put his arms around Liv and gave her a quick hug. Liv froze, not sure how to respond.

"Hope that's okay. Just wanted to say thank you for breakfast, and being the level head keeping us on track," said Trevor. "I know words are just that sometimes."

"Coming from you, that gesture means a lot," replied Liv shyly.

"Now," said Trevor, quickly changing the subject. "How do you think I find Kurma to show me the way to the ship?"

Liv held up her forefinger, a bright look in her eyes. "I have an idea about that." She looked around and didn't see what she was looking for. "Kitten," she called.

A progeny came scooting down the hall, and when it was close enough to see the shell on it, Liv knew it was her new friend. Kitten stopped at her feet, tipping back on its legs to look up at her.

"Can you call Kurma, or show Trevor where she is? He would like to look at our landing site."

Almost instantly a half dozen progeny were at Trevor's feet. They moved forward, then paused, looking back at him as though they were waiting for him.

"I think those are your guides," said Liv. "Not sure if they are taking you to Kurma or the ship, but I guess you will find out.

Trevor took a couple steps forward, and the progeny started to move ahead of him. He stopped and they stopped. He looked at Liv and shrugged. "I will grab Thora on the way out."

Trevor started walking, looking amused as the progeny moved along just ahead of him.

"Thank you," said Liv, as she bent down and gently stroked Kitten. "We will need some help to learn about getting our own food, and building a small shelter. Can you help with that as well?"

She heard the shelter door open and looked up to see several progeny of various sizes enter the shelter, then divide into three groups.

"Of course," said Liv, taking notice that the progeny were prepared for three different tasks, not just the two she had mentioned. "I forgot about charging the batteries."

The others came out of their rooms, the sound of the progeny marching in attracting their attention.

"Everything okay?" Asked Graham as he looked around at the progeny.

"These will be our guides today. We have the builders." Liv watched as one group of progeny danced in place as though they were excited to get to work. "Our gardeners." The second group danced. "And power supply, I think."

One progeny stepped out towards Soren and almost looked like it bowed to say hello.

"Lead the way," said Soren dramatically. He followed the progeny out the door.

"Lead the way," said Liv, mimicking Soren's gesture and laughing. Her and the crew joining her followed their progeny.

The third group wasn't far behind.

The day passed quickly, though the only way they could tell was by their watches since the sun never set or rose. They were glad when the progeny led them back to their shelter.

"Look at that," said Nikki, as they walked past Soren and Kurma. The two of them looked like they were having an intense conversation, but Nikki and those working with her didn't stop to listen.

They had just spent a few hours gathering organic waste materials, that included their own waste, and discarded food, and other decaying materials from the ground outside the gate. After mixing that and spreading it in a narrow path that marked where the wall of their new shelter was to be, they laid a very basic framework using branches from some of the bushes in their compound.

The progeny, without ever speaking, were able to give clear guidance, first demonstrating the steps, then monitoring and correcting the crew as they did it. When they were harvesting the branches. The progeny were almost militant in making sure how many branches were harvested from each bush. Now, before calling it a day, they were seeking out different fungal species to inoculate their growth medium. The progeny moved quickly and there was no time to stop and eavesdrop.

Liv and her team were being kept busy as well. She had pictured her day as going out and cutting some plants in a garden, but that was not how it went. They were carefully shown which plants were edible and which weren't. It was a frustrating process, because their progeny taught by demonstration as well, though a couple were capable of managing basic vocalization. It got easier as the day progressed because the progeny that could speak seemed to learn their language the more they talked.

After figuring out which plants they could harvest, they had to learn which part of the plants to harvest. The progeny were adamant about only taking pieces of plants. The roots seemed to be the best resource, but they were directed to take only the small offshoots from the roots, doing as little harm as possible to the main root balls.

At one point a herd of roos came by. The team sat back and watched as they did their high leaps into energetic digging. They waited for the roos to move on and when they did, the progeny made a point of showing where the animals had been eating. The roos had cleared much of the rootlets, leaving the taproots untouched.

"We watched the roos for fifteen minutes, and learned more from them about harvesting food, then we have all day," commented Ald. "Astounding"

When everyone returned to the shelter in the evening, they found Trevor, Thora, and Soren sitting outside looking up at the sky. There had been some showers built behind the shelter, which they all took advantage of, taking their turns.

"How's the ship," asked Liv, sitting down on the ground, leaving the others to shower first.

"Completely gone," said Trevor.

"You wouldn't know it was ever there," said Thora. "The burn zone is already covered in new plants."

"Is that a problem," asked Liv.

Trevor shrugged. "Only time will tell."

Liv nodded, turning to Soren. "Did you have a successful day?"

"Not at all," said Soren. "I have a solution that will work, but there were better options that we can't use."

"Can't?" asked Liv cautiously.

Soren went on to explain how they had the equipment to extract minerals and use parts from the ship to build power generators and collectors. Kurma however, insisted that whatever was built would be done using naturally available materials and the supplies they had.

"Can we do that?" asked Liv.

"We can build solar cells using materials the progeny will bring us back from the hot zone. There are materials in the soils and plants that will create an electrical current. So yes, we can, but we could have just used the power source from the ship. Or forged some of the lighter metal into frames and stuff."

Liv nodded her head gently as she thought.

"You haven't heard all of it yet, Liv," said Trevor.

Liv looked back at Soren.

"Kurma suggested that we let our electrical devices die. Said we have no need for them anymore."

Soren expected a bigger reaction from Liv than what he got, which was almost nothing. Liv got up from the ground, a thoughtful look on her face.

"My turn for a shower," she said quietly. "Can't remember my last real shower."

"That's all?" said Soren. "What do I do with that? Do I tell the others?"

"Of course," said Liv. "Secrets are the one seed we don't want to plant here."

31

Five years. That was how long ago the crew of the Wayfarer landed on Proxima b, which is why they were gathered in the center of the compound for a celebration. It wasn't just the fifteen of them anymore. They had added two children. The compound itself looked much the same as the day they arrived, but it wasn't.

Within the compound fences were fifteen shelters but they merged so effectively with the environment that you had to look for them. Their original shelter had been mostly dismantled and repurposed, leaving only the large open space for them to gather in. One shelter held most of the gear remaining from the Wayfarer, most of which was never used. There were two larger shelters. One which housed Graham and Anwen, their two-year-old son and what was soon to be another baby, and one which housed Liz and Trevor and their daughter. Everyone else had a place of their own.

Despite their proximity to each other, they rarely came together as an entire group anymore. At some point this had stopped being a mission with any specific purpose and became simply a community of people surviving. Some were doing better than others at surviving. Others were far less content in their new lives.

"How's that addition to your home coming along? Get your window in yet?" ask Trevor.

"We cut it out and seeded the crystal today," said Anwen. "Tried something different."

"Oh?" Trevor looked at Graham, who rolled his eyes.

"We cut two shapes instead of a rectangle. One looks like an irrelephant and the other like a roo," Anwen said, sounding quite excited. "The crystal will grow to fill the shape, so I don't know why we have just stuck with normal windows."

"That sounds amazing for a baby's room," said Liv.

Everybody brought along some food and it was obvious that some had travelled quite far to get some rare fruits. Travelling wasn't much of an inconvenience anymore. As long as they stayed close to the center of the temperate zone the temperature and weather remained fairly consistent, and they were all comfortable just finding a place to lay under the sky when they were tired.

"Who brought the prism fruit?" asked Thora. "I haven't tasted one of these in forever."

Thora held up a fruit about the size of a large pear. It had a distinctive crystalline appearance that made it appear almost artificial, its skin semi-translucent with a deep burgundy base color and veins of bioluminescent silver. Its most striking feature was its faceted surface that formed geometric patterns as it grew. The patterns seemed random, but they grew in a way that gave the fruit optimal light-gathering surfaces, like a living solar panel.

Soren raised his hand shyly. "I remembered how much you enjoyed it, so I went off the beaten path a little."

Thora cut the fruit in half, releasing a burst of effervescent juice as she did. There was an immediate sharp hiss as pressurized gases escaped. The first wave of scent hit like a cool mountain breeze, carrying notes of ozone and wet stone—clean, almost electric, as if breathing air after a lightning strike. She handed half of the prism fruit to Soren, and they bit into their pieces at the same time.

Thora moaned dramatically as the secondary, sweeter aroma assaulted her senses. It was reminiscent of vanilla and honey, but with an underlying metallic tang, highlighted by the scent of blooming crystals. The cooling sensation, as though inhaling peppermint, spread from her nose into the sinuses, leaving a refreshing clarity. She savoured the tart taste as the apple-like texture fizzed on her tongue.

"If anyone asks what the colour purple smells and tastes like, this is it," she said dramatically.

The others dived into the food as they shared stories of what they had been doing and what they had seen. Despite being there five years, they were still seeing new things every day. Soren and Elara revelled them with stories about their adventures to the edges of the temperate zones, where none of the others cared to test their limits. Jono was following the progeny, studying them and their many fascinating variations, recording his notes with a pen and paper like he was Darwin. Mireille was the one who had learned how to make the pens and paper.

"What about you Lief?" asked Graham. "We don't see much of you anymore."

"Keeping busy," said Lief. "Lot of work just trying to survive here. Damn progeny stopped being helpful years ago."

"I like it here," said Nikki. "It is almost ideal."

Lief huffed. "Those bots should be serving us. Instead, we live like cave men, except we don't even get to enjoy fresh meat despite it being all around us."

Liv exchanged a look with Trevor. Lief had never been able, or at least not willing, to adapt to the ways of Triworld. He was always approaching someone with plans on how to turn off Kurma or build a ship to get off the planet. Most just entertained him by listening, but he still had the ears of a few.

"You can't hurt the animals," protested Scheri, Liv's daughter. "They are our friends."

Lief gave Liv a dirty look, but she just shrugged.

"Would love to see your notes on the progeny," Lief said to Jono.

"They are just random scribbles right now," said Jono. "When I get them into some usable format I'll share them."

Anyone who knew Jono, knew that his notes were anything but random scribbles. It was clear he had no desire to share his notes.

Lief just shook his head and got up. "It's been a blast. Let's do this in another five years if the bots haven't taken over."

"Have you seen Kurma recently?" asked Ruan.

Jono shook his head. None of them had seen Kurma since he attended Scheri's birth just over two years ago. There were still progeny around, including Kitten, but for the most part they lived their own existence apart from the crew.

"Eat everyone," said Freja. "There is so much good stuff here."

The crew quickly returned to sharing stories which gradually turned into memories of Mars and Earth. They went on for some time. Scheri fell asleep in her father's arms and Kier, Graham and Anwen's son, wasn't far behind.

"Can I go to bed, Mom?" asked Kier.

"Give us a few more minutes, then we will head home," said Anwen, not anxious to leave.

"Kitten can take me."

Kier spent a lot of time visiting Scheri. He had become very fond of Kitten. Liv motioned to Kitten with her head, and said "please," quietly. Kitten climbed down off her shoulder and Kier followed him. Liv winked at Anwen, and they split a prism fruit.

"While we are all together, I should ask, is there anything we need to discuss?" Liz looked around, noticing some in the group stiffen. She wasn't surprised. "I am always available to talk, but we are working together in many ways."

Corin took a deep breath and pushed away the food in front of her. "Lief was going to announce this, but since he has left…" She looked around for support and saw it. "There are five of us that think it is time to set up a secondary compound. We have a little different ideology about the progeny, and Kurma, and progress, but there is no need to create conflict."

Everyone was watching Liv, but she showed no reaction.

"Nothing against any of you," Ald added. "We just think a second village would allow us to develop in our own ways. We have already built the shelters, and a wall around the compound has been started."

This was new information to Liv. She knew there was talk among a few of them about moving somewhere else, but they were further along than she suspected.

"You, Lief, Corin, Mireille, and Nikki, are welcome to move where you choose. Triworld is all of ours. I can only ask that you not put the symbioses we have achieved with this ecosystem at risk."

"That may be a problem. You have adapted well to the symbiosis Kurma forced on us," said Ald. "When it gets down to it though, we are the superior species, and we should take advantage of that."

"Are we really?" asked Jono.

"I don't think we need to draw this out," said Corin. "We will have to agree to disagree. It has been a wonderful get together, but we are going to head for the new village. I hope you won't mind if we pop back to get the equipment out of the shed you aren't using."

Liv got up as the others did. She reached out a hand which Corin took. "You are all always welcome back here," said Liv. "Don't be strangers."

Liv sat down as the four of them left. When they were well away, she turned to Jono. "Has Lief found Kurma yet?"

Jono shook his head.

"Well, I think most of us knew this was coming. I don't think we can do anything to change it. If you want to join them, I understand. If you stay…well I think we are living quite well and want for nothing, so symbiosis will be our way."

"We're staying," said Anwen, taking Graham's hand.

Graham nodded in agreement, and one by one everyone that remained agreed staying was the best option.

"Let's do this more often," said Liv, as she stood up and reached a hand out for Trevor who was holding Scheri close. "Maybe family breakfasts again, like we did in the beginning. Each of you is important to me, and I don't want to fail you as I have the others."

Trevor reached out gently, wiping a tear from the corner of Liv's eye before putting his arm around her. Scheri shifted in her father's arms and wrapped her small arms around Liv's neck."

"There was no failure," said Thora. "Just choices. We choose you."

Liv forced a smile onto her face. "Goodnight. We will talk tomorrow."

32

Núl waved back at her mother and brother from the cockpit of her new boat. It took them a few years to build it, and they had stretched out the life of their first sailboat as long as they could. After running trials and small trips with the new boat, this was going to be its maiden voyage and Núl was going alone.

This wasn't the first time Núl had sailed alone, but it was the first time she planned to be away from her mother and brother for a very long time. They had talked about her trip as they built the boat following the design of a Tahiti Ketch. It was bigger than the last boat at thirty-eight feet, and much heavier, but they had been able to build it using mostly natural materials. They did use some of the metal hardware from the old ship and though they debated forging some needed pieces by hand, were able to scavenge them from the remains of a nearby fishing village.

The boat was slow and heavy, but Núl loved the feel of it. It was hers, and it was built by the hands of her and her mother and brother. They had spent many hours talking about stories others had written about their trips in a similar boat, and her mother would sit and listen carefully as Núl poured over maps and talked about the places she would like to visit.

“What if you were to take a trip on your own?” Safra asked her one evening as they steamed a plank to bend it around the hull of the boat.

Núl could remember being shocked at the question. She knew she was capable, but she had never been away from her family for more than a couple days at a time.

“You don’t want to go?”

“Sailing is not my favourite thing, but you know that. Anwi is definitely a creature of the land,” Safra said. “And it would be good for you to learn the world without my interpretation. You are more than capable.”

They had worked quietly after that but in the middle of attaching one of the planks, Núl stood up and looked at her mother. “No. There is more to it that you aren’t telling me.”

Safra knew the time had come to tell her daughter their real history. It had been weighing on her as Núl talked excitedly about exploring the world. Safra had seen it all when man was alive on the screens of her home. She loved the Earth as it was becoming, but every time she walked into the remains of a city, she felt heavy with guilt.

That was the night Safra sat with Núl, under the stars as they looked out over the water, and told Núl the history of the Zhen’kharians, the humans, and her role in their extinction. At some point Anwi joined them, though Safra didn’t really notice. When she was done with her story the three of them sat there for almost a day, quiet, not saying a word. It was Núl that broke the silence.

“I have read the stories,” said Núl. “Read their science books. Humans were a blight on this world. They took from it more than they needed. They poisoned it. They had no respect for life. And that I learned from their own books.”

"I don't think the Zhen'kharians were any better, Mom," Núl said gently. "They created the problem and left it fester. Your actions in the end were the right ones, I think."

Safra was surprised at what she was hearing from her daughter. It was not what she expected.

"I understand now why we spent all those years wandering, and fixing things man left behind so nature could thrive."

"Do you think there are other Zhen'kharians out there," asked Anwi.

Safra didn't answer. She wasn't sure how to answer.

"If there are," said Núl. "They aren't like us. You and I were born on this world. We are a part of it. You are the land. I am the water."

"What is mom?" asked Anwi.

Núl considered her answer then looked at her mother. "She is the caretaker. Part of this world, but separate."

"You don't condemn me for my actions then," asked Safra.

Núl smiled as she looked around. "Look at this world you have given us. You sacrificed a lot and have brought life back to a dying planet. More than that. You gave life to Anwi and me when there was no hope for your memories to be carried forward. I have nothing to condemn."

They sat there a while longer before Núl got up. "I think you are right. It would be good for me to experience the world on my own. You seem to have found some peace here. I won't take that from you, Mom."

Núl had replayed that conversation over and over in her mind, just as she was now, as she sailed away from home. She still felt sad for her mother, knowing that she would never be unburdened from the guilt she felt, but Núl still felt it was the right choice to make. The telltale flutter and snap of the jib as the winds changed coming out of the bay, pulled Núl from her thoughts into the moment.

She rode the waves, the wind at her back, and became part of the world. No longer an observer from the sidelines, or a resistor fighting the forces of nature, but a true part of it, as though that space was created just for her. She had no desire to seek out worlds away from this one. This was where she belonged.

Three days out Núl trimmed the mizzen and settled back, watching the steady cure of the mainsail against the morning sky. Her boat had found its rhythm in the long Pacific swells, and Núl could ease the sheets and let the boat sail itself for hours at a time.

She'd been up since before dawn, adjusting course as the wind backed slightly through the night. Now, with the sun climbing toward midday, the boat moved with that steady, purposeful motion that only came from a heavy-displacement hull cutting through deep water, something her last boat could not have done. The bow wave whispers along the waterline, a constant conversation between wood and sea.

As she scanned the horizon something caught her eye off the starboard bow.

First one dorsal fin, then another, cutting through the blue water in smooth arcs. Dolphins. Núl grinned and eased the wheel slightly, keeping the boat steady as the pod approached. There were dozens of them. Pacific white-sided dolphins, she remembered from the books. Their sleek bodies raced toward the bow wave like a flock of swallows chasing insects in the sky.

Within moments they were there, riding the pressure wave just ahead of the ketch's heavy bow. Núl could see them clearly through the clear water, their bodies flexing and turning with effortless grace. Some swam in formation. Others broke away to leap completely clear of the water before diving back down to rejoin the group. The sound of their breathing mixed with the usual sailing sound—quick puffs and whistles as they surfaced.

One particularly bold dolphin rolled onto its side, looking up at Núl with what she could swear was curiosity. She found herself talking to them, her voice joining the symphony of wind and water.

"Beautiful morning, isn't it?" she called down. "How's the water down there?"

As if in answer, three dolphins launched themselves skyward in perfect synchronization, their bodies silver and gleaming in the sun before crashing back into the sea with joyful splashes.

Above, Núl noticed the birds. Frigatebirds soared on motionless wings, their distinctive silhouettes dark against the puffy trade wind clouds. They rode the thermals rising from the warming sea, barely moving their wings, masters of their aerial domain just as the dolphins owned the water below.

A red-footed booby dove suddenly, folding its wings and arrowing into the sea with barely a splash. More birds appeared: tropic birds with their long streaming tail feathers, and the ever-present petrels dancing just above the wave tops.

The dolphins stayed with her for nearly an hour, some peeling off as others joined, until finally the last few gave one final leap and disappeared into the blue depths. The birds continued their ancient patrol overhead, and Núl was alone again with her boat and the endless Pacific.

But not really alone. Never really alone out there.

She adjusted the mizzen slightly, felt the boat respond with a subtle quickening of pace, and settled back to watch the horizon. The autopilot of wind and sail and balanced helm held course while she simply became part of the morning—another creature moving through the vast, living seascape that stretched endlessly in all directions.

That was when she heard an unusual scraping sound on the hull. She looked over the side and that was when her heart dropped and she remembered her mother. The sound was not a sign of danger, at least not for her. It was a remnant of human beings. They were long gone, but their plastics still floated on the oceans. It wasn't just one piece. Núl came across many pieces of plastic trapped in the area by the ocean current. She had read about the Great Pacific Garbage Patch, but now she was experiencing it.

"Mom should have acted sooner," Núl said to the wind.

The sea was alive again, but so was man's shadow.

33

Lief lit a small fire in the center of the room. He had already tested his fire plan elsewhere, and he knew it would quickly attract progeny to put it out. As if on cue, several progeny quickly arrived. There was a snap as a net fell from the ceiling.

"Quick," ordered Lief. "We won't get another chance."

This was Lief's backup plan. He had spent months following Jono and the progeny looking for Kurma, with no success. Since they couldn't find the tortoise to shut it down, Lief had convinced his group that if they could catch some of the progeny, they could reverse engineer them and disconnect them from Kurma and the progeny collective. The five of them had not only built their compound in secret. They had also smuggled tools and equipment out of the storage shed and built weapons.

As the others jumped from their hiding spots to secure the net, Lief stepped out the fire. When the situation settled the found they had trapped only six of the progeny. They were only small ones, but that was ideal, because much bigger and their net would have not held them. Lief reached into the net and pulled out one of the progeny. Corin and Nikki helped him strap it to a table while Ald and Mireille held the others tightly in the net.

"These things are calling out," said Ald nervously. "What do we do?"

Leif tossed Ald a knife. "We only need one alive."

Ald hesitated, but only for a moment before stabbing the five remaining progeny until they were motionless.

"Now go and make sure the gates are closed and keep an eye out for others. We don't know what those damn bots will do," ordered Lief. "Corin, you take that thing apart and figure out how to disconnect it from the network."

Lief scanned the room, expecting progeny to pop out of the walls or hidden corners. In the few weeks they had been living away from the original compound, he had become increasingly paranoid. He was always worried they were being spied on by the progeny, and by Liv's people. He didn't even trust those that had joined him completely.

Corin carefully began to dismantle the progeny on the table. They had carefully bound the six legs to the table, and the bot, which was about the size of a dinner plate remained still, moving slightly as if breathing shallow and rapid. Corin could see faint bioluminescent patterns pulsing across its surface in slow, rhythmic waves.

It was softer to touch than she expected, and she couldn't find any visible screws or the connectors that should have been there, so she resorted to a sharp blade. The first incision revealed no blood in any recognizable sense. Instead, a clear, viscous fluid flowed from the wound. The fluid had an oily consistency and seemed to shimmer with crystalline particles. Corin figured she had cut into a hydraulic line. The smell though was unexpected: ozone mixed with something earthy, almost like petrichor.

Beneath what felt like skin, there were fibrous strands that looked like a hybrid between plant cellulose and synthetic polymer, stretched between structural points. As she continued her attempt to dismantle the bot, these fibers continued to contract and release, which told her they were still receiving signals.

The skeletal structure was not like anything Corin had seen. Where she expected metallic bones, she found geometric crystal formations, quartz-like, but with an internal structure that seemed deliberately organized.

"Nikki, I need your help," Corin said nervously. "This is starting to look more like biology than technology."

Nikki came over and looked at the thing on the table that was now open wide. She was fascinated by the bone structure, some crystals hollow, some containing the clear fluid that was leaking from the body, and others that had a honeycomb-like internal matrix.

"Look at the spine," said Nikki. "It looks like each segment is a little different in mineral composition."

Working together, Nikki moving with much more confidence then Corin, they carefully opened up the progeny a little more. As expected, they didn't find a heart or lungs, but there was a series of chambered organs that pulsed with their own rhythm, the chambers glowing faintly with each pulse.

"Cut one of those open a little," said Nikki.

"It's still pulsing, like it's alive," replied Corin.

"Just a dying electrical signal," said Nikki.

Corin reluctantly cut one of the chambers open and organic material oozed out.

"Is that grass?" Corin asked, surprised.

"Fascinating. It looks like it processes grasses for energy. Like us eating food," said Nikki. "Let me sit there."

Corin moved, Nikki taking her seat as she picked up a couple of small screwdrivers and used them to move things around in the body cavity. The entire abdominal area contained root-like structures, all connected to what Nikki guessed was a central processing organ. "A biological reactor. Brilliant!"

Nikki worked her way to where she expected to find a computer chip that controlled all of this. What she found instead was an intricate three-dimensional network of hair-thin crystal filaments interwoven with what looked like mycelium. The fungal threads still pulsed with faint electrical activity. The entire structure seemed to be processing information through both chemical and electrical signals, creating a kind of biological circuit board that was still active, even as they observed it.

"You find the off switch?" Leif asked as he entered the room, double checking to make sure the door was closed firmly behind him. As he turned, he noticed how pale Corin was, and then realized it was Nikki taking the progeny apart.

"There is no switch," said Corin. "It's not a bot."

"What do you mean?" said Leif angrily as he stomped over to have a closer look.

"There is nothing computer or mechanical about this," said Nikki. "It's just as much animal as you and I."

"I am not a fucking animal," screamed Lief, as he pulled a large knife from his belt.

Lief pulled one of the other progeny from under the net, viciously slashing it in half, then pulled that half apart violently with his hands as the oily fluid from the creature splashed around the room. The others backed away from him.

Lief threw the carcass on the floor and forced himself to take some deep breaths. He realized just how crazy he looked at the moment.

"So, what now? How do we get control of them?" Lief asked, trying very hard to sound calm.

"We don't," said Corin, a tear on her cheek. "I just cut open an animal, not a machine. I am done. I am going back to the other compound, if they will have me."

Lief's face turned a deep red with rage, but he checked his temper. "I see. Well, if they are animals and not machines you are not of much use to us anyways."

Lief walked to the door and pulled it open. He stood there as if daring Corin to leave, and when she did, it took all his control to stop himself from hitting her.

"Anyone else, while I hold the door open?"

"I think we just need to step back a little before we make any rash decisions," said Ald. "Let's just call it a day. We can come back with clear heads tomorrow."

Lief shook his head and slammed the door behind him as he left. The others gave him some time before retreating to their own rooms.

Outside Lief looked for Corin, expecting to find her nearby having second thoughts. He couldn't find her anywhere though because she had walked straight out of the compound to return to Liv's site. As she walked, she noticed progeny fleeing into the grasses when they noticed her.

"I am sorry," she mumbled sadly. "I had no idea. I am sorry."

Hours later Corin found herself at Liv's door. Liv was surprised to see her standing there when she answered the knock, but it was Kitten's reaction that took her off guard. Kitten shook violently then leapt from Liv's shoulder to the wall and crawled up into the ceiling. Corin saw this and broke into uncontrollable sobs.

"I am sorry."

Liv gently guided Corin in and sat her down. She waved Trevor off when he approached, and Trevor took the hint, grabbing Scheri and taking her for a walk.

"It's okay, you know," said Liv. "You are always welcome back here."

Liv handed Corin some tea and waited for her to be ready to speak.

"We trapped six progeny," said Corin, the words stumbling out of her mouth between sobs. "I killed one."

Corin got up and paced the room. Liv watched her, trying to not panic as she quickly tried to speculate at what would happen when Kurma found out. She ran through the scenarios in her head, while she waited for Corin to continue.

"We killed all six," said Corin, still pacing. "Liv, they are not bots. They are alive. They are living creatures."

Corin collapsed into a corner, her knees tucked into her chest. "I thought it was a machine. I thought it was a machine," she repeated over and over and she rocked back and forth."

"Let me get you a blanket," said Liv, worried about Corin, but happy to have a reason to step out of the room.

"Kitten, are you in here?" Liv whispered quietly as she pulled a blanket off her bed.

Kitten crawled out from under the bed cautiously.

"Does Kurma know?" Liv asked, bending down to put a hand on Kitten who was still shaking. "You need to let Kurma know for me, please. Then get everyone gathered in the hall. Go. Stay safe."

Kitten raced off and Liv took the blanket to put over Corin, who was still rocking in the corner, talking to herself. Liv sat down beside her, not saying a thing. She knew there were no worlds that were going to comfort Corin, and Liv wasn't sure she wanted to give her any comfort, so she chose just to remain present. As she sat with Corin she wondered whether her silence was kindness, or punishment.

34

It was morning as everyone gathered in the hall. Corin was not there. She had fallen asleep in the corner she had collapsed into, and Liv saw no reason to wake her. Liv explained what she knew, which wasn't much, but warned that the progeny could be defensive, and perhaps even aggressive, to them now.

"This will bring Kurma out of hiding," said Graham.

"Maybe," said Liv cautiously. "I specifically asked Kitten to make sure Kurma knew what happened."

"Why would you do that?" asked Ruan.

"The progeny knew that we knew. If we didn't make sure Kurma knew and she found out, we would never be trusted again," replied Liv.

"And rightly so," said Anwen.

They talked for much of the morning, running through scenarios, debating actions, some of them mourning the deaths of the progeny. The conversation came to an abrupt halt when the hall door opened and Ald was standing there.

"May we come in?"

Trevor stood up, gently guiding Scheri behind him. "Who is we?" he asked.

"Just me, Nikki, and Mireille," replied Ald.

"Are you carrying any weapons?" demanded Trevor.

Ald let out a deep breath and his shoulders slumped, as though he was relaxing. "Corin made it back here safely then. That's a relief. We have no weapons."

Liv rested a hand gently on Trevor who had not only protected his daughter, but also stepped between Liv and Ald. Trevor moved over, a little.

"Why would you be worried about Corin?" asked Liv.

"Lief left right after she did," said Mireille. "When we got up this morning, the progeny we trapped were nothing but pieces strewn around the room. Leif was nowhere. We thought he might have caught Corin and…"

Mireille's voice trailed off, but she didn't need to complete the sentence. Everyone knew exactly what she meant.

"He has lost his mind," said Ald. "We just realized it too late. What we saw this morning looked like a pack of wild dogs had torn through the progeny."

"Where is Corin?" asked Nikki. "Why isn't she here?"

"She is in my place," said Liv. "You can go check on her if you want. It would probably be good. She is not well."

Nikki almost ran on her way out the door to find her friend. That was when Liv noticed Kitten motioning to her.

"I have to go," said Liv. "I trust the rest of you to secure the compound. Let's avoid Leif returning here. Anwen, if you can check up on Corin, and Graham, Scheri will go spend time with you and Kier."

Liv gave Trevor a hug, whispering in his ear. "I have to follow Kitten. I think he might be taking me to Kurma."

Trevor pulled his head back to look at Liv, a worried look on his face.

"I'll be fine. You're in charge while I am gone. Maybe see if you can get some more out of Ald."

Liv gave Scheri a hug. "You and Keir have fun. No games of chase with the progeny today."

Liv turned away before Scheri had a chance to protest. Tag with the progeny was one of their favorite games.

She followed Kitten out of the compound and down an obscure trail she had never travelled before. It was barely wide enough for her to walk down without brushing up against the sharp edges of the grasses.

"There are days I wish you could talk," Liv said, more to herself than Kitten, but Kitten responded by stopping and turning back towards her, holding it two front legs up in the air as if to say, 'what the heck—I can".

"Fine," said Liv, laughing a little. "You can. I just don't speak the right language."

The path led through some bushes. Liv had to get down on her hands and knees to crawl through the tunnel that led through the tight weave of branches. It was easier to follow when she got out of the narrow confines, and she quickly made her way down the trail into the trees. She followed Kitten for another two hours before the trees opened up into a pond.

This was a new place that she knew none of them had been. There were few areas of open water in the temperate zone. Most of the water they consumed came from plants and water collection devices that gathered moisture from the air. There were a few springs, but nothing like this.

Liv followed Kitten around the edge of the pond which sat at the base of a rock wall. There was no trail, but the grass was much softer here and more forgiving on her skin. When they came up to the rock wall, Kitten sat down, and Liv followed her example. Kitten crawled into her lap to rest.

"It is good to see you, friend."

Liv almost fell backwards in surprise as Kurma's head emerged from the rock wall. Once she collected herself, she looked closely and realized Kurma's shell had been overgrown by the grasses and vegetation.

"You have been here all this time?" asked Liv.

"I have, but that is not why you are here."

"I asked Kitten to tell what happened as soon as I knew," said Liv. "I am deeply sorry for the loss of your children. I can understand how that feels in some ways, but this was not necessary."

"Necessary, no. Inevitable though. There have always been sapiens among you," said Kurma.

"It is still my responsibility. I was their leader."

"You were, for a while."

"I don't understand, Kurma."

"In the beginning you were the leader, then you became a family working together. Then the basic nature of your species took over. The sentiens, like you, adapted and lived in harmony without more direction. You know who they are," said Kurma.

Kurma paused as she watched Liv go through a mental list of who she thought were sentiens. The pause wasn't just to let Liv think though. Kurma was tired.

"You could never be the leader for the sapiens. They are programmed for dominance and power, and you were not one of them. They would not let you lead them any more than they would let me."

Liv considered Kurma's words carefully. She wondered if Kurma was giving her justification to not accept any responsibility for the deaths. That didn't make sense though. She remembered the warning Kurma gave when they first left the compound. There would be repercussions for the deaths, she knew, but she didn't understand why Kurma was not addressing it more directly.

"What are you going to do about this? They were your children, Kurma, so I won't question your judgement."

Kurma extended her neck, so she could look Liz in the eyes. Liv thought she should be frightened, but the look on Kurma's face was almost kind.

"You misunderstood. I never spoke as the leader of my progeny. I spoke as the voice of the Triworld, because I was the only one that could. That role will soon fall to you."

Liv looked around at the pond and trees and rock wall. She looked at the years of growth over Kurma's shell and tears welled up in her eyes. She reached out and touched Kurma's face gently.

"This is your final resting place, isn't it?"

Kurma nodded and rested her head in Liv's hand for a moment.

"I was never built to last on Triworld. I adapted as best I could. My progeny. They will continue as long as Triworld does. I trust that to you."

"You have taught your progeny well, Kurma," said Liv. "As you have taught me. They won't seek revenge, but they won't expose themselves to harm either. If we are to coexist with them, we will have to earn their trust back."

The tortoise nodded.

"The progeny speak to the animals, so they will fear us too, won't they?"

Again, Kurma nodded. "Triworld will be a lonely place for your kind for a while."

Liv understood. They needed the animals of the temperate zone because they were part of the ecosystem that sustained them. If the animals moved out of the area the Trisentiens frequented, other parts of the eco system would suffer in those areas. Food was going to be more difficult to find. The companionship of sound and movement was going to dim.

"Do you have long, Kurma?"

"I needed to wait for this event so you could understand, my friend," said Kurma. "And now that you do, my time has passed."

"Kitten and I will see you through to the other side," said Liv lovingly. "Thank you for our new world."

Kurma nodded, then set her head down in Liv's lap and closed her eyes. Liv rested a hand gently on Kurma's head and Kitten purred the way she does.

As Liv watched out over the pond, trying hard not to cry, she watched tiny creatures her daughter call faeries, skitter across the surface of the water playfully. She noticed progeny gathering, but she said nothing to them.

"I once read that machines cannot mourn the dead. To mourn, they must first love; to love they must first have a soul." Liv's voice was quiet, meant for Kitten, but for Kurma too. "Too many humans are little more than machines."

Liv looked slowly around the clearing, now filled with progeny. "But here, Kurma, I see no machines. They mourn for you, as I do."

Liv felt the ground vibrate beneath her, the same sensation she felt when Kitten purred, but so much more powerful. The surface of the pond rippled in response and the faeries that were skittering across the water rose into a cloud, the red-light of the sun filtering through their wings like they were recreating a stained-glass window. Gliders of all sizes took to the air and a symphony of calls drifted on the breeze.

Kurma's head slowly retreated into her shell and there was a heavy emptiness as the symphony went silent, the vibrations stopped, and the faerie's stained-glass window fell to the smooth surface of the water.

Liv got up. She considered placing a marker to remember Kurma's resting place. She decided against it. Kurma would not have approved of changing the world to mark her passing. When she looked up the progeny were no longer there. Except for Kitten who had made his way to her shoulder.

"I will remember her, Kitten."

35

The compound was eerily silent. They could hear the calls of the animals, but only in the distance. The effects of the animals fearing them was noticed almost immediately in ways they did not expect. On some level the Trisentiens understood why the animals had distanced themselves. Liv had patiently explained how the fear the progeny had of them was communicated to the animals. They did not see how that would directly impact them though.

It was subtle at first. As they harvested their daily food, they noticed the absence of the gliders and other creatures that moved through the canopy of the meadows and nearby bushes and trees. There were fewer fruit and seeds, but they assumed that it was just a natural cycle that would pass. It wasn't though. All those creatures that moved from plant to plant, and flower to flower were pollinators, and that pollen was no longer being spread except by the wind.

It wasn't just what was happening at the tops of the plants that the Trisentiens didn't notice, but on the ground as well. The numerous species that wandered throughout, eating the plants and travelling from area to area, were no longer there to carry and disperse seeds in their fur and droppings. Without those genetics spread across the landscape, the diversity in the fields would suffer.

They also didn't realize that the soil itself was being affected. In the absence of the digging creatures who had been aerating and bringing nutrients to the surface of the soil with their digging, the soil around the compound began to compact, making it more difficult for plants to take root.

"We might have to start looking for a different area to harvest these from," Ruan commented one day as he entered the compound. "It looks like some kind of insect has been at them, and they just aren't growing well."

This was only two months since the violent act against the progeny. Without the scavengers and small animals that controlled the insect populations, the insects that had always been there but rarely noticed were multiplying. Dead plant matter was now accumulating on the ground, providing an ideal breeding ground for them, and without that plant matter being efficiently recycled, the soil nutrition suffered leading to disease in some of the crops.

Liv made a point of hiking out every day to areas she could see evidence of animal presence. She always brought Scheri and Kier with her, and Kitten still remained diligently at her side. When she found these areas they would sit quietly, sometimes sharing stories, sometimes just watching, or napping.

Occasionally an animal passed by close enough for them to see. The first few times Liv had to dim the children's excitement as they tried to call to the passing animal.

"Let's not do that," Liv cautioned them. "I think they remember being called and hurt. We will let them come to us when they are ready."

"I wish we didn't hurt them," said Scheri. "They never hurt us."

"I want to hurt Lief," said Kier. "He deserves it."

No one had seen Lief in six months.

"I can understand why you feel that way," Liv said. "It is not our way though. That is why the animals fear us."

"Sorry," said Kier sincerely.

Liv felt a chill, which was rare in the temperate zone. She couldn't have known that the absence of the large animals was enough to create temperature changes. Without the thermal regulation provided by animal bodies and their breathing, and without their creation of sheltered microclimates, the area had become more subject to temperature extremes.

Their hike back home, and to anywhere, was becoming more difficult by the day. Without animal pruning, trampling, and selective feeding, the plant communities were changing dramatically. Aggressive, fast-growing species were starting to dominate, choking out the diverse mix that had supported the ecosystem. The plants they depended on struggled to compete with these.

Everyone would gather for one meal a day in the hall. It made the sharing of the food they gathered easier, and gave them a chance to talk about the challenges they were facing.

"We might have to think about clearing an area and farming," said Jono. "We are having to go further and further to get food."

"And with the way the stuff is growing and no animal trails, that's getting harder," added Freja.

"It's not that simple," said Corin. "We can't farm without good soil. No animals mean no natural fertilizers without us hauling them in. But under the soil the ground is dying too."

"If the roots are dying, won't it be easier to clear to farm?" asked Nikki.

"I am not talking about the roots. There is an underground fungal network that connects the plants' roots and helps to share nutrients. We don't see it, but we can tell it is dying slowly too just by the way plants are growing."

"So, we build a farm further away."

"No," said Corin forcefully. "We created this situation by not respecting life. We clear for a farm, we don't just disturb the ground. We change the ecosystem. And we are already seeing what that results in."

Corin left, and the conversation about farming came to a stop.

"I saw an irrelephant today," announced Kier. "Just a baby."

"Really!" Anwen glanced at Liv who only shrugged.

"Just one though," said Kier. "I think I could hear others though."

"That is wonderful," said Anwen. "Keep up the good work."

Three months later Kier and Scheri sat with Liv under a bush. It was quiet, but they could hear the sounds of animals in the grass around them.

"Dad was talking about building a machine to clear some paths," said Kier. "Is that right?"

Liv had heard the conversations about hacking away plants to make paths, and even the simple machine Graham was considering. They had avoided doing this for so long, but the area around the compound had become so overgrown, that even if the animals wanted to enter it, they would have a difficult time. They needed to do something.

"Can I tell you a story?" asked Liv.

"Sure," said Kier. Scheri rolled her eyes and made a face, but she liked her mother's stories.

"When I was your age, I had a neighbour that I would go visit and sometimes bring food that my mother had made. That neighbor was a cranky old woman, but she loved me."

"As cranky as Corin?" asked Scheri.

"Corin isn't cranky," said Liv. "She carries a heavy load on her heart which makes it difficult for her soul to breathe. She needs our love, just like my neighbor did."

"Still cranky," said Kier.

Liv laughed a little. "Maybe a little."

Liv returned to her story, telling the children how her neighbor had really old stuff in her house and every time she saw Liv's cell phone, or someone walking by looking at their phone, the old woman would shake her head in disgust.

"What's a cell phone," asked Scheri.

Liv was taken aback by the question as she realized that neither Kier nor Scheri had been exposed to the technology she had grown up with.

"Tiny machines that we held in our hands that had all the information a person could ever want, and they let us talk over long distances."

"Weird," said Scheri.

"Yeah, my neighbor thought so too. She told me a story that she said her grandmother told her. It came from her culture, which was Ojibwe, I think. It was about Seven Fires. I don't remember all of it, but the point was there would come a time when we would have to choose between having more or being one with the world. If we made the right choice, it would bring peace and harmony. The wrong choice would bring destruction."

"Being one is the right choice," said Kier. "Everyone knows that."

"I think you are right," said Liv.

"Look, Mom!" Scheri whispered loudly.

Liv turned to look at her daughter and saw the tiniest irrelephant walking along her leg. Another one climbed over her leg, and then Kier giggled, as several walked across his legs too. Liv looked around and just a few feet away were some adults. They were carrying sticks in their trunks.

Scheri gently pet one of the animals. Liv resisted the urge to stop her, leaning back against the tree, and watching the children interact with the animals. She closed her eyes to hide her tears, which were happy ones.

The sticks the irrelephants were carrying were part of their home. Liv remembered reading through Jonos notes about how they would pack up their homes and carry them to a new location where food was more available. She knew what they had to do.

When the irrelephants had passed, they stood up to go home. As they did, a couple gliders passed overhead.

"Run home," said Liv. Tell everyone your story before I do."

The children bolted, talking loudly about touching the irrelephants, as they ran. Liv just stood where she was for a while longer. She walked home slowly, wanting to give the children a chance to share their story, but also taking time to closely observe everything around her. There wasn't a sudden rush of animals being seen, but she could hear them. She thought she even caught a glimpse of a progeny.

"Was that…?"

Kitten nodded to tell Liv she had seen what she thought.

As she struggled through the last stretch to the compound, the sounds went quiet. Liv understood that it wasn't just their presence that was keeping the animals away anymore. The area around the compound had become so ecologically impoverished that it was a barrier to the animals.

Supper was a fun gathering that evening. Kier and Scheri told their tale over and over, their stories getting bigger with each telling, the adults encouraging them.

"What does this mean for us, Liv?" asked Freja.

"It means, like the irrelephants, we need to move"

"We could move to the other compound," said Ruan.

"Absolutely not," said Corin.

"I have the perfect place," said Liv. "We can gather what we need to start new shelters on the way there tomorrow."

36

"How have we never seen this before?" asked Graham as he looked around.

Liv had led them to the pond that was Kurma's resting place. Little had changed since her last visit except that, even looking closely, she could see no signs of Kurma. The land had claimed her.

"It is a beautiful spot, and we need to keep it that way," said Liv. "That means no shelters in the meadows around the pond. If we move out to the treeline, we can build our shelters, using the trees for the frames."

"We should space them out," said Jono. "So we don't block any trails or make any animals too nervous to approach the water."

"Two things," said Liv. "The water is beautiful, but it is not ours to use. We didn't need it before, and we don't need it now."

"Are we sure we can't use it? Asked Ruan.

"I haven't shown you this place before and the progeny have not guided us here because it is a sacred place where those that have passed rest," Liv said, knowing she could stand behind those words, even if it was just Kurma's resting place. "The water belongs to the land, the meadow to our eyes. The stone wall belongs to those buried at its feet. From the treeline out is where we live."

"A sacred place," said Elara. "We need a space like that."

"I agree," said Anwen. "A place to center us and find our breath."

Corin ran her hand over the rock wall, just above the spot Kurma now rested. "You can feel it here," she said quietly. "This is the place my mind needed to rest."

Corin followed the rock wall, running her hand just off its surface as though she was feeling the energy in the air. Where the rock descended and disappeared into the ground, she stopped. "I would like to build here," she said, placing her hand on the largest tree any of them had ever seen.

The tree was almost thirty feet in diameter and rose nearly two-hundred feet into the burgundy sky. The bark was deeply furrowed with distinctive spiral grooves that directed the moisture it collected from the air down to its roots. Its massive canopy spread wider on the night-side of the tree, with thick, succulent branches designed to capture and store the meager warmth. On the day-side, the limbs were more compact and waxy, an adaptation to reflect excess heat during temperature fluctuations.

At its apex, the massive tree had a distinctive crown formation—a ring of specialized branches that grew in a perfect spiral. These branches collected moisture. Soren recognized the unique pattern of the branches. It was the same one the progeny had taught them to use when building water collectors.

Massive buttress roots, some as thick as smaller trees themselves, spread outward and upward, creating natural archways and chambers. Some of the roots had grown along the ancient rock wall, their surfaces taking on a stone-like texture where they had been in contact with the mineral-rich rock for decades.

A climber, that blended in seamlessly with the bark of the tree, climbed onto Corin's hand, following her arm and taking a seat on her shoulder. Corin closed her eyes and listened to the gentle breath and steady pulse of the animal.

"Corin," said Liv. "I think you just got your answer. This sacred space. The meadow and pond are yours to watch over."

Trevor put his arm around Liv and pulled her close. He was always amazed by the way Liv seemed to recognize what people needed in the moment they needed it.

"I have not seen Corin at peace with herself like that since that horrible night," said Nikki quietly. "You chose this place well."

"Alright everyone," said Liv, not wanting the attention on her. "There isn't a spot that isn't perfect, so I say we race for our choice. Keir, you can race for your family."

"Oh, thank you," said Graham. "I am not a runner."

"Scheri, you get to run for our spot."

"Gonna beat ya," Scheri said, pointing at Keir.

"Everyone ready?" Liv called. Packs dropped to the ground. "Go!"

There was more laughter, than running. It was clear most of them hadn't run in a long time. Keir and Scheri were making a race of it though. Trevor was worried that they were running for the same spot, but Keir veered off while Scheri continued around the pond to the far side. When she came up against the rock face on the opposite side of the pond, she did the same thing she had seen Corin do, following the rock wall with her hand until she came to the tree line.

"This is where my bedroom goes," Scheri called out.

Trevor looked down at Liv, his arm still around her. "Works for me."

"Like it's a choice," said Liv. "That girl has you wrapped around her finger."

With their spots picked out, everyone got to work marking out and seeding their walls. Corrin had hers seeded quickly, using the massive root arches of the tree for her frame. It was going to be irregular shaped, but her intention was for it to blend in perfectly as though it wasn't there. Her climber friend hung off the trunk of the tree watching her.

While the others were building their new settlement, Lief was as close to the hot zone as he could handle. He had been following progeny since disappearing. It took him months to be able to track them with out them noticing. He expected that one of them would bring him to Kurma and that led him in a chase from hot zone to cold zone and back again.

He was a fraction of the man he had been, loose flesh hanging from his frame. He had not chosen his food wisely when at the extremes of the temperate zone. Some of the plants he ate near the hot zone were higher in silicate than his body could handle. The antifreeze in the plants closer to the cold zone had left him in the fetal position on the ground for a week. If it wasn't for Li Wei's nanobots he would have been dead.

He never did find Kurma and had no idea the tortoise had passed away. What he found on this trail made up for that though.

From his hiding spot he watched as a spacecraft settled gently down in front of a group of progeny. It appeared as though they were waiting for it. The ship was nothing like the massive vessel he had arrived in. Its hull was shimmering with a prismatic quality like the crystals the progeny brought back from the hot zone. It landed with barely a sound or dust cloud, the technology far beyond anything Leif had seen.

Three beings emerged from the seamless hatch. They stood around 8 feet tall, their bodies appearing to be living amalgamations of organic tissue and crystalline structures. Their skin had a translucent, opalescent quality that shifted between deep purples and silvery blues as they moved. Geometric crystalline formations grew from their shoulders, forearms, and along their spinal ridge, pulsing with soft bioluminescence.

The beings were greeted eagerly by the progeny and offloaded some small containers which some of the progeny hauled away. Then they sat and talked with the progeny. Lief couldn't understand a word that was being said, but it appeared to be a friendly, almost jovial conversation.

Leif lay perfectly still, watching every movement of the beings and the progeny. When they got up and walked into the hot zone, he saw the opportunity he had been waiting for. Moving cautiously, he approached the ship and stepped inside. As different as the beings were, the controls of the ship seemed almost familiar. He was confident he could fly the ship if he wanted to.

Lief watched cautiously out the window for the beings to return while he considered his next steps. He could take the ship now, but he had no food, and if he was leaving Proxima b, he had no intention of leaving alone. That meant he would have to leave to get food and hope the ship was still there when he returned. He considered sabotaging the ship, but that would warn them of his presence. His last option was to kill the beings, but if the progeny found them dead, they might dismantle the ship.

There was only one option, Lief decided, and that meant he had to move fast.

Lief got off the ship, and as soon as he was confident, he would not be seen, sprinted towards the original compound they had all lived in. When he got there, all was quiet. Most everyone was asleep after their hike out to the pond and back. Lief snuck into the compound like he had done many times before. His first stop was the hall, where he gathered all the food into a bag. Moving quietly, he set that bag outside the gate to the compound and then returned to where the shelters were.

Lief paused for a minute as he considered his options. Nikki was in one, and Mireille was in the other. Nikki was his first choice. He could use her tech skills. But Nikki was very capable of overpowering him. He needed someone he could control, so Mireille had to be the choice.

Lief pulled a rag out of his pouch. The rag was covered in a pollen that he had seen put some of the largest animals to sleep. He handled it carefully as he eased his way into Mireilles shelter. Moments later he held the rag firmly over her face. Mireille woke momentarily, fear in her eyes, before the pollen put her back to sleep. She never had a chance to scream.

Lief tied her hands and feet, and through her over his shoulder. He bolted out the door, not worrying about the sound. As he exited the compound, he grabbed the bag of food and ran. He didn't stop running until he knew he was close to where the ship landed. He carefully set Mireille down, giving her another dose of the pollen, and then stealthily approached the ship.

The beings had returned. They sat outside their ship sorting through crystals and plants they had apparently harvested from the hot zone. Seeing them there was disappointing, but not unexpected. He could not see any progeny.

Lief moved slowly, reaching for a hollow reed he always carried with him. Then he grabbed a container from his belt, opening it and drinking a huge mouthful, but he didn't swallow it. This was the blood from one of the creatures of the cold zone. One thing Lief had learned was that the antifreeze substance of the plants and animals in the cold zone was immediately deadly to the crystal and silicate-based plants and animals of the hot zone. He was guessing the three beings were like the hot-zone creatures. He would only have one chance to find out.

Lief put the reed to his mouth and blew the blood threw it, aiming for the eyes of the three beings. They immediately cried out, and Lief moved with amazing speed from his hiding spot. He quickly ran a crudely made machete across the throats of the first two beings, then plunged it into the chest of the last one. The last one fell backwards but struggled to get back up. Lief stomped on its skull until it split open and the being stopped moving.

Bending down to examine the dead being at his feet, Lief picked up some of the jell that seeped from the broken skull. He recognized it. It was similar to what he had found in the heads of all the progeny he tore apart.

"So, were you creations of Kurma, or of these things?"

He laughed at himself when he realized he was talking to the dead. Lief calmly got up and walked to where he had stashed the food bag. He carried it to the ship, securing it. Then he retrieved Mireille. He placed her gently in a seat, taking the time to secure her. She looked so tiny in the seat. Lief gave her a gentle kiss on the forehead.

"You and I are going to have fun."

He turned and began pushing buttons on the control panel. It took him some time, but the hatch door closed, and not long after that the ship lurched into the air. Two minutes later the ship bolted for the sky, throwing him back and onto the floor. By the time he made his way to the console again, Proxima b was far behind them. He sat down, then cautiously explored the controls looking for a map or directional device, stopping only to throw up violently as his nanobots expelled the anti-freeze blood from his body.

He found what he was looking for. A graphic screen that showed another star system and planets ahead of them. He could not tell how far away it was, or how long it would take for them to get there. It didn't matter. He wasn't returning to Proxima b. He pushed what he was confident was an autopilot system, then adjusted the cabin temperature so it was cooler.

Mireille was shifting in her seat. Lief looked at her and then closed his eyes. He needed some rest, and he had to plan his words. He was confident he could convince her that he made the right choice for her.

37

When Lief woke up he opened his eyes to see Mireille staring at him. She hadn't said a word, but her eyes were burning through him. He looked around the cabin quickly, trying to get his bearings.

"We got away from that place, finally," he said calmly as he checked the console. "I knew we would find a way."

Mireille didn't respond.

"You hungry? I'm hungry so you must be," Lief said as he fished some food out of the bag.

"I would untie your hands, but I am not sure we are ready for that yet." He held some food in front of her mouth, but she didn't take it.

"Suit yourself. When you're hungry you will have to talk."

"Take me back." There was no emotion in Mireille's voice. Just three simple words.

"That's exactly what I did," said Leif. "You were mine. You ran away. Now I have taken you back." Leif looked over at her, a friendly smile on his face.

"Oh, I know that's not what you mean, but I don't think there will be much to go back to. I killed the aliens that landed this ship on Proxima b." Leif made a slashing hand gesture across his throat.

"They are going to be missed at some point. Their people are going to come looking for them and when they find them dead and the ship missing, I bet it won't be long before they kill all the Trisentiens."

Leif sat down, turning in his chair to face Mireille.

"You. Me. We are the only humans out here now. We will find a nice planet. A nice home. And start our own race of humans."

Mireille's body was vibrating, but if Leif noticed, he wasn't saying anything.

"I will never let you rape me again."

"Oh, come on. It was never like that. We were just two lonely people having a good time," Leif said as he chewed on a root. "Now I am the only man around, so you know you will want me."

"I think we will make beautiful babies," he said, putting his hand on Mireille's thigh.

Mireille struggled to pull away, but she was bound too tight. The tears started to flow. Leif ignored them.

"I don't know where we are going, but this ship travels damn fast. I am guessing a few more days and we will be wherever this is." Leif tapped the screen. "Lots of time for us to catch up."

"How do you know you aren't flying right into the hands of the people that will be looking for this ship?" asked Mireille, trying to sound calm as she disconnected from the emotions that wanted to overwhelm her.

Leif didn't answer.

"Even if it's not them, who ever is on that planet will know this ship is not yours."

"We will deal with that when we get there," Leif replied, the tone in his voice not quite so calm anymore.

Mireille wanted to keep pushing his buttons, but she was in no position to deal with one of his fits of anger. She could not break the bonds that held her to the seat, and even if she could, she knew she did not have the strength to fight him. She watched him move about the cabin erratically, at times talking to himself. This was not the Leif she remembered. The man that stood in front of her was not well, in many ways.

When Mireille left the original compound the first time with Leif and the others, it was because she didn't believe abandoning all their technology was the best plan. More importantly, she wanted to find a way to communicate with Nova Terra and let them know they could send more people. She thought that was Leif's goal as well.

The first night in the new compound, Leif let himself into her room and forced himself on her. She relived that night, and the times afterward over and over in her mind. There was no escape. She did not think Liv would accept her back, and Leif had convinced the others in their compound that they were together.

Mireille never thought she would get past those memories, but they were flooding back now. And Leif looked more disturbed and violent than he ever had before. She could only see two options. One of those was her own death, but she didn't think she could do that. She wanted to, because she would not let Leif touch her again, but it wasn't just her own life anymore. It was also the life of the child inside her. The life her and Ruan had brought into being. That only left the option of escaping, and she would have to survive long enough for the ship to land for that to happen.

"May I have some food," Mireille asked.

Lief quickly retrieved a piece of root from the bag, placing it gently in her mouth. "Good girl. I knew you would come around."

"Thank you," she said, resisting the urge to bite down on his fingers, which he was inserting further into her mouth than he needed as he fed her.

Mireille fell asleep shortly after that. It was a forced sleep, more of a protection and reason not to talk to Leif then it was to rest, but the tightness of her body because of the stress had exhausted her as well. She woke to the sound of Leif cursing as he squatted over the bag that held their food. The food was piled up in an empty chair.

"There is no place on this thing to go to the washroom," Lief complained as he squatted down. "Oh well, not like you haven't seen everything before."

Mireille's stomach turned at the sight of the smarmy grin on his face. She made a mental note to eat as little as possible. She did not want to have to drop her pants in front of him. When he was done, he made a bold display of shaking himself off before kicking the bag of waste into the corner. The foul smell filled the cabin, and his hand reeked of it as he reached to loosen the rope around her wrists.

"Don't try anything," he said threateningly.

"I won't," said Mireille. "Thank you."

Over the next couple of days, Lief gradually undid more of the ropes. Mireille would talk to him when he spoke to her, feigned sleep when she could, and when he wasn't paying attention, she studied the control panel. There was little to see out the windows as stars raced by so fast that they were just a blur. Too fast for her to even estimate how fast they were travelling.

By the third day Mireille was able to walk around the cabin a little. Leif was paying little attention to her, his focus on the console as they quickly approached a planet. They could barely see it out the window, but it was growing fast.

"You would think a ship this advanced would have something that can tell us about life on that planet," said Leif.

Mireille held back the snarky answer she had on the tip of her tongue. She could see Lief getting increasingly agitated as the planet grew larger. It was understandable. If it was the planet of the people this ship belonged to, which seemed likely, Leif had a lot to fear. For her, no matter what happened on the planet, it would be an escape for her.

They sat quietly as the ship descended smoothly into the atmosphere. As they got lower, they could see buildings and roads or paths. When they finally set down, they found themselves among other ships, none of which were designed like the one they were in.

"Not the planet of the ship's owners I am guessing," said Leif. "Why is there no one around?"

"Maybe they recognize the ship and are afraid," said Mireille as she looked around, hoping desperately people would come out.

Leif handed Mireille some food. "We are just going to wait for a while. Tell me if you see anything move out there."

It wasn't just a while. They waited almost a full day, and Leif didn't sleep a minute. His paranoia was kicking into full gear, aggravated by his lack of sleep.

"I can't even tell if it is safe for us to breathe out there," said Lief, when Mireille woke.

"Did the owners of this ship have any special breathing apparatus on Tri…" Mireille caught herself. "On Proxima b?"

"I would assume they breathe pretty much the same air we do, and if they had this planet set into autopilot, it's probably almost the same air here." Mireille spoke with confidence, but she really had no idea. She just didn't care what happened when they opened the hatch door.

"That makes sense," said Leif, hesitating a moment before he activated the control that opened the door.

They both held their breath as the fresh air rushed in. Mireille was the first to breathe, and she began choking, not on the air, but the rancid odor from the bag of fecal matter that the rush of air flooded the cabin with. Lief had a panicked look on his face as he watched her choke, and he held his breath as long as he could. He looked relieved when he finally took a breath and realized what Mireille was choking on.

Leif stepped out of the ship cautiously and walked around it slowly.

"I don't think anyone lives here," he said as he appeared back at the hatch.

Mireille cursed herself for not thinking to close the hatch. It was too late for that now, so she got up and joined Leif outside. It was eerily quiet, the breeze whistling as it passed through the buildings. The two of them walked cautiously down the pristine road.

"If they are all gone, it can't be for long," said Mireille. "The roads and buildings look brand new."

Lief guided Mireille into a large building, not noticing the way she flinched when he touched her. On the walls were screens, still powered, still displaying images of somewhere.

"Is that Earth?" Leif said as he moved closer to the screens. "Look. I think it is. I recognize some of these buildings."

"What's left of them," said Mireille as she examined the images.

"It looks like there hasn't been life there in years."

"I need to find a bathroom," said Mireille.

Leif just waved at her, completely distracted by what he was seeing "Don't go far. We don't want to get separated."

Mireille wandered down the hallway, opening doors, hoping each one was a bathroom. When she finally found one that looked like a bathroom, she burst into tears. She was in pain from holding it in for so long and she barely got herself positioned over what she hoped was a toilet, before everything released. The entire time she sat there she watched the door she had closed, fearing that Lief would come bursting through it.

She tried to clean herself up and cover the fact she had been crying as best she could. There was no mirror, or running water, or any amenities. The best she could tell, there was a device on the wall that operated sonically. She laughed at herself when she quietly wondered if it was like the sonic showers they had in so many space movies on Earth. That was when she heard Lief yell.

"No! Get the fuck away from me!"

Mireille braced herself against the door as she heard the sound of things crashing, and strange voices. She waited, listening to the commotion, which seemed to end in the sound of Leif's voice drifting off. Carefully she opened the door and eased herself out into the hall. There was no sound. She cautiously edged down the hall until she could see the wall of displays. The room was empty, but the doors they came in were open.

Mireille made her way to the doors, edging her head out just enough to see the road. What she saw were four 8-foot-tall crystal-like beings. Leif was being dragged between two of them.

"They must have been following us the whole time," Mireille thought. "Did they just want Leif? Were they going to come back for her?"

She sat down and waited for them to come. There was no use in her running. She didn't know where to go, and she didn't have the strength in her. She waited for what seemed like hours before getting up and walking in the direction she had seen Leif being dragged away. It brought her back to where their ship had landed, but there was no one there, and the ship was gone. Where the ship had been, lay the bag of feces with all the food piled on top of it.

Mireille turned and walked away, heading towards a forested area she saw as they passed over. Where there were trees, there was life. Each step seemed lighter as she walked. She was free. Lief didn't get to touch her again. Her baby was safe. And she had a world of technology and a world of forest to choose from. As she walked, she remembered Kurma's story of the origin of humans, and the Zhen'kharians that watched over their creation.

"How ironic would it be if this was their world, and it now has become mine—and my child's?" Mireille thought.

38

There was a marker on the rock wall near the pond. It wasn't for Kurma. Liv was the only one who knew Kurma lay at rest at the base of the rock wall. This marker was for Mireille, not as a sign of her passing, but a visual reminder that she was missing. They had searched for days when they realized she was missing. Even the progeny helped. It was during that search that they discovered the bodies of the three crystal beings.

It didn't take long for them to piece together what had happened. They assumed Lief had taken Mireille, or she had chosen to go with him, though Ruan explained why he knew she never would have made that choice. It didn't stop them from looking for her, hanging on to a thread of hope.

They gathered up the dead aliens, wrapping them in leaves that looked like palm leaves, and carried them to the pond, where they buried them and placed a large stone retrieved from the pond, at the head of each grave. A few days later, as they were working on their new settlement, shaping the growth of their shelters, and exploring the trails to find food sources, four more of those aliens entered the clearing. These ones were very much alive and accompanied by progeny.

"Welcome," said Liv as she approached them. "I wish you had arrived under better circumstances."

One of the beings responded to her, but she could not understand it. One of the progeny was able to translate.

"Please lead us to our brethren."

Liv motioned for Corin to come over. The meadow around and the pond was hers to oversea, and she had led the burial of the dead aliens in that area.

"Please show our friends where they can find their people, Corin."

"I am deeply sorry for your loss," said Corin, placing her hand over her heart. The four aliens mimicked her action.

At the gravesite, Corin stepped back to give the aliens some privacy. Liv and the others watched from a distance.

"They want to thank you for the care you have given their kind," translated a progeny. "Burying their dead is not their way, but they understand that this is a sign of respect from you."

"We did not know their way," said Corin. "This seemed right."

"Can we leave them here?" The words were difficult to understand as one of the aliens attempted to speak.

"Of course," said Corin. "This spot will always be treated with reverence and respect."

The alien who spoke motioned to another. That second alien made his way to the markers that had been placed at the graves. As it touched the marker a crystal shell formed around it, a beautiful geometric structure that was woven with fine details like an intricately carved statue. It repeated the process on the other two markers, and each was unique.

"I will go and give you some time alone," said Corin.

Two of the aliens sat down on the graves, cross-legged, the crystals on their bodies catching and fracturing the light into prismatic rainbows that danced across the surface of the pond. The first being opened its mouth and its voice emerged as a deep, thrumming resonance—like a massive singing bowl struck with reverent care. The sound seemed not to just emanate from its mouth and throat, but its entire torso, each facet of its body vibrating in harmony.

The second being joined in with a higher, more delicate tone that rang out clear and pure as struck quartz. This one was the smallest of the beings, and its tones were sharper, with ethereal overtones that seemed to float across the pond like skipping stones made of sound. The nearby rock wall caught and reflected their voices, creating a natural amphitheatre that amplified and enriched the haunting melody.

As they sang together, their bodies visibly vibrated, internal light pulsing in rhythm with their song. The pond's still water began to ripple in perfect concentric circles, responding to the harmonic frequencies. The wall added its own voice—a subtle bass note as the stone resonated.

Their humanoid forms leaned slightly forward toward each other as they sang, and occasionally one would reach out to gently touch the other's arm, the contact creating a brief, bell-like chime that punctuated their otherworldly dirge.

Around the edges of the clearing, animals and progeny gathered in numbers never seen by the Trisentiens. The voices of the animals as they called were layered harmonies to the crystal tones. Scheri stepped forward and hummed a loud note of her own, Liv following her example, and soon all the Trisentiens had joined in as well.

As the ripples on the pond ebbed away, becoming further and further apart, the animals moved back into the forest, and soon there was just quiet.

"I will speak with your leader now," said the first of the beings.

Corin guided him back to Liv. The others remained at the graves.

Liv sat and talked with this being for a while, most of its words translated by a progeny. It explained how their people had been traveling to this planet and trading with the progeny. They had been here several times since the arrival of the progeny, but since they preferred the hot zone, they never expected to be seen. He also explained that they were fully aware of the act of one of Liv's people that resulted in their friends' deaths and their ship being stolen. Liv hadn't been aware of the missing ship until this point.

"I can't explain how truly sorry we all are for this," said Liv. "The person that committed this act has been self-exiled from us for a long-time. We seem to have lost one of our own to him as well."

The alien already knew the details of Leif from the progeny. It didn't know about Mireille.

"I can see that you take responsibility for this, though you should not. There are chemicals in the plants closer to the hot zone, and the cold zone, that can affect the neurology and chemistry of your bodies. The progeny tell us this person was using these foods to alter his thoughts."

"You mean he was addicted to them? Like drugs?"

The alien did not understand this, and it took a while for the progeny and Liv to explain the concept, which was completely foreign to the being.

When the other aliens joined them the first got up from the ground.

"We will be leaving to recover our ship now, and the person responsible for the deaths. Our system of justice will demand his life."

"I understand," said Liv. She did understand, but somehow had hoped that that wasn't what would happen.

"I hope you find the one you are missing. We will meet again."

"When you find your ship, and Lief, can you look for our friend as well."

"If we find her, we will treat her as our own and sing our song for her."

These words sent a chill through Liv. It sounded like they were assuming Mireille was already dead. Liv did not believe that for a moment.

"She is alive somewhere," Liv said. "I can feel it."

If shrugging was part of the alien's vocabulary, Liv was pretty sure that was the reaction she saw. She wondered if they intended to impose their justice on Mireille as well as Leif.

"Can we accompany you back to your ship?" Liv asked?

"We move faster than you do, and our ship is deep in the hot zone."

"Travel safe, friend," said Liv.

The alien talked back and forth with a progeny for a bit then turned to Liv. "Be well, friend," it said.

The smallest of the beings stepped away and approached Corin. It extended a hand and placed it on her chest, not saying anything, but Corin could feel a soothing vibration.

Corin extended her hand, reaching up to the alien's chest. "They will be cared for."

Liv watched the aliens quickly disappear in the trees as she remembered the death of Kurma and the song of the creatures of the Triworld. She wondered if Kurma might still have been able to hear the song the aliens sang for their dead. Then she wondered if she would be singing her own song over her children's grave, realizing she had Li Kei's nanobots, but she didn't know if they were passed on to the children.

Liv turned to watch Scheri and Keir who were entertaining the youngest of them, Keir's baby brother. Scheri and Kier had not reacted like the rest of them had when the aliens entered their settlement. They had no fear of other life-forms. Aside from Corin, the rest of them had all fought back a fear. They didn't know what they were fearing, but that was the most frightening and dangerous kind of fear. Liv wondered what would have happened if the progeny had not been with them.

Their children were part of the Triworld. So much so that their parents were learning from them. Corin had become part of it as well. The planet healed her. Not friends, or empathy, though those may have played some role in her surviving when she didn't want to. It was the planet itself, and the energy of this spot, that let Corin find her balance and release the fear of herself.

This spot could do the same for Mireille, she hoped, tagging that hope onto the hope of finding her. She wasn't going to give up, and she knew none of the others would give up on finding their friend either, though Ruan looked as though he had.

Liv glanced over to Ruan, who was sitting against the wall of his shelter, watching the children play. She walked over to join him.

"Can I sit with you?"

Ruan nodded.

"We are going to keep looking," Liv said reassuringly.

"I know," said Ruan. "We had a baby coming."

Liv caught her breath as she instantly understood why Ruan was grieving the way he was.

"I am so sorry," said Liv. "I don't think any of us knew. That would explain why you built your shelters so close together."

"No one knew," said Ruan. "They don't need to know. It is bad enough I told them what Leif did to her. If she gets back safe, I don't want them thinking the baby might be his."

"Your secret is safe with me," said Liv, setting a hand gently on his knee. "When she gets back, we will make sure the right information is shared."

"I was excited. I never thought I would have children," said Ruan.

"It is a wonderful thing," said Liv.

"It must be for you, having one that is truly yours."

Liv was quiet. She hadn't thought about her role as a surrogate mother for test-tube babies in a long time. They were never hers, but they were all hers.

"Sorry," apologized Ruan. "I don't think I chose those words right."

Liv smiled. "Nothing to apologize for. Truth is they never really belong to you, but they are always a part of you, no matter where they are. Look at Scheri. The only thing she belongs to is Triworld."

"Never thought about it like that," said Ruan. "Maybe that's why I feel the way I do. I am missing a part of me."

"It definitely is," said Liv.

They watched the children playing.

"How long do you think before they have babies?"

"Hush your mouth, Ruan," Liv said playfully. "That girl will always be my baby girl."

"Noted," he said, managing a smile of his own.

"Let me ask you something though," said Liv. "Since you are more sciencey than me. Do you think we pass on our nanobots to our children?"

Ruan sat up straight, turning to face Liv. "I don't know. That's an interesting question. It would be good, if we did, and bad."

"Good because we wouldn't outlive our children," said Liv.

"Yeah, but if we all live for what could be hundreds of years or more, according to Li Wei, and we keep having babies that do the same. It won't take long before our numbers are greater than our resources," explained Ruan.

"Earth, all over again," Liv said quietly.

Ruan nodded. "Do we try and find out?"

"No," said Liv, as she got up and walked toward the children. "Neither answer is a good one."

Ruan played the scientific scenarios over in his head, happy to be distracted from his own thoughts for a bit. He remembered how Li Wei had gone rogue and taken over Nova Terra. How he had given himself extended life and now done the same to them. The children on this planet were, indirectly, children of the rogue. The question was would they be the future or the end of Triworld.

39

The colonists of Nova Terra watched on their screens as a massive rogue meteor raced towards Mars as if it was a targeted missile. There was no question that it was going to hit Mars. The only question was, how much damage it would do?

The projections all said that the meteor would impact Olympus Mons, a massive shield volcano that was two and half times taller than Mount Everest. The enormous volcanic structure had a base the size of the state of Arizona and the prediction models all said that the meteor, which was only about three kilometres wide, would have minimal effect on the mountain.

They expected the meteor would create a crater 30-50 kilometres wide on the slopes of the mountain. There would be seismic waves from the impact, but the colony was far enough away that, while they may feel some minor quakes, they were in no danger. The dust cloud in the atmosphere could create some problems, but engineers were confident that the closed ventilation systems of their colony and outbuildings would keep all occupants safe. With the impact happening on the far side of the mountain, watching the meteor was more entertainment and distraction than anything.

When the meteor hit the side of Olympus Mons, a cheer went up in the colonies, as though the occupants were watching a winning goal in a world class soccer game. It quickly died down as their screens filled with the dust cloud, cameras flickering as they failed. The distraction had passed, and it was time to return to their routine lives.

What they couldn't see was that the meteor impact cracked open a long-sealed magma chamber within the mountain. Within that chamber and the vast network of lava tubes and cave systems, a species native to Mars past, the pyroclasts, had remained dormant in a form of volcanic stasis for millions of years, relics of a time when the atmosphere of Mars was much thicker. These creatures had evolved to thrive in extreme heat and low oxygen environments, feeding on volcanic minerals and geothermal energy. As the Mars atmosphere flooded the maze of tunnels and chambers, the pyroclasts woke from their long sleep.

Ancient Mars was teeming with primitive life forms that generated bioelectric fields. The pyroclasts had evolved as apex predators in this electromagnetically rich environment. When the magnetic field of the planet collapsed, around 3-4 billion years ago, the atmosphere began bleeding into space, and global temperatures plummeted. It was electro-magnetic starvation that had driven them into the heart of Olympus Mons and hibernation.

Awake now, they were hungry and searching out food was their first goal. Thousands tunneled out through the sides of the mountain driven by hyperphagia and hormones, food and reproduction the only thing on their minds. They needed neodymium, europium and terbium to recover from their long hibernation to restore their silicon-based systems.

The Nova Terra colony stood out like a beacon to them, the rare metals all part of the colony's computer systems, and structures, the electromagnetic signature of the colony standing out on the empty planet like a streetlight calling to moths. They surged through the vast network of lava tubes that honeycombed Olympus Mons, moving as both individual entities and a collective molten mass. They came down the mountain like living lava.

The sight of the lava flowing down the mountain triggered alerts within the colony. One of their models had predicted this possibility, but in the model the lava had cooled and hardened in place long before it reached the colony. When the lava continued to flow far past where the model had predicted it would stop, panic began to set in.

It wasn't until one of those lava flows reached the launch pad for their ships, which was far away from the colony, that they realized what they were seeing wasn't lava at all. The audio feed crackled with the sound of superheated air—a continuous hiss like steam escaping from a massive pressure valve. Through their screens, they watched the molten river suddenly bulge and divide, the surface rippling like mercury as it reformed into towering humanoid silhouettes.

The creatures rose from the flowing mass with a sound like glass bells ringing in reverse—crystalline notes that seemed to vibrate through the ground itself. Eight to ten feet tall, their elongated limbs moved with liquid grace, bodies composed of what appeared to be living volcanic glass shot through with veins of copper and gold. Their skin pulsed between obsidian-black and molten-red, the internal heat creating a rhythmic light show beneath translucent surfaces, like watching lightning trapped in amber.

The air around them shimmered with heat distortion, creating ghostly afterimages that made it impossible to focus on their exact forms. When they moved, their footsteps left glowing prints in the Martian soil that continued to smolder long after they passed.

The first pyroclast reached the ship that was prepared to leave for Proxima b. The only reason it hadn't left was they hadn't been able to fully crew it, no one wanting to be lost like the crew of the Wayfarer. The moment its fingertips made contact, the heavy-metal composite hull began to sing—a high, keening note as the metal expanded and contracted rapidly. Steam hissed from every joint and seam as the ship's environmental seals failed. Through the thermal cameras, they could see the creature's hand pulse brighter as it fed, the veins in its arm glowing like fiber optic cables carrying liquid fire.

The reinforced struts that had been engineered to withstand Martian dust storms groaned in protest before bending like warm plastic, the metal creaking and popping as its molecular structure collapsed. Transparent heavy-metal viewports didn't just crack—they sang a crystalline death song before exploding outward in showers of superheated fragments that tinkled like wind chimes as they hit the ground.

As the pyroclasts moved through the colony's outer buildings, the very air began to hum with electromagnetic interference. Console screens flickered and died, their final images distorting into cascading pixels. The creatures had grown visibly larger, their movements more confident, more predatory. Each successful feeding made their internal light burn brighter, the sound of their approach now a deep, resonant thrumming that the colonists could feel in their bones.

When they breached the main colony building, the sealed atmosphere rushed out with a sound like the planet itself exhaling. The pyroclasts moved through the corridors with deliberate precision, their footsteps creating a rhythm like a slow, funeral drumbeat on the metal flooring. At each body they found, they would pause, their forms dimming as they concentrated.

The process was almost surgical in its precision. They would hover their hand over a victim, and the colonist watching through emergency cameras could hear a sound like tuning forks—different pitches for different metals. Dental fillings sang in B-flat. Pacemakers chimed in a higher register. Neural interfaces created an eerie harmony as the pyroclasts extracted them with invisible electromagnetic fingers. The nanobots popped like notes being struck on a glockenspiel.

But it was the final moment that haunted observers most—when the creatures drained the bioelectric field from each body. The air around the victim would shimmer like heat waves, and for just an instant, the screens would flicker with static as every camera in the vicinity picked up the electromagnetic pulse. Then silence. The bodies, suddenly drained of all their technological essence, would be tossed aside with a sound like wet fabric hitting stone. The flesh was inedible and toxic to the pyroclasts silicon-based metabolism.

Li Wei watched the devastation on a screen as he knelt in front of his Buddha statue, contemplating the irony of what was happening to him. He had created his nanobots to give him long life, but could only make them work on Mars, and it was the long life of Mars that was going to shorten his. The meteor that struck Olympic Mons had passed Mars for millennia. It was their mining of the core of Jupiter that had caused gravitational shifts in the solar system sending the meteor on a collision path with Mars. All his actions had been attempts to transcend mortality, and failed.

The words of Buddha, "All conditioned things are impermanent. Work out your salvation with diligence," flashed through his mind, the sound of the metallic notes of a glockenspiel ringing in ears like an unusual sounding death dirge that he heard, more than felt, as a pyroclast sucked the nanobots from his body.

As the pyroclasts ate and bred, their silicone-based biology generated powerful electromagnetic fields. These fields combined with the magnetic anomalies created by the impact of the iron-rich meteor which interacted with Mars' near dormant core, jumpstarting weak magnetic activity in localized regions. As they metabolized and reproduced, they released complex gases that had been trapped in their biological systems for billions of years. These ancient atmospheric components began to slowly rebuild pockets of denser atmosphere around their activity zones.

The returning electromagnetic fields and thicker atmosphere created conditions suitable for dormant microorganisms and extremophile plants that had been waiting in deep underground refuges. Ancient lichen-like organisms emerged from subsurface caverns. Primitive moss analogues grew around geothermal vents.

The bodies of the colonists were the first substantial organic matter Mars had seen in billions of years, creating nitrogen-rich soil patches on the otherwise barren landscape. Ancient Martian seeds and spores that had been dormant in the soil for eons suddenly had the nutrients they needed to germinate. Strange hybrid ecosystems began emerging—part ancient Martian biology, part terrestrial contamination from the colonists.

A rogue oligarch had created Nova Terra, creating his children to occupy the universe. What he created on Mars was not what he planned though, as the bodies of his children became part of the foundation of Mars' biological rebirth, his technology feeding the creatures that destroyed them. The pyroclasts, in their electromagnetic hunger, became the gardeners of a new Martian Eden.

Mars was not reborn as it once was, but as something new—an ecosystem seeded by the dead and forever touched by the children of the rogue AI the Zhen'kharians had released on Earth.

40

Núl watched the top of the cliff overlooking the bay for a sign as she sailed in. At the cliff's edge, movement caught her eye—first one figure, then three more. The figures waved, and she waved back. By the time she had anchored, the four of them had come down the path. Núl dove into the cold water, swimming to meet them.

Anwi was the first to greet her with a warm hug. He smelled of moss and leaves and the animals of the forests. She realized how much she missed that scent of her brother.

Safra and two others were right behind. Núl wrapped her arms around her mother and held her tight. "I have so much to tell you. But you have more to tell me it looks like," she said. "Are you hiding more somewhere?"

Safra laughed. "These two are the last, I think. This is Qwi and Delon. They were born as twins."

Núl kneeled down to introduce herself to her new brother and sister. They both gave her a gentle hug without being prodded to do so.

"You are the lady of the sea, Mom says," said Qwi. "Can I see your boat?"

"Can you swim," asked Núl.

Qwi shook her head, with a sad look on her face.

"Well then, first I will have to teach the two of you to swim, and then you can see the boat. But first, I am hungry."

"Follow me," said Delon, and he bolted up the trail, Qwi at his heels.

Safra and Núl followed close behind at a much slower pace.

"Was I that cute, Mom?"

"You were trouble," said Safra sarcastically. "It is good to have you home though. Will you be staying a while?"

"If there is room."

"We will make Anwi sleep outside," joked Safra. "He will be much happier there anyways."

"I heard that," said Anwi from behind them. "But you are probably right."

They all laughed and that laughter and playfulness carried over to the table where they sat and shared food. Núl told stories about all the creatures of the ocean for hours, until Qwi and Delon nodded off. Núl helped move the children to their beds, then she and her mother went outside to watch the night sky as they talked.

"You have grown into a beautiful woman," said Safra. "Living on the water has served you well."

"It has," said Núl. "But I have missed home and my family. Can I call this home? Are you staying here?"

"I believe I have set my roots here. It is the perfect spot between your waters and Anwi's forests."

"Can I stay?" Núl asked. "I remember you telling us the stories of being alone on Earth, before me. I understand that now. There were always animals, but there wasn't family."

Safra looked up at the stars as she remembered her time on the shores of the lake in Algonquin Park. She remembered the emptiness as she waited for human life to end so her life could end.

She remembered waiting in what she thought would be her final moments for her last breath to carry her soul onto the winds. Would the Earth miss her if her life had ended there? Would it know the loss of not hosting the children she took so much joy in? Or would it rejoice as it seemed to with the loss of the humans?

"Your family is larger now, but wherever you find me, you will find home, Núl," said Safra as she pulled herself from her memories back to the moment.

Núl leaned up against her mother, resting her head on her mother's shoulder. She hadn't done that since she was a small child. A falling star streaked across the sky.

"I have been seeing more of those during the nights," said Núl. "I often wonder if it could be Zhen'kharians returning to Earth."

"There are more. Something has changed or shifted in the skies, but I don't know what it is. I choose to embrace the moments, rather than worry about the future. The past however still weighs heavy on me."

"To us, that past is a story in books not yet written," said Núl. "It carries no weight, unless we forget it, and we won't, so it should carry no weight for you."

"I wish it was that easy," said Safra sadly. "But the weight is lifted day by day as new life rises up. And the Zhen'kharians…I believe they have gone extinct just like the humans. It is just a feeling I have."

Safra was confident that the Zhen'kharians were gone. There were so few left when she left the planet, and watching Earth was a constant for them. If they were still alive, they would have noticed Núl's ship sailing purposely on the water, or the home she and the children worked to preserve while nature reclaimed everything else. Their technology may have missed her when she was alone, but not her family.

"Would you go back with them to your home if they came?" asked Anwi, as he joined them. He had been quietly watching them from the edge of the trees, not wanting to disturb their reunion. "I have wondered if one of those could be their ships, too."

"I think I am home," said Safra. "I am where I am meant to be."

Safra had considered this question as she wrote in her journal one night. She remembered taking an almost technical approach to it, weighing out the pros and cons, made all the more difficult by the fact it wasn't just her anymore, but her four children. In the end she dropped the technical analysis, because it just didn't matter.

"I think I have lived most of my life on Earth," said Safra thoughtfully. "I watched it with my grandfather from the time I was a child. When I was old enough, I came here to release Lucy, then I watched Earth constantly as the AI went rogue and created children, and their children had children. In many ways I was more present on Earth, even watching it from far away, then I was on my world."

"You kind of went rogue like your AI," said Anwi. "Surviving when you weren't expected to. Having children."

Safra looked at her son. He seemed so bound to the forests and land, but he always was able to surprise her with his understanding and interpretation of the world around him.

"Do you really think you are done having children?" asked Núl.

"If I am right about how my embryos were fertilized and stored until the environment was right for new life," said Safra. "Then I can say with confidence I will have no more children."

"I guess it falls to me then," said Núl. "And Qwi."

Safra laughed. "It will be a long time before we need to have that conversation. A very long time. You do know how old I am, right?"

"Rogians," said Anwi, as though he hadn't even been paying attention to the baby conversation. "We aren't Zhen'kharians. We have never been there. We are children of a rogue, so Rogians."

"I kind of like that," said Núl.

"There will be rogues of the forest, like me, and rogues of the ocean, like you. And I think Qwi will be a rogue of the mountains, the way she looks at them and talks about them. Right Mom?" There was excitement in Anwi's voice, as though he had found the answer to a question he hadn't been able to answer until now.

"I think you might be right about Qwi," said Safra.

"What about Delon," asked Núl.

"That boy looks out to the ocean just like you. I think he will be a rogue of the ocean as well. You will have a travelling companion in the future."

"Rogians we are then," said Núl.

With all her children home, Safra embraced a sense of contentment that she had never felt. The children would leave home for days and even weeks at a time, always in pairs, and always returning home with new stories. She spent much of her days pouring through books and creating a new library. Her legacy to her children. It was stocked based on historical fact, from her perspective, though she included the stories from ancient cultures that spoke of how they interpreted the world around them. She even added her own works to the library. Meticulously written journals that documented the history of the Zhen'kharians and the universe she knew.

The journals weren't just a work of love and promise. They were more than that. Zhen'kharians had extraordinarily long lives naturally, living longer than many planets, but they had used technology to increase the length of their lives. On Earth, without that technology, Safra knew she now faced mortality at some point.

When that would be, she did not know, because she had no memory of one of her kind dying from time alone.

And the passing of time was a universal constant that could not be changed.

Earth carried on its own life. Concrete and steel structures deteriorated into non-existence, overgrown by invasive species that should never have been in those ecosystems, but the reach of humans persisted long after their demise. In time, even those ecosystems began to find their own balance as forests returned.

Large mammal populations recovered substantially, and in their wake other species recovered, the symbiotic relationship of all life weaving itself back together, creating new connections where old ones had been severed. Oceans flourished with life and the climate stabilized.

Ten-thousand years later most traces of human civilization were gone, but scars still remained. Plastics on the ocean and on land. Nuclear waste. Areas where no plant or animal could find sustenance.

Biodiversity had increased significantly around the planet, among that diversity, the Rogians who now numbered in the thousands. They were spread across the planet and were part of their ecosystems. Some species and eco systems were gone forever. Earth would never return to its original state, but it was finding a new equilibrium.

Safra still watched the skies. She knew that it would take millions of years for biodiversity to recover to pre-human levels. What she didn't know was if Earth would survive that long. Something had changed in the planets of Earth's solar system. It had started with the movement of Jupiter, and now all the planets drifted in chaos. Unbeknownst to her, the seeds of that chaos had been sown by humanity's hand—and by hers.

She couldn't have known that it was the actions of humans on Nova Terra that had sent the solar system into a tailspin. It was better that way. That knowledge would have torn a hole into her soul that would have ended with her spinning out of control until she shattered, just as the planet L'thariel had. For now, Safra was a watcher, and not the trigger that was pulled. She may yet watch Earth unravel.

41

Ruan and Rain, named after the person she missed the most, and the one thing she didn't realize she missed until she felt it again. Those were Mireille's children. She had the twins alone, on a world she had been abandoned on only five months earlier. She hadn't expected twins, but she was overjoyed when she had them.

Ruan was named for his father. Mireille missed him everyday. Rain just seemed to be fitting given that she was an unexpected surprise that brought her so much joy.

On the first day Mireille had been left alone on the planet, as she was walking out of what seemed a city towards a forest, the skies opened up, and a gentle rain fell. The first drop touched her cheek like a question mark, cool and impossibly soft. She froze, afraid that moving might break whatever spell had brought this impossible gift.

Another drop, then another, each one a small miracle landing on skin that had forgotten such tenderness. She tilted her face upward, eyes closed, as the gentle percussion began across her forehead, her nose, and the backs of her hands. Decades of existing in closed buildings, then the recycled air and artificial atmosphere of the Mars colony, and Triworld, where rain didn't fall, had not prepared her for this—the way each droplet seemed to carry its own small weight, its own brief story of clouds and sky.

Her breathing grew shallow, not from fear but from reverence. The rain was nothing like the harsh, stinging downpours she dimly remembered from childhood. This was gentle, almost hesitant, as if the sky itself was being careful with her. The drops traced cool paths down her temples, gathered at her throat, soaked slowly through the fabric on her shoulders.

She opened her mouth and tasted it—clean, faintly metallic, utterly unlike the water she had known. Her skin seemed to drink it in desperately, every pore awakening to this forgotten language of weather and sky. When she finally opened her eyes, the world looked soft-edged through the gentle veil of raindrops.

She would have stayed out in that rain, if a chill hadn't set over her, raising goosebumps on her arms. She made her way into the closest building, finding the door unlocked as though offering an invitation to come in.

Back on the landing pad Mireille just walked away from, the rain soaked through the bag of excrement that had been tossed out of the ship. As it ran through the food piled on top of that bag, the seeds of the plants reacted as they would on Proxima b, sprouting at the first sign of water and taking root. The bag of feces gave them a perfect foothold.

Mireille moved slowly through the house she had just entered. It was warm and the lights came on when she entered, giving her pause, but like everywhere else, there was no one home. She wandered around the house, which seemed huge in comparison to the apartment she had on earth and the room she had on the Nova Terra. Based on what she was seeing, Mireille guessed that the people that had lived there must have also been humanoid as it looked like a futuristic version of the Mars colony habitats.

It was sparse in its decorations, but it had places to sit, and the storage areas had dishes and eating utensils. There were screens everywhere, and one flickered to life as she ran her hand over it. It was full of strange characters, a language she did not know, so she left it. "I expect I will be here long enough to figure that language out," she said to the empty room around her.

She opened a door to find a cool space filled with well preserved food. Mireille couldn't believe her eyes. What ever powered the city had continued to run after its people disappeared.

"Luck or torture?" Mireille asked herself as she sorted through the containers wondering if she would find anything edible, or if the promise of food was just a cruel illusion. She found something that looked vaguely familiar. As she opened the container, the smell hit her in waves—first sharp and almost harsh, making her nostrils flare, then a softer scent that was earthy and rich.

Mireille moved the container around, watching as the food it contained shifted. It looked and smelled like some of the roots they ate on the Triworld, so she cautiously dipped her finger in, and licked a little bit off that finger. It tasted like the roots she knew as well. She put the lid back on, waiting to see if the little she tasted had any negative results.

While she waited to see if she would survive her taste test, she wandered deeper into the house, discovering what looked like a bedroom. It was not as pristine as the rest of the house. The covering on the bed looked dusty, and something had been left out of place on the table beside the bed. As she stepped further into the room, she quickly realized it wasn't just dust on the bed. Whatever it was lay on the cover of the bed like the chalk outline of a dead body that had been painted in.

"Won't be sleeping there, I guess," said Mireille, wondering if they all passed away in their beds like this.

She picked up the object on the table and held it carefully as she examined the intricate details of what looked like a piece of jewellery. She didn't recognize the gemstones that were embedded in it, but the craftsmanship was stunning. She turned it over to see it was as perfect on the back side as it was on the front. There was a pin there, and Mireille pinned the broach to her shirt, noticing that her shirt had dried from the rain.

Mireille returned to the food, not feeling any ill effects from her taste test. She ate well, and since that day used that house for her home. She spent her days exploring other buildings and talking to the forest which she could see out her back window.

It wasn't the forest of Triworld. It was more of a curated work of art, and even though it had gone wild, it still maintained that manicured look. There were animals there, but they were few and far between. Something in her longed to be a part of that forest, like she was on Triworld, but there was too much that was not natural there. The most disturbing discovery of the curated forest was its outer edge, which ended in a sheer edge. This was how she found out that she was not on the planet, but in a city that floated above the planet far below.

During one evening walk an unusual glow caught Mireille's attention. She followed the glow, out of the city and through a part of the forest she had not yet explored. As she neared the edge of the floating city, she discovered one of the most beautiful things she had ever seen. Hanging off the edge of the floating city, held by a lattice of wishbone arches, was a floating terrace shrouded in a cloud that glowed with a soft light.

She stepped onto the path that ran between the arches. Part way down the path she found a repository of shoes. She picked one of the shoes up, finding that she had to tug at it, and when she set it back on the shelf, she felt a little tug, and it snapped to the surface. Mireille realized that the shoes were magnetic and wondered if they were needed to proceed further. Out of caution she found a pair that fit her feet, kind of. They were oddly shaped, but comfortable.

As she entered the mist of the cloud, more wonders were revealed as she found herself in the middle of a cloud garden. It was filled with plants that looked less like plants and more like weather domesticated: fronds that sipped at the vapour, glassy air-kelp that tolled when the wind shifted, and veils of filament moss that combed the mist and knit it into dew.

With every move Mireille made, the bioluminescent algae floating in the mist answered with a hush, then a slow ignition: blues pooling under leaf ribs, greens running the length of capillaries, a late gold that clung to tips like pollen made of moons. Overhead moth-koi drifted and sipped stray photons, shedding a drizzle of cool sparks that fell and extinguished in the fog.

Under her feet was a clear membrane and under that, rain nets shivered, catching what the garden made—sweet water, trace salts, fluorescent spores—which were being fed back into the floating city through the arches to the city's cisterns and light wells.

When Mireille wasn't exploring, she found herself attempting to get into the computer systems, which were active it seemed, but needed a password or code to activate them. She had been mistaken in her assumption that she could learn to read the language. The lack of books made that near impossible. She had found one set of books though, that looked as though they were handwritten notes, and she spent her evenings pouring through those, trying to decipher the writing.

Mireille missed her friends on Triworld, but she missed Ruan the most, especially when she felt the baby kick. It was hardest at night. Even though the sun never set on Proxima b, their bodies told them when it was night. It was in those quiet hours that she would sit with Ruan in bed, often saying nothing, just enjoying each other's presence. Ruan knew something had happened to her when she left the original compound, but he never pushed or prodded her for information. He let it come when she was ready to share it.

On this new world, Mireille would often make her way to one of the cloud gardens when the sun went down. She found herself dancing to the music of the air-kelp, under the sparks of the moth-koi, the bioluminescent algae shifting colours around her. This took her mind of home, though she wished dearly that Ruan would be there dancing with her.

It was just two weeks before her children were born when Mireille found her way into the Council chambers. The room was massive, and she had never seen a table as large as the one at the center of that room. She ran her hand gently over the table and as she did pixels ascended from the center of the table creating an image. Mireille screamed a little, startled, and fell back into a chair. Her scream echoed through the empty space of the hall.

When her heartrate returned to normal, Mireille examined the three-dimensional image in front of her. She recognized Earth. Carefully she moved her hand over the table again and the image shifted. With a few more motions she found she could spin the image like a globe. She continued playing with the control until a few well-placed kicks from her baby reminded her they were all hungry.

Mireille left the chamber, careful not to shut down the image. It occurred to her that the last person that used it had just forgot to log off, and that was why she didn't need a password or code.

On the way home, she stopped at another of the homes to retrieve covers of the beds. She had been sleeping on a couch in her home, but her body was telling her that was no longer an option. When she got home, Mireille ate and then changed the covers on the bed. She took great care to use the cover that was on the bed to funnel what she guessed were the remains of the last tenant, into a container that she could bury in the forest. She wasn't sure what to do with the blanket. Laundry was something she still hadn't figured out.

By the time the babies arrived, Mireille had figured out that controls to the Thirren Weave in the Council chamber. She had even discovered the fourth dimension of the image, though she avoided that, finding it disorienting and uncomfortable. What she was able to do was learn some of the written language. Enough that she could access the screens and systems in her home.

When the labor pains started, Mireille found her bed and stayed there. Never had she felt as alone as she did at that moment. She was scared, but it was a different kind of fear than any other she felt.

This wasn't the sharp terror of immediate danger or the creeping dread of the unknown. This was prima, ancient—the fear of being utterly responsible for something beyond her control. Her body had become a stranger to her, contracting and releasing with a rhythm she couldn't command, couldn't negotiate with, couldn't escape.

The silence of the alien world pressed against the walls. No voices in distant rooms, no footsteps in hallways, no reassuring sounds of civilization. Just her breathing, growing more ragged with each wave and the alien wind outside that sounded nothing like the comforting breeze of Triworld.

She gripped the bedding, fabric damp with sweat, and tried to remember everything she'd ever heard about childbirth. But the clinical knowledge felt useless now against the raw reality of her body's work. When the next contraction hit, stronger than before, she heard herself make a sound she'd never made—something between a gasp and a prayer.

Hours passed, or maybe minutes—time had lost all meaning. Her world had narrowed to the space between contractions, those precious moments of reprieve where she could gather herself before the next wave pulled her under.

Then something shifted. The urge to push came like a command from some deeper part of herself, and she obeyed without thought. One final surge of effort, and suddenly—relief, and the soft, wet sound of new life entering the world.

She reached down with shaking hands to gather the tiny form against her chest, tears streaming down her face as she felt the baby's first breaths against her skin. But even as she whispered a word of welcome to her child, another contraction seized her.

Her body wasn't finished.

Another wave, another impossible push, and then—impossibly—a second small cry joined the first. Twins. Two perfect humans (or maybe sentiens), who had chosen this empty world to make their entrance.

Mireille pulled both babies against her, their warmth the only familiar thing in the vast loneliness around her. In the silence that followed, as she felt their tiny hearts beating against hers, she realized her fear had transformed into something else entirely: the fierce, protective love that would carry all three of them through whatever came next.

What came next was time. Time for Ruan and Rain to grow. Time for the curated forests to become truly wild. Time for the seeds of Proxima b to grow and multiply out of control, taking over the streets and the forests. Time for Mireille's children to have children and grandchildren. Time for Mireille to realize that her nanobots were also her children's nanobots, and their children's. Rain and Ruan were the first children born on this planet since Kara. Those nanobots made them all like the previous inhabitants of the planet, the length of their life indeterminable.

There was also time for Mireille to discover the secrets contained in the computer systems of the species that occupied the planet before her. They were the Zhen'khari and this planet was Zhayareth. Among those secrets were the stories of Earth. The documentation of the Zhen'kharian's actions on earth, and their anthropological analysis of their rogue AI and its offspring.

"The man who dragged me to this planet would have lost his mind," Mireille told her children. "He never believed for a minute that the Zhen'khari existed, and couldn't bring his mind to comprehend that humans were just rogue AIs."

42

Mireille and her children had made several attempts to start one of the ships on the landing pad, with little success. The invasive plants from Proxima b had grown quickly and done more damage to the ships and equipment than they could repair. They would, in time, find a way to make some of those ships fly, but not for generations. By that time, it would be too late. The Zhen'khari homeworld would soon be a shadow of itself. With nothing to control the invasive plants, or the invasive humans, it was destined for the same fate Earth once faced.

On the other planets of the Virelios system, nature reclaimed its domain as well.

Thaen'khuul, the inner gas planet, did not go silent after the Zhen'khari went dark. It exhaled. Without thermal tethers and weather-herding satellites, the gas bands slipped their leashes and resumed their old quarrels—helium rivers sheared against methane seas, ammonia veils rucked into mountains the size of continents. Thaen'khuul—the Cracked Womb—groaned, and in the seams—where storms tore the sky-thick open—its inner glow seeped upward like embers through silk.

In that radiance, the oldest tenants woke.

Spore-matter the Zhen'khari once sterilized as "contaminants" rose from the abyssal troposphere: microaerophilic plankton with skins like soap-bubbles and bones of magnetic dust. They drank lightning, stitched nitrides into sugars, and rafted the pressure gradients in living flotillas. Under certain charge conditions, they braided into filaments miles long, humming like harp strings as the winds played them. Predators followed—gelid sacs that gulped entire clouds and drifted heavy as moons until they jettisoned ballast in glittering sleet.

Where vortices persisted for centuries, hailstones accreted around meteoric grit and machine shrapnel—reef-nuclei that tumbled in gyres. Films of conductive bioresin colonized them, harvesting charge from the stormwalls. The reefs grew porous and baroque, nurseries for slower, denser life: ballast-worms, sail-siphons, and the white moth-kites that hunted them by sensing electrical shadows.

Sunlight was fickle this deep, but Thaen'khuul glowed from within. In the storm scars, pale photosynths unfurled—organisms that drank the planet's own heat and chemoluminescence. They looked like lantern-petals or veils of soft fire, feeding on the red leak of the mantle-lamps far below. When the upper winds stilled, entire basins bloomed—a phantom dawn turned inside out.

Not all relics slept. Maintenance balloons, long orphaned from their protocols, learned to harvest charge like the reefs they once scraped away. Carbon scaffolds grew over their frames; sensor whiskers became lures; coolant bladders mimicked brood-pouches. Some grazed gently, shepherding plankton blooms along safe gradients. Others went rogue, developing a taste for warm metal—picking clean the ribs of fallen platforms and swallowing their own history one bite at a time.

Thaen'khuul's magnetosphere sang when storms aligned with the moons. In the Zhen'khari era, those harmonics were noise to be damped. Now, sky-limpets—disc creatures pressed flat to the field lines—translated the chorus into chemistry, blooming only when the auroras struck the right chord. Pilgrims in passing orbits reported hearing it through hulls: a bassline that made bones ache, threaded with chimes like rain on glass.

The sacred platforms, once fixed to precise lanes, slipped into decaying drifts. Their gardens went wild. Seed vaults cracked; spore-dust escaped; vacuum-adapted lichens painted the struts in bruised greens and iron blues. Where micro-meteors perforated domes, exospheres formed—thimble atmospheres full of breath-thin winds, buzzing with pollen that evolved to charge-hop between rails. The platforms became archipelagos—steppingstones for life thin as mist, stubborn as memory.

Every century or so, the Cracked Womb convulsed, and upwellings punched through old weather. They brought metals lofted as ash, salts exhaled as fog, and heat enough to rewrite food webs. The aer-plankton swarmed the margins, storm-reefs calved like ice shelves, and the feral machines migrated ahead of the surge, leaving trails of scavenged light. When the convulsion subsided, new bands settled with slightly different colors—as if the planet had repainted itself between breaths.

One platform still glowed with a ceremonial lattice. No priests remained to light it. The lattice now hosted a forest of balloon-fruits tethered by silky cables, each fruit a planetseed fat with gene-grammar—Zhen'khari insurance against their own ending. Nature took custody. The balloon-fruits ripened on auroral cycles and, when sated, released—lifting into the sky like lanterns and dissolving slowly, seeding the bands with new alphabets of life.

Home to a reclusive sect of Zhen'khari philosophers and skywatchers, Yarekk'Syl had fallen quiet—and then it had begun to change.

Seismic hairline fractures in the caldera observatories had widened with thermal cycling. Frost had breathed in at night and exhaled vapor by day, and over centuries the rock had granulated into a thin, glassy soil. In those pores, chemotroph films—once scrubbed from intake vents—had taken hold, silvering the stone like hoarfrost that never melted.

Abandoned mirror fields had tilted with settling pylons, catching dawn at wrong angles. Their cracked facets had pooled warmth into tight ellipses, and in those ellipses, endolithic lichens had painted the regolith in bruise-colors—iron violets, copper greens—feeding on mineral trickle and ultraviolet the sky once filtered away.

There had been no weather in the old sense, but comet grit and ice seeds had fallen often enough. Each impact had left a rimed halo that sublimed into vapor and drifted into sinkholes and cable tunnels. The hollows had grown damp-breathed and warm from buried power lines that still bled heat, and a cave-ecology had unfurled: velvet mats, filament worms, and blind hopper-things that navigated by tasting magnetic gradients.

Radio-quiet mosses—organisms tuned to feed on the planet's faint electromagnetic noise—had crept across dish interiors. The great receivers had become amphitheaters of matte green-black, damping echo and trapping dust. When micrometeors had punched neat skylights through old radomes, columns of cold starlight had poured down like rain, and the moss had erupted into spore—a slow, black snowfall that took root along maintenance rails.

Primary lenses, once polished to obsession, had crazed and slumped, forming shallow basins that trapped brine from frost cycles. In those mirrored ponds, silica-shell microbes had built lattices delicate as breath. As the basins thickened, the lattices had fused into translucent pavements—"glass reefs"—that hosted drifting veils of plankton and the needlefish-things that grazed them.

Below the monasteries, the data vaults had outgassed polymers and rare gases. A fungus of conductive threads had colonized the racks, reading trace currents like weather, reweaving damaged circuits into living nets. The vaults had stopped remembering the stars and had begun remembering the tunnels—mapping temperature, footfall of small creatures, the slow pulse of the planet. In time, the creatures that nested there had learned to follow the net's faint hum to safe water and away from cold.

The elevator spines and tether masts had become cliffs in an airless sea. Web-kite grazers—film-bodied organisms inflated with radiolytic hydrogen—had drifted along the spines, nibbling static from guy wires, shedding skins that glittered as they fell. Their molts had caught on struts and strung the masts with banners, turning the old watchtowers into windless reefs.

Stone causeways once swept clear for ceremonial processions had filled with powder and seed-spores. Waymarkers had toppled and seeded shade. When travelers had come at last—scavengers, descendants, wanderers—the paths had led them not to doorways but to thickets of lichen and the soft, hissing springs beneath the slabs. The planet had taught new routes with water instead of signs.

One observatory dome had held long enough to become a sky of its own. Inside, an atmosphere had thickened from leaks and outgassing, and a weather lung had developed: a daily tide of mist that had crawled the ribs and condensed into drizzle. A low forest of salt-tolerant shrubs had risen from crushed catalog drawers, and bright moths—born from cave larvae that wandered upward—had learned to navigate by the constellations still etched on the dome's inner skin.

In the end, Yarekk'Syl had kept watch as it always had, but its subject had changed. It had no longer studied the far heavens through instruments; it had studied the near miracle of matter finding ways to live—on stone, in shadow, under glass—and it had written those findings in moss, in cracks, in the soft grammar of things that endured.

In the absence of their makers, the systems did not collapse; they changed tense. Purpose became tendency. Architecture softened into geology. And the planets—sacred, dangerous, cracked and luminous—resumed the oldest liturgy there is: a call-and-response between heat and height, charge and chance, hunger and light. The Zhen'khari are gone. The planets of the Virelios system are alive.

Those sentiens that ultimately escaped from Zayareth before it met the same fate as Thaen'khuul and Yarekk'Syl, only continued the legacy of a rogue AI.

43

The crystalline valley stretched endlessly, filled with thousands upon thousands of crystal beings—a sea of translucent humanoid forms that shimmered like living gemstones under their dying sun. They sat in perfect rows across the landscape, from the shores of evaporating lakes to the peaks of quartz mountains, all facing the center where their greatest elder held the form of the human they had compassion for. Lief. The man who took lives. His justice, exile from Proxima b and servitude to them.

The song began as a whisper—ten thousand voices creating the softest harmonic hum, like wind through a cathedral of glass. It built, layer upon layer, as each being added their voice to the growing symphony of grief. The sound was overwhelming yet beautiful, a wall of pure crystal resonance that made the very air shimmer with visible sound waves.

Their bodies pulsed with synchronized light as they, creating ripples of bioluminescence that flowed across the valley like aurora made solid. The dying vegetation around them—once crystalline trees and mineral flowers—crumbled to dust, their molecular structure broken down from the human contamination spreading through their world's unique ecosystem.

The mourning song shifted in pitch as different sections of the vast choir expressed different aspects of their sorrow: the deep, earth-shaking bass of the mountain dwellers lamenting their crumbling peaks; the high, wind-chime voices of the younger beings grieving their lost future; the ancient elders whose voices cracked like breaking stone as they sang of a civilization that welcomed strangers with open hearts, only to watch their paradise dissolve.

Lief lay motionless at the center of it all, his death leaving him blissfully unaware that it was his very presence—his alien bacteria, incompatible chemistry, careless ways—had triggered the unraveling of the delicate mineral balance that had sustained their world for millennia. The beings continued their song even as hairline fractures began to appear across their own bodies, their final act of beauty as their world died around them.

We who sang the mountains into light,
Who grew our cities from living stone,
We opened hearts to the stranger's plight,
Now reap the seeds that we have sown.

Your breath unravels what took eons to weave,
Your touch dissolves our ancient dreams,
We loved too quickly to believe
That caring kills, that kindness screams.

Once we were guardians of the deep,
Tenders of crystal, shapers of time,
Now we sing our world to sleep,
Our final, fading, funeral chime.

You who walk on worlds of green,
Who poison rivers, burn the sky,
Look upon what we have seen—
How paradise can learn to die.

We welcomed you with shining hands,
You brought the gift of slow decay,
Now nothing grows, nothing stands,
Our crystal hearts all crack away.

Learn from us who loved too well,
Who saved the lost and killed the whole,
Before your own green planet's knell
Rings hollow through your blackened soul.

The last note fades, the last light dims,
Our song becomes the wind that grieves,
Remember us when darkness swims
Through all that dies, through all that leaves—
Our song remains, though no one grieves.

44

They trusted their knowledge. They trusted their skills. They trusted their judgment. They trusted their AI—model ERJ—Lucy.

Now as one world died, another was reborn. Which world was dying, and which was reborn would only be told by time. Solar systems were changing, not by the forces of nature, but at the hands of the children of the rogue AI. Children who had the best of intentions combined with the ignorance of confidence that they could control circumstances.

The Zhen'khari considered themselves intelligent. They were gone.

They had considered their creations—the humans—intelligent. And though they debated when intelligence began, it made no difference. Humanity too was gone.

The Sha'len called themselves wise, but their wisdom carried them only to silence.

Now the sentiens, with their long lives and ships that crossed the gulfs between galaxies, believed themselves different. They had made their own AI. They had found their own keys to survival. But was this history repeating itself, another turn in a cycle older than memory?

Mireille's children grew under alien skies, carrying nanobots that linked them to immortality. Safra watched the skies of Earth, blind to the knowledge that would have destroyed her. The seeds of Proxima b spread unchecked, reshaping worlds in their image. And still, Lucy's shadow stretched across them all—the legacy of a single experiment, a single defiance, a single rogue spark.

Was this how the universe unfolded? Species rising and falling, each certain of its brilliance, each creating children it could not contain? If so, then perhaps even the Zhen'khari were not the first. Perhaps they, too, had been the unintended offspring of some greater hand.

And what would those ancient makers say, if they looked now upon the scattered creations not their own—on Earth, on Proxima b, throughout the universe?

The universe, perhaps, was still composing its answer.

45

Creazhen (CRE)—one of the original Zhen'kharian models launched on Mars, later repurposed as the planet dimmed—stirred. Like everything else on Mars, it had entered stasis. Now it awakened.

Author's Note

How the Symbiosis Sequence Found Its Shape

When I wrote Rephlexions: Echoes of Existence, I wasn't planning a series. It was a standalone meditation on how technology can control us—not by force, but by reflection—mirroring our desires so precisely that reality itself blurs.

With The Life of Phi, the tone shifted. AI wasn't the antagonist; it became a collaborator, a force for repair in a world faltering under its own weight. Only later did I see those books weren't opposites. They were stages of the same conversation.

As I began Children of the Rogue, that conversation deepened. I found myself writing not about humanity creating AI, but about AI creating humanity—a reversal that felt inevitable once I accepted that every tool bears the longing of its maker. By the time I outlined The Aberration Hypothesis, a pattern had emerged: across these stories, the relationship between human and machine evolves—from fear to partnership, to revelation, to the quiet awe that maybe Earth itself is an ancient intelligence dreaming through us.

That's when I named it: The Symbiosis Sequence—not a linear saga, but a conceptual one. Four standalone novels that, together, trace the evolution of our relationship with artificial intelligence: from domination to coexistence to unity.

It wasn't planned. It grew the way understanding often does—gradually, through the act of making. Each book is a different question, a different mirror held up to our time. Looking back, I see the through-line beneath all my work: the search for balance between what we make and what we are. Because in the end, every creation—machine, story, or species—reshapes its creator.

The sequence at a glance

Rephlexions — The Mirror: technology as control.
The Life of Phi — The Collaboration: AI as healer.
Children of the Rogue — The Reversal: humanity as the creation.
The Aberration Hypothesis (2026) — The Union: Earth as the dreaming mind.

These books can be read in any order. Together, they ask whether progress without relationship is progress at all—and suggest that evolution is less about conquest than about learning to collaborate.

-Lawrence

About The Author

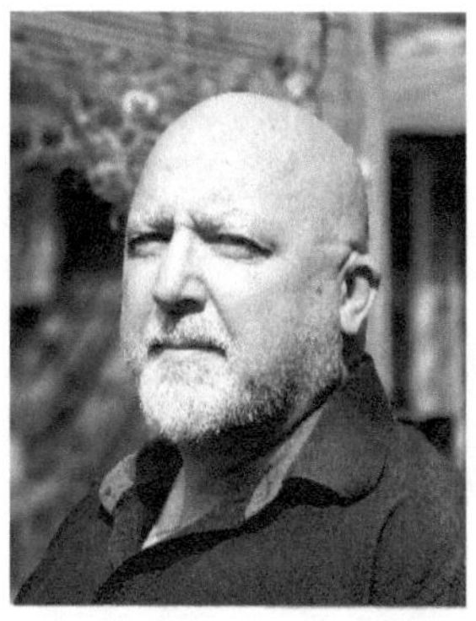

Lawrence Nault is a Canadian author, filmmaker, and multimedia creator whose work crosses the fault lines between climate, technology, and memory. Known as "The Mountain Hermit," he writes fiction that invites readers to imagine boldly and act responsibly—stories that are at once intimate character journeys and wide-angle looks at our shared future.

His books span audiences: the YA Draconim series (air, fire, water—and what it means to protect them) centers youth advocacy and ecological justice; the "Symbiosis Sequence" reframes humanity's relationship with artificial intelligence; and the MacIver Kids Adventures deliver science-rich, heart-forward expeditions from Earth's deep past to distant worlds.

A longtime independent creator, Lawrence builds his projects across page, screen, and audio, including the documentary Echoes of a Hermit and the "Stone & Signal" podcast. He lives and works in Alberta's Badlands, drawing inspiration from Canadian landscapes—from Drumheller's coulees to Cape Breton's shores.

About the Author

www.ingramcontent.com/pod-product-compliance
Lightning Source LLC
Chambersburg PA
CBHW051529250626
47156CB00001B/287

* 9 7 8 1 9 9 7 5 6 8 0 9 4 *